RALPH COTTON'S

FRIEND OF A FRIEND

BOOK 1: THE GUN CULTURE SERIES

D1519471

FRIEND OF A FRIEND

BOOK ONE OF THE

GUN CULTURE SERIES

BY RALPH COTTON

He may be reached at **www.ralphcotton.com**

Cover photo and interior art from **123RF.com**

Cover design & book layout by Laura Ashton
laura@gitflorida.com

Author's photo, p. 295, by Mary Lynn Cotton

ISBN: 978-1508616009

Printed in the United States of America

Some Reviews by Amazon Readers

By *Patrick Naville* – Bestselling Author of *Cripple Creek*

Ralph Cotton has consistently been an outstanding writer in the Western genre, but I believe he's hit upon a whole new talent for modern day literary fiction. This was one of those books that you hate to put down because you're afraid something will happen and you'll miss it! It's fast-paced, the characters are well developed and story hooks you from the first page. Ralph describes the seedy side of the Florida drug underworld and does so in such a way that you hope you never cross paths with any of these people. The bad guys are as nasty as they come! Ralph throws some plot twists in there that the reader never sees coming. I won't give the ending away other than to say, you WILL be surprised! Great job, Mr. Cotton! I look forward to the next one in the Gun Culture Series. Keep 'em coming!

By *Cheryl* –Amazon Reviewer

Mr. Cotton's first book in his new Gun Culture series: Friend Of A Friend does not disappoint! His gift for capturing the subtle and not-so-subtle nuances of his characters -- from seedy, psycho criminals to everyday heroes is flawless. There is a realism and a familiarity of his characters that draws the reader in from page one. His ability to weave riveting plot twists is one of the reasons I have trouble putting his books down when I know I should be turning out the light to get to sleep! I'm anxiously awaiting the arrival of Book 2 in the Gun Culture series: Seasons of the Wind.

By ***Bob H*** –Amazon Reviewer

I finished Ralph Cotton's new book last night and would recommend it to anyone who thinks of Ralph as strictly a western writer. You will thoroughly enjoy his new book. I thought I had it figured out and at the end was completely wrong. Outstanding writing as usual. I am waiting for his new book which is due to come out shortly.

By ***Bridget*** –Amazon Reviewer

OMG, he has done it again!! this is a awesome book, and a whole new brand of series. Once you start reading, you can't seem to put it down. JUST AWESOME!

By ***FloridaGal*** –Amazon Reviewer

Mr. Cotton's stories never disappoint, I look forward to the next in his Gun Culture series. Anyone on the gulf coast will recognize the locations and the outrageous characters. Nobody does it better!

For Mary Lynn ... *of course*

PART I

(HAPTER ONE

Chicago, Illinois:
Temperature 36 degrees:

Christmas music played from an overhead speaker in the grilled metal ceiling. Dylan gazed up from beneath his hat brim at the floor number lights above the stainless steel doors. The elevator climbed; he watched the digital floor numbers click higher, feeling the upward push of the carpet beneath his feet.

> *Here we go ....*

He wore black-rimmed drugstore glasses with dark tinted lenses. A tangle of wild blonde hair bushed up under his hat brim covering his ears. He looked anonymous enough, easily unnoticed he liked to call it, yet the getup put him in mind of some street performer embarked on some sort of skit.

This was no skit.

Outside, a dusting of light snow had blown through the city overnight. Wind off the lake pulled the temperature down into the low thirties. Cold, but not unusually so for this time of year, he thought, remembering the brutal winters he'd survived here years ago. In front of him an elderly woman stood only inches from the closed elevator doors. She wore a heavy coat and a dark green feathered hat. She stared at the doors as if waiting for instructions. Two rolls of wrapping paper stood up from a shopping bag in her gloved hand.

A bell gave a soft single ring when the elevator whooshed to a halt. He watched the woman step out and walk away as the doors closed behind her. Alone now, he stared at the closed doors himself, holding gloved hands in the pockets of a black down-filled hooded jacket. He knew a security camera lay somewhere up in the grillwork overhead, but it wasn't working this morning. *Not this morning ....*

When the bell rang again, the elevator stopped at the top floor and opened its doors. He stepped off, started walking. At the end of a carpeted hallway he looked down at a small unoccupied desk where a morning paper laid spread open beside a half cup of coffee. He removed a gloved hand from his left pocket and opened the unlocked door. He stepped inside the penthouse suite and closed the door behind him without a sound. Then he moved quietly across the carpet, pulling a silenced .22 caliber pistol from inside his coat.

He seated himself in a high-backed chair and listened to a shower running in a bathroom down the hall. When the water stopped, he heard the far end of the apartment grow silent for a few minutes. Then he heard the bedroom door open and close. He waited, poised. A few seconds later an elderly man in a white terrycloth bathrobe walked into the room barefoot. The man crossed the carpet without seeing him and bent over a glass-topped coffee table.

He picked up a silver six-tube cigar case and a small aluminum emergency medicine container from atop the tinted glass. He straightened, opened the cigar case and started to drop the medicine container into his robe pocket. But he froze when his eyes went to the figure standing up quietly from the chair twelve feet away. A streak of surprise and outrage came over his face, but only for a second. It went away as a cool hardness set in. The man recollected himself and started to put his hand and medicine container down into his robe pocket.

Dylan shook his head slowly, stopping him.

"Hunh-uh, lay them on the table," he said in a low even tone.

Before doing as told, the man gestured toward the cigar case in his hand. With a nod from Dylan he took out a cigar, snapped the case shut and pitched it onto a small catchall tray sitting atop the table. He pitched the medicine container down on the tray with the cigar case and let out a breath.

"How did you get in?" he asked, his voice was gravely, but carried the same low even tone as the man who had come here to kill him. His stare had turned to cold gray granite.

Dylan only stared back at him.

The man glanced away toward the front door, then back. He shook his head as revelation set in.

"Figures," he murmured. "After all the money I pay that son of a bitch …." He let it go and looked Dylan up and down. He said, "What are you in that getup, some kind of street clown?" He eyed the hat, the large black-rimmed glasses, the curly hair. "You look like Harpo Marx for God sakes."

Dylan didn't answer.

"That's a rug you're wearing, right?"

Still no answer.

"Jesus, I hope it is," the man said, getting in a dig even under the circumstances. "All you need is a handful of balloons."

Letting the man work his situation out in his mind, Dylan only continued to stare—some quiet doctor here to deliver bad news.

"Is my son behind this?" The man stuck the fresh cigar between his teeth.

Dylan still gave no reply. Supposedly the room had been swept for sound and video surveillance, but you never knew. He stepped slowly over to the man, gun aimed and ready. Reaching down into the man's bathrobe pocket, he pulled up a small shiny pistol and held it on his palm for the man to see.

"That? I've carried that for years. I can't even tell you if it's loaded." He gave a half shrug and brushed the matter aside.

Dylan put the pistol into his coat pocket. He stepped back and motioned his gun barrel toward the sofa.

"What about money? Will cash do me any good?" the man asked quietly as he stepped around the coffee table and sat down. "I can lay a hundred thousand dollars in your hand this minute. You can walk out of here."

Here came the negotiations. Dylan watched him take the unlit cigar from his mouth and hold it forked between two manicured, arthritic fingers.

"What do you say?"

Instead of answering, Dylan took a syringe from inside his coat and laid it on the table in front of the man.

The man looked at the syringe, then back up at him.

"Go fuck yourself," he said.

Dylan understood. He took a calming breath and motioned his gun barrel toward a framed picture of a young boy in a baseball uniform, a bat propped over his shoulder. At various places in the room, Dylan had already seen other pictures of the same boy, several more pictures of a slightly older girl.

"Grandkids?" he asked quietly. He gestured toward the pictures.

The older man studied the pictures with him.

"What's it going do to them, you checking out this way?" Dylan queried.

"Leave them out of it," the old man said. "My *son of a bitch* son does this to me? Let him deal with it." He appeared to stiffen with resolve. "My own *son* for God sakes," he grumbled under his breath.

"It's not your son," Dylan said, still keeping his voice low and even.

The old man stared at him as if deciding whether or not to believe him.

"Who the hell else, then?" he asked, showing no sign of giving in. "He's the one who gains the most." He paused and said. "You do know who I am, don't you?"

Dylan only stared, waiting, studying the closed face. He wasn't going to answer—wasn't going to say he knew who he was, wasn't going to mention that he had in fact even worked for him twice over the years. He'd said all he needed to say here. He'd given the man a choice. After a silent moment, he said, "Have it your way …," and he leveled the gun an inch from the man's left eye.

"Wait," the man said sharply. "You're telling me he's not behind this?"

"What did I say?" said Dylan, his hand still poised, his finger ready to press back on the trigger.

The old man reminisced something in silence for a moment.

"Jesus, all my life it's been for him—" He caught himself and stopped and shook his head.

Dylan waited, watched. He was used to this, hearing how hard a guy like this had worked, always for his family. He'd never heard one admit in the end that they'd really been a greedy, self-serving prick. It was always about their sacrifice for the good of something, someone. Good family men these guys, they liked to claim. Dylan didn't judge.

"All right," the man said, still in a quiet tone. He flipped open the right bottom edge of his robe revealing a graveyard of needle marks a few inches above his knee, some older, some more recent.

Dylan backed up a step. His information on the man was right. Everything was going as it should. He stood watching the man pick up the syringe and uncap it. The man closed his eyes for a moment. When he opened them, without another second of hesitation he slid the thin needle into the patchwork of insulin marks and plunged the syringe's clear contents into his thigh. He removed the needle from his thigh and looked up at Dylan as he relaxed back and pitched the syringe back atop the glass coffee table.

"What now?" he asked.

Dylan didn't answer. He took a step farther back and stood relaxed, lowering the gun a little.

"Baseball, huh?" He nodded at the boy's picture.

"Yeah. The kid's always been good at everything," the old man said. "He's older now, going on seventeen—already getting offers. The girl's planning on law school."

"That's nice," Dylan said in a quiet tone.

"Yeah, real nice ...." The man gave a tired little smile, leaned his head back and closed his eyes. "Do me a favor? Don't tell my son what I said, even if he *did* do this," he half whispered.

"No problem," Dylan said almost soothingly. "Go to sleep now." He looked at his watch, took note of the time and let his gun slump a little more.

(HADTER TWO

And that's how it's done ....

Dylan watched, listened as the man murmured final words to a white ceiling in the silent room. Then the man's head gave a single exit bow and he fell as silent as the room itself. His purple-veined foot had drawn up tight on the carpet, then twitched, relaxed, and slumped over on its side.

Good and quick, no mess, no fuss ..., Dylan told himself. Nothing like it used to be. He stood up, walked over and pressed two fingertips to the side of the old man's throat. No pulse. Okay. He looked all around the room, put his gun inside his coat and went to work, setting things up.

He picked up the syringe and capped it and put it in his coat pocket. He picked up the unlit cigar from the sofa where the old man had let it fall from his fingers and laid it on the glass tabletop. He pulled the old man forward at the waist and laid him face down on the thick smoke-colored glass beside the cigar. Standing back examining the scene as he set it up, he noted for the first time the heavy smoked glass rested on the palms of two dark metal mermaids. They gazed up at him through the dark smoky glass with brassy smiles, their bare breasts loosely covered by cascading ringlets of hair.

Mermaids ....

He picked up the aluminum medicine container, twisted the top off of it and shook out a few tiny white glycerin tablets atop the table near the dead man's face. He stopped short of placing one of the pills between the man's lips. He didn't need to go that far. He let the container fall from his hand to the floor and looked around again.

Everything looked good. The man was diabetic, had a bad liver, a bad heart, carried glycerin for emergencies. There it was. The man was alone. He'd walked in here feeling bad, sat down on the sofa, even tried to grab for his pills—never made it. End of story.

He pulled the dead man's gun out of his coat pocket and reached out to drop it into the man's bathrobe. But before he turned it loose he heard a sound of music and a shrill pulsing alarm spring to life down the hallway from the master bedroom. Loud, but not too loud.

He froze and listened and waited for a second. *All right. This would work ....* The alarm had gone off after the old man walked in here from the shower, sat down and died. It was believable; leave it alone. Walk away. He clicked back into motion.

But again he stopped short when he heard the music and the alarm suddenly cut off. This was getting worse; he pictured a hand reaching out from the bed, hitting an *off* button. He froze and listened. After a tense moment, he laid the dead man's gun on the glass tabletop above the two mermaids and straightened and looked down the hall. He glanced toward the front door, wanting to reach for the knob. But then he looked back down the hall. No, he had to check it out. Who was there, what had they seen, what did they know?

Taking out his gun from inside his coat, he crept down the hallway, staying close to the wall on his left, keeping his right hand ready, the gun raised. When he got to the half-opened door, he stopped and listened again. Nothing. He opened the door an inch farther, enough to peep in and look back and forth into the wide shadowy bedroom.

In a glow of morning sunlight seeping in from the edge of a drawn curtains he saw a naked young woman stretched out on her back, only the corner of a sheet drawn across her waist. She held a hand outreached to the side, resting on the nightstand near the radio. A thin gold chain bracelet hung from her wrist. Dylan studied her face for a moment, then looked around the room again in the silence. Was she asleep or feigning it? Only one way to know. He eased forward and stood over her and pointed the gun barrel down an inch from her eye.

Everything stayed the same, her breathing, her sleeping expression.

"I know you're awake," he whispered. His voice was barely audible, but loud enough to draw a response from anyone who knew they were about to die. He held his trigger finger poised and ready. But her eyes didn't open. Nothing changed. Not the slightest twitch of nerves, not the slightest change in her breathing. If she was faking, she was the best he'd ever seen. A pointed gun revealed more truth about nerves and breathing than any polygraph.

He backed away.

A few feet away he saw a purse resting on a leather ottoman. He stepped over, picked up the purse and backed away through the door. He closed the door without a sound and went back to the living room.

He rummaged through the purse and pulled out a pearl-blue lady's wallet and opened it. He pulled out a driver's license from inside the soft leather and looked at it. *No harm done,* he told himself. She hadn't heard him, hadn't seen him. In a few minutes the alarm would go off again. She'd find the old man here dead. *Good enough ....* Everything still moving along like it should. He compared the face on the driver's license to the sleeping woman in the bedroom.

It was her. *Jill Markley,* he told himself, reading the woman's name and the address of an apartment complex over in Oak Park. He committed the information to memory, shut the wallet and slipped it back down into the purse.

He pictured the place an hour from now, provided she didn't find the man dead and slip out of here. There would be uniformed police in and out, a detective or two. Lots of questions for her, a coroner. *Enjoy your day, Jill Markley ...,* he said to himself.

He left the apartment and boarded the elevator without looking around. The desk outside the apartment door would remain unoccupied for another few minutes. *Plenty of time ....*

Outside in the chilled morning air, he walked a block and turned off the street into an alley. He stuffed the hat down into a full dumpster, dropped the small syringe into some debris on the ground and crushed it underfoot. He took off the wig and carried it inside his coat. He walked back out and along the sidewalk going over what had happened.

The girl being there wasn't his fault. The old man was supposed to be there alone. Whoever had set this up would have to explain how they'd overlooked the woman. For his part, he'd handled it the right way, he thought, still walking. Nobody had died who wasn't supposed to die. That meant a lot.

Three blocks farther, he dumped the wig and he pulled a knit skull cap from his coat and put it on. Another block, he stood in another alley, unscrewed the silencer from the gun barrel and dropped both pieces onto a sewer grate at the edge of a curbing. He actually could have kept the gun and silencer, since he hadn't used them. *But no* .... He scooted them both into the sewer with the toe of his shoe.

That part's over ....

He took a deep breath and walked a block farther, to where he'd left the car. He got in the late model Ford, started it and drove away. Two miles along the parkway, he pulled off and drove down an exit ramp. A moment later he pulled into a sprawling motel parking lot where he left the Ford with the key lying under the front seat. He left the parking lot in a black Lexus he'd rented in Atlanta under an assumed name. At no time did he look up at the cameras mounted on the edge of the brick building. Cameras were everywhere these days. You had to live with them, give them as little as you could.

Pulling away from the lot he took off his gloves and shoved them back under his seat. He would leave them there until he crossed water somewhere. The lake, the canal. He didn't care. He'd pitch them out without stopping, not even slowing down. He was done here.

Next stop Atlanta ..., he told himself, then south in his own car, back down to the Gulf. Back home— *Get out of this cold ....* He relaxed behind the wheel and headed south out of town.

CHAPTER THREE

Two days later:
Hernando Beach, Florida:
Temperature 81 degrees:

On Sami Bloom's lanai, overlooking the Gulf of Mexico, Sami and Ray Dylan watched a red sun sink into the gulf. They lay half-entwined in a rope lounge hammock drinking vodka tonics, Ray with his eyes half-closed, still a little weary from the road.

"Welcome home, Ray," Sami whispered, even though he'd been there with her most of the afternoon. Much of that afternoon they'd spent in her bedroom just inside the sliding doors behind them. She lay with her head on his chest.

"Um-hmm," Dylan nodded. "Good to be back. Anything going on around here?"

"No, not really," Sami said. Then she said, "Oh, Henry Silky, my pool man scared the bejesus out of me the other day. He was here cleaning the pool, 5:30 in the morning. It was still dark out. I heard a noise, went to see about it—walked into him coming around the side of the house before I saw his truck back there."

"What were you doing up at 5:30?" Dylan asked.

"I just told you, I heard a noise," Sami said. "Anyway, he told me he thought I was out of town, like that made it okay." She shook her head. "Poor Henry, I know he's old, and he needs the business. But sometimes …." She let her words trail for interpretation.

Dylan smiled.

"I've heard this one," he said. "You can't get rid of him, because he and Sidney had an exclusive agreement for years."

"It's true. Silky Pool Service wouldn't exist if it hadn't been for Sidney. Henry's been coming here for years, like clockwork." She breathed out a sigh of resolve and changed the subject.

"So, how was Sarasota?" She asked. He'd told her he was driving down to Sarasota to check on the sale of a property he owned there. The less she knew about his work the better.

"Warm and busy," he said.

"How do you like the new agent?" she asked.

"He's okay."

"He …?" Sami looked at him. "I thought you said the agent's a woman."

"I meant she," Dylan corrected. "She's okay. Very efficient, seems like. She and her husband work together—both brokers, that's why I said he."

"Do they have names?"

Dylan detected a tone.

"Diane and Max Foster," he came back quickly. "She's the listing agent. Her husband brought in the buyer."

"What're they like, the Fosters?" Sami asked.

"Max is easygoing, a quiet guy," said Dylan. "His wife is all real estate. Long nails, big rings and coffee jitters. Pushy."

"But she brought you an offer fairly quick."

"That she did. I'm happy," Dylan said.

"So, the place sold and you're through dealing with it?" Sami said.

"Yes, I should be." Then he said, "I might have to go back for the closing in a couple of weeks. Depends on how things go." He let his eyes close more. "Did you miss me?"

"Yes," Sami said. "I've gotten used to us being together."

"Me too, I like it." Dylan smiled a little. "I thought about you, about back when you were a mermaid."

"You realize I wasn't *really* a mermaid, right?"

"No kidding?" He gave a faint smile.

"Really though, I'm flattered," Sami said. "Thank you for thinking of me."

"My pleasure," Dylan said, his eyes closed now.

A quiet moment passed while Sami drew little circles on his chest. Dylan's chest was still a little damp from earlier in the pool, and from the shower moments ago.

"I've been thinking, Ray …." She let her words trail. There was more coming; he waited for it. "Will you teach me to shoot a gun?" she asked.

Dylan cocked his head a little.

"That depends. Who are you going to shoot, Henry Silky some morning?" he asked.

"I'm serious." She gave him a friendly little slap

on his chest. "Will you? It's something I think I should know how to do, the way things are these days. What could I do if someone forced their way in here?"

"Call me …?" Dylan smiled, still playing it light. "I'll come over and shoot them for you?"

"It's not a joke, Ray," Sami persisted. "What if that wasn't Henry the other day, but some creep? What if you're *out of town?*"

There it was. Ray liked the slightest pout she put in her tone. It was something about him not asking her along on his made-up trip to Sarasota, he told himself.

"If I'd asked you to go with me, would you have gone?"

"No, probably not," said Sami. "But it's always nice to be invited."

"Next time then, I promise," Dylan said.

"Anyway, we could go to the gun range out off nineteen," she went on. "You could teach me. We could go tomorrow, make a day of it. I mean if you're rested up."

He considered it. She wasn't going to let up.

"You mean it …?" He looked at her, swirled his glass of Ketel One, ice and tonic.

"Yes, of course I *mean it.*" She gave a push on his side. "Why would I say it if I didn't mean it?"

"Sorry," he said. He collected himself. "Sure, I'll teach you how to *fire a gun.* But you know they'll have instructors there who do that sort of thing—"

"No, I want you to teach me," she said, cutting him off. "I trust you, somebody I know. I don't want some stranger behind me, up against me. I've seen how they do."

"On television?" he said.

She smiled.

"Golf lessons, years ago. But that's what these *instructors* do, isn't it? Always trying to cop a feel, as they say?"

Cop a feel ...?

"I don't know, I've never *instructed* anybody," Dylan said. "But maybe I should. You make it sound interesting."

"Anyway, I'd rather you teach me," she said. "I know you carry a gun."

"Everybody in Florida carries a gun," Ray said wryly. "It's a state law."

"Sidney once told me you were in law enforcement a long time ago. Said you were some kind of undercover cop?"

Undercover cop ... He gave it a thought before answering.

"No," he said, "I was nothing like that. Sidney was mistaken."

Sami pondered the matter for a moment, a finger to her lip. "Of course, he once told me he thought you were a hit man."

Dylan stared at her, bemused.

"Jesus, Sidney said that? About me?"

"He did," Sami said. But then she played it off. "Later he took it back. He said he shouldn't have told me. Said he didn't know why he'd ever thought it in the first place."

"Man ...." Dylan shook his head. Then he said, "Okay, I spent some time in *law enforcement* a long time ago. I wasn't cut out for it. I never talked much about it back then." He smiled a little. "Who cares anyway?"

"I do," she said. "I can understand you didn't talk about it back then, if you worked undercover," she said. "But you can talk about it now, can't you?"

"I'd as soon not," he said, liking the way he was handling this, neither confirming nor denying a thing.

"You *did* carry a gun, though, all those years back then?" She kept at it.

"I did carry a gun back then." Dylan answered as if admitting to something pressed upon him. "I still keep one in the car."

Sami smiled coyly.

"You still know how to point it, aim it, and all that?"

"Yes, I can do all that," he said. Again he relaxed, sipped his vodka.

"Wow, that was like pulling teeth for you, Ray," she quipped. She returned his smile. "Can we do it then? Tomorrow, if you've got nothing else planned?"

Dylan thought about it again, gave a slight shrug.

"We'd have to get you some ear plugs, a gun to use—maybe a range rental."

He figured the next thing, she was going ask to use his gun. She'd seen the big .45 semiautomatic once when she'd opened the console in his Buick. He was ready for her: The .45 was too much gun for her, too big for her hand, too heavy, had too much recoil ….

But Sami didn't ask.

"I've bought one, a brand new one," she said, sounding excited at the prospect. "I picked it up the other day at the gun store on Cortez. Want to see it?" She was up from the hammock swinging a gauzy beach robe around her before Dylan could answer. "Don't move," she said, "I'll be right back." She walked away into the shadowy house, evening sunlight turning her loose.

Dylan stood up and slipped into his trousers and sat down in a cushioned aluminum chair and raked his fingers back through his hair. He hiked the chair around from facing out onto the gulf and sat half-facing the lanai sliders as she came walking back, a black and gray gun case in her hands.

She laid the case in front of him on the glass tabletop and opened it.

"Nice," he said. He looked at a compact two-tone stainless and black Sig Sauer .380, lying in a hard foam rubber bed. An extra stainless steel magazine lay beside it. "But you didn't have to go buy a gun."

"You mean I could have used yours?" she said, as if she'd read his thoughts. "I was afraid it might be too much gun for me to handle, starting out."

He just looked at her.

"Anyway," she went on, "You said it's nice. *Nice, how?*" She stood with a hand parked lightly on her hip.

"What do you mean, *nice how?*" Dylan countered. He picked up the gun, dropped its empty magazine clip into his hand and racked the slide, pinned it back and checked it. The gun chamber wasn't loaded; it appeared to have never been fired.

"I mean is it nice and *chic?* Nice and *accurate?* What?" she asked. "Did I do well, choosing it?"

"A Sig Sauer is a good choice. A little expensive maybe. As far as *accurate,* you won't know until you've shot it." Dylan said. "As far as it being *chic,* I've never heard anybody describe a gun that way." He smiled a little.

He turned the compact .380 on his palm, inspecting it, hefting it, judging its weight. It was a handsome gun, he had to admit—a little small for his hand, about right for hers, and a nice backup either way. "How does it feel to you?" He looked up at her.

"It's a good fit," she said. "It feels comfortable." She held her hand out and he laid the pistol in it. She gripped it a little tight, then loosely; but she kept her finger on the trigger.

Dylan said, "It's a good habit to keep your finger off the trigger unless you're getting ready to fire."

"Why?" she asked. "It's not loaded, is it?"

Jesus ....

He gave her a look. "You have to ask?"

"Oh—" She got it. She smiled and took her finger out of the trigger guard and let the gun lay on her palm, the tip of the barrel pointed loosely at him. He reached out turned the barrel away from him.

"Well, anyway," she shrugged, "it's just the two of us here."

"Right," Dylan said, "so odds are if you accidently shot somebody it would only be me … or yourself."

She sighed a little and handed him the gun.

"See? I do need someone to teach me."

"We'll go tomorrow, if you want," Dylan said. He shoved the empty magazine back into the .380. He laid the pistol inside the case down in its hard rubber bed and closed the lid.

Sami slipped into a chair beside him.

"Is it the right caliber? The fellow at the store said for personal protection, it is."

"It'll do," Dylan said. "It doesn't have the knockdown power of a .40 or a .45 caliber, but I wouldn't want to get shot with it."

"Ted said some cops carry the .380 for backup," Sami said.

"*Ted ...?*" said Dylan.

"Ted, the fellow at the gun store," Sami said.

"Ted." Dylan nodded; he considered it and said, "He's right, some cops probably do." He gestured at the Sig Sauer. "But this would be an expensive backup. "For less money, you can get a compact .40 caliber that gives a harder punch. Cops like .40s."

"If you were a cop today, what would you carry?" Sami asked.

"A cop *today?*" Dylan said. "I'd carry a flame-thrower, maybe hand grenades."

"I mean it, Ray," she said. "I'm trying to understand all this. I want to be able to take care of myself—in case I ever need to."

"I know," Dylan said, getting more serious. "Police need something that can take a person down, quick. A backup for emergencies, in case something happens to their regular sidearm." He stopped and looked at her, and said, "Sami, is everything all right?"

"Yes, of course," she said, "why wouldn't it be?" Dylan let it go.

"No reason," he said. "We'll go to the range tomorrow, see how it goes. Florida has some rules you need to know if you're going to go heeled. Keep you out of trouble."

"*Heeled ...?*" she smiled. "Now there's an old term I haven't heard in a long while. Anyway, I'm not going to go *heeled.* I just want to keep a gun around the house. Know how to protect myself."

"Got it," Dylan said. "I've been watching too many Turner Classics," he said. "Still, if you're going to own a gun you need to know the Florida gun laws—to protect yourself." He looked at her again. "Are you sure everything's all right?"

"Everything's *fine*, Ray, I promise," she said; but he wasn't convinced. Women like Sami Bloom weren't usually interested in guns. *Unless something happened that caused them to be,* he told himself.

He'd see.

(HAPTER FOUR

Ray Dylan had met Sami Bloom back when she and Sidney Augio were together. This was back in the eighties. Back then she'd been a hostess at the Kapok Tree, a huge upscale restaurant and nightspot on the highway coming up out of Clearwater. Before the Kapok Tree she'd been a mermaid in Weeki Wachee. There's where she got the legs, he figured. All that swimming, underwater acrobatics, her twenty-one, twenty-two at the time. He pictured the bronze mermaids he'd seen in the dead man's apartment holding up the smoked glass tabletop. Their hair, their brassy bare breasts, that was Sami.

He let the image go and eased the silver-gray Buick along the Suncoast Parkway just over the speed limit. And he pictured Sami back then, in her mermaid days. She looked good now, *real good*. But back then hosting at the Kapok, wearing a long black evening dress showing the right amount of thigh up one side, a nice white flower in her hair. *Jesus ... What a looker. Still is ....*

He cruised under a perfect Florida sky.

Of course once Sami had hooked up with Sidney Augio her hostess days were done. Sidney was connected high up in the Outfit. Connected, but never what Dylan would call a wise guy, or anything close. He was a financier—a money man. He'd come from big French-Canadian money, and for three generations the Augios had made an art form out of sliding large chunks of their money around without it being seen. Their pockets were so deep, the leaders of the Outfit went to them on a moment's notice and got straightened out between the peaks and valleys that came with this line of work. By the time the Augio money passed down to Sidney, he wouldn't have had to deal with the kind of people he dealt with.

So why did he? Who knew? Some people had to get their action off the grid, Dylan figured. All he knew was that everything Sidney Augio did, he did it with Detroit, Toronto and the Chicago Outfit's blessings. Money he put out always came back, just like it should.

Dylan and Sidney Augio had known each other from a respectable distance. They knew what each other did, sort of; they knew the same people, heard things through the same grapevine. But they'd traveled in different circles, Sidney way up there at a higher level. He'd worked and played where big money worked and played. Ray Dylan? Well. He wasn't exactly a grunt. He'd gone his own way and done all right for himself, he thought. He considered it as he put the Buick into the exit lane and came down off the Sun Coast onto Cortez Boulevard. He was still alive, that had to be worth something.

Sidney Augio? Sid was dead, had been two years

now, Dylan reminded himself, cruising through light traffic along Cortez headed west toward the homes along the water. Outside of his will which directed the bulk of his estate to his wife and children, Sidney Augio had made discreet arrangements for Sami to be taken care of, off the books so to speak. He'd seen to it she got the summer place they'd shared all those years on the Gulf near Weeki Wachee; and he'd left her plenty of cash—*unreported cash,* both Canadian and US. Dylan never knew exactly how much money Sami had been bequeathed. For the most part he wasn't even curious. Nothing between them was about money. *That made it nice,* he thought.

The two of them had hooked up when a good friend and *associate* of Dylan's in Chicago, Phil Rodell, had asked Dylan to look in on Sami—*you know, see she's doing okay, make it look coincidental.* Dylan had been happy to do so. He arranged to run into Sami *coincidentally* at a shopping mall the following week. This was around four months after Augio's death, and Ray could tell Sami had already been alone too long—not that she would have had to be, a woman like her. She was paying respect to Sidney, which Ray thought was classy.

Being asked to check in on her, Ray Dylan saw an opening for himself. To be honest he'd always had a thing for Sami. He knew if he was going to make a move he'd better make it. So he did; and now, here they were. How was that for luck? He smiled to himself.

"She's okay then, the mermaid?" Phil Rodell had asked him on the phone a week later, when he'd called it in.

"Seems okay," Dylan replied. "We talked a few minutes." He'd listened close, wondering why all the interest in the *deceased* Sidney Augio's girlfriend.

"Doesn't need anything?"

"Not that I could tell," said Dylan. "I didn't come out and ask."

"No, of course not," said Rodell. "Just wanted you to check. Sid Augio was thought of highly by some of us—a friend of mine you could say."

"I hear you," Dylan had said, and maybe that was all there was to it. "You want me to check again, a few weeks?"

The phone went quiet for a second.

"No, that's enough," Phil said.

"The thing is," Dylan said, making it up now, "We're meeting for coffee, her and I. Is that a problem? If it is …." He let his words trail.

Again the silent phone.

Phil finally said, "Go ahead, have coffee the two of yas. Enjoy yourselves."

And that was that ….

Ten minutes down Cortez Boulevard Ray steered the Buick off the main road and out toward the water. Two rights and a left later he eased onto Sami's driveway. He turned the car off, got out and walked to the front door thinking back to a year ago when they'd started seeing each other for more than a dinner date now and then.

"As far as any serious commitment," she'd told him one night, the two of them dancing slow and close in a little jazz restaurant over in Hernando Beach, "I want to be honest with you, Ray, it's not going to happen. We have needs, desires. I want to enjoy your company, I want us to enjoy *each other*." She'd smiled. "For me that's as far as it's going to go." They swayed as she talked, Dylan liking the feel of his hand there on the small of her back.

Granted, the dance floor was not the time or place to be having that conversation, but that's how it went, and it fit just right, he thought. He had listened, and nodded, and listened and nodded some more, until she finished her say on the matter and came in closer and rested her cheek against his shoulder.

"What do you think, Ray?" she'd whispered. "Do you agree?"

"I *hear you*, Sami," he'd said close to her ear. "I couldn't agree more ...."

After a cup of coffee and a cinnamon Danish, they were headed out Commercial Way, north to the gun range, Sami's brand new gun, box and all in a Macy's shopping bag in the trunk. A box of ammunition Dylan had picked up lay beside it.

"I got standard range loads," Ray said, maneuvering the Buick along in the morning traffic.

"Range loads?" She just looked at him.

"Practice bullets," Dylan said. "If this all works out we can get you something with a little more punch."

"You think I'm not going to stick with this, don't you?" Sami asked. She sounded a little defensive.

"That's not it," Ray said. "Some people carry range ammunition all the time. I'm saying there's plenty of options the kind of bullets you want to carry." He looked at her. "Nervous, huh?"

She sighed, relaxed, gazed straight ahead.

"A little, I suppose …." She paused then said, "I was thinking about what you said last night—*knockdown* power?" She shook her head. "I can't believe we were talking about what bullet most effectively kills a human being."

"That's the nature of shooting, Sami." He gave her a sidelong look as he drove. "You don't have to get into all this," he said quietly, watching the road ahead. "I can turn around here, take us back—"

"No." She cut him off. "I'm going to do it, Ray. It just takes some getting used to—terms like *knockdown*."

"*Stopping power's* a better word for you," Ray said. He offered a thin smile. "Want some history?"

"Sure." She continued gazing straight ahead.

"In the early 1900s, US troops used the old tried and true .38 caliber pistols, fighting the Moro in the Philippines. The Moro would get hit by the .38 sometimes two or three times and keep on fighting. They kept killing American soldiers before they finally bled out."

Sami listened, staring straight ahead.

Ray went on, "So the Americans decided on the .45 caliber, a bigger round—a heavier powder load, something that would knock a person off their feet, leave them down and out."

"*Knockdown power …,*" Sami deduced.

"After the war, police officers wanted to carry the big .45 but their departments wouldn't allow it," Ray said.

"Oh?" she said, looking around at him.

"Because of innocent bystanders," Ray put in. "Local and state governments figured with any caliber bigger, more powerful than a .38 special, if a cop missed hitting their target they could end up killing an innocent person a few blocks away. Finally everybody compromised, went with the .357 magnum once it got popular. There's more to it, but this is it in a nutshell."

"I see," she said stiffly, clearly uncomfortable with the subject matter.

"Not a very pleasant conversation, is it?" he said.

"No, it's not," Sami replied without hesitation.

"But if you're stepping into the world of shooting for personal protection, I think you need to know the terrain, okay?" Ray studied her expression as he drove.

Sami sat quiet for a moment. Then she sighed silently and took on a resolved look and said, "Okay, you're right. Tell me more. Why is it today's police can carry the larger caliber guns? Do innocent bystanders not rate as highly as they used to?"

"That's a good question," Ray said quietly. "I don't know the answer." He gave a glance into his rearview mirror and drove on.

A moment later he said, "I suppose the feeling is, if John Q Public, as well as all the hoods and crazies can carry the big stuff why can't I, if I'm a cop? That's how I would look at it anyway."

"Makes sense," Sami said. She let the conversation go. Looking away she idly watched the roadside where cabbage palms swayed and wild palmetto crowded in close around runaway oak, pine and cherry laurel. As the foliage streaked by she watched a pair of sand cranes, one of them bent and picking at the concrete's edge while the other appeared to keep watch.

"They say when those birds mate, it's for life," Dylan said, glancing away from the road for a second.

"You see them, they're always together. You see one by itself, it means something has happened to its mate."

"I've heard that," Sami said. "It's sad, or I should say, bittersweet."

Ray saw her continue to gaze out at the passing roadside after the cranes were out of sight. He reached over and pressed a hand on her knee.

"Hey, Lady, I didn't say it to spoil your day," he said. "Who knows, maybe you see one by itself it means they just had a fight, they'll make up later."

Sami looked around and smiled and laid her hand over his.

"I like that much better," she said. She relaxed and watched him turn his attention back to the road ahead. She was comfortable around Ray Dylan. *No, wait* …, she reminded herself. She was more than *comfortable* with him. She liked him … she liked him a lot.

(HAPTER FIVE

A range officer had called a fifteen minute break in the firing when Sami and Dylan walked down from the Buick, Sami with her gun case in hand. Standing back a few feet from the firing line, the waiting shooters eyed Sami. Not disrespectfully, and not that they weren't used to seeing women at the range, just that Sami had the kind of poise and good looks that drew attention wherever she went. Even with some mileage starting to show, she still turned heads. The looks and all the attention from other men were things Ray had resolved himself to dealing with. Sami handled it well; she'd had a lifetime of getting used to it. If she was cool with it, so had he better be.

Besides, moments later after they'd gotten set up and he stood behind her, his arms forward around her, the two of them close together, so what if they got looked at a little now and then. Sami Bloom looked as good in her designer jeans as any woman half her age.

Well, almost as good ....

Anyway, this thing between them was not all about looks. Ray cared about more than her appearance.

He liked her company, the touch of her, the way she made him feel.

Stop it, pay attention ..., he told himself.

Standing behind her, against her, he reached out around her and raised her hands and adjusted her left hand down farther, cupped under her right, letting the Sig rest on her palm.

"Remember what I told you?" he said quietly. "If you hold both hands wrapped around the gun, when you fire it the slide will come back over your left thumb—cut it, if you're not careful." He spoke with his face up close to her ear, feeling her hair soft against his cheek.

"Oh, I did it again," she said, hearing him through her orange earplugs.

"But you're learning," he said, encouraging her. "Lay your left palm out flat, until you start remembering." He adjusted her left hand just right. "Then rest your gun hand down on your open palm, like this." He liked having his arms round her this way.

"Okay, I've got it," Sami said.

"I should have been an instructor all my life," he whispered.

"See? I told you this could be fun," she whispered back.

Ray took a breath and got serious. He let his arms down slowly.

"All right, stay that way, take aim." He watched her focus down the three white dot gun sights. "Now let out a breath, hold it. Let the sights sit steady, squeeze the trigger. Let the shot come as a surprise."

Following his advice as he gave it, Ray heard the shot explode as his words left his mouth. The compact pistol gave a slight buck in her hands.

"Go again," he said, before she had time to let down and get out of position.

She caught herself, steadied the gun out at arm's length. Ray smiled watching her.

When the gun fired again, he could see she'd held herself steady, not jerked her hand anticipating the shot.

"Good," Ray said, "now reach your right thumb up, set the safety and let the gun down in front of you with both hands."

She did, holding the gun out above the top of the shooting stand in front of them. Up and down the range guns fired sporadically. Ray reached around her and picked up the small pair of binoculars he'd laid on the wooden stand. At range this close the binoculars were for convenience rather than necessity.

"How did I do?" Sami asked, watching him look out at the two paper targets hanging side by side. She'd fired at the target on the right.

"Not bad," Ray said. "One shot is almost dead center, the other is only a few inches off." He lowered the binoculars and held them at his side. "Either way, you hit your target both shots."

"Let me see," Sami said. She started to lay the gun down.

"Not yet," Ray said. "You've got four more rounds before you empty the clip. I want to teach you what's called a *double tap*."

"Sounds like a dance step," Sami said.

"Now who's fooling around?" Ray said.

"All right, I'm ready," Sami said. She raised the gun in both hands.

"You're going to do everything like before," Ray said, "only this time, instead of making one shot, make two, one right behind the other."

"A double tap," Sami said, getting it.

"Yes," Ray said. "In a self-defense situation, think of the second shot as *insurance*. The trick is to keep your hand perfectly steady. Two shots. Don't hesitate, don't think about it. Just squeeze the trigger back twice instead of once. Keep your arm steady."

He watched; she took aim. When she made the two shots, he noted a slight hesitancy, but not a lot. She sighed and let the gun down with both hands.

"Put the safety on," Ray said. "Get in a habit of doing it every time you lower the gun, unless you're in a *situation*."

Sami set the safety switch on. Ray stood looking at the target through the binoculars.

"How bad was that?" she asked, looking toward the target on the right.

"Not bad for the first time," Ray said. "Your first shot was only off-center a couple of inches. The second went a little wild on you."

"It's harder than it sounds," Sami said.

"If it was easy you wouldn't have to practice." Ray reached over and laid the binoculars on the stand. "Let's try it again."

"Here," Sami said, "you show me." She held the gun over to him with the barrel pointed down range.

"This is all for you, Sami." Dylan glanced back and forth along the line of shooters. He held his hand out as if to keep her from handing him the gun.

"Please, Ray," she said. "Watching you shoot

before I started helped me see how to stand and aim." She smiled and coaxed. "Come on, just one little *double tap* …?"

Ray took the gun and stepped over behind the stand as she stepped aside and picked up the binoculars.

"Ready?" he asked. He gave another guarded glance along the shooters, then raised the gun arm's length, one-handed.

"Yes, ready," she said, binoculars half-raised. Noting his left hand at his side, she said, "But aren't you going to—" Her words stopped short at the sound of two sudden bursts of gunfire from the pistol. "—use both hands?" she finished, staring at him.

Ray glanced back and forth again as he dropped the empty magazine from the gun and laid both pistol and magazine on the stand.

"There you are," he said. "I'll watch while you reload this time."

But Sami had raised the binoculars to her eyes and stood gazing at the paper target on the left.

"Don't you want to know how you did?" she asked sidelong.

"Okay," Ray said, "how did I do?"

"One hit and one miss," Sami said. She lowered the binoculars a little. "Sorry," she said.

"Look again," Ray said. "See if the bullet hole is a little lopsided."

"Lopsided …?" She put the binoculars back to her eyes. "How can it be lopsided?" She paused, then said, "Wait, *actually* it is lopsided."

"That's what I thought," Ray said. He turned to the box of bullets and started picking out six of them.

"You mean …?" Sami let her words trail. "You hit the target in the same spot both shots?"

"Not exactly the same spot," he said. "That's why the hole looks lopsided." Ray gave her a short smile and laid the bullets on the stand beside the gun and magazine.

"But still …." Sami gave him a look. "That was *good* shooting, Ray," she said, impressed.

"Thanks," he said matter-of-factly, dismissing the matter. "Want to reload, the way I showed you?"

But Sami wouldn't let it go. She stood staring, surprised and impressed at what she'd seen.

"Does *everybody* shoot as well as you do?" She glanced along the row of targets as if checking everyone's aim.

"I hope not," he said wryly, taking a step back out of her way. He gestured a hand toward the bullets.

A whistle blew. Sami stood a moment longer, still staring as along the line of shooters, guns fell silent. Some shooters took off head gear; some took out ear plugs. They laid down their guns and stepped back behind a white line on the concrete deck.

"Now we step back away from the gun," Ray instructed her, nodding down at a white line on the concrete deck behind them. "Range safety rule," he added. "The firing will shut down for fifteen minutes."

Sami stepped back with him, leaving the bullets, the Sig and its magazine still lying on the wooden stand. Quiet ensued along the line of shooters. Some of them walking out to their targets to inspect and replace them.

"Okay …," she said with in a determined tone, "I want to be able to shoot a gun the way you do, Ray," she said. "Think I can get there, I mean with practice?"

Dylan looked at her. No matter how casually she played it, he still saw a trace of tension, a masked urgency in her cool blue eyes. But he wasn't going to ask her again if anything was wrong.

"Sure, with practice," he said. "Anyway, I'm just fair. I'm not *all that*." He smiled, looked her up and down, always liking to look at her—at times finding it hard to take his eyes off her.

Be cool ..., he warned himself. If something *was wrong*, she didn't want to tell him; and if this was how she wanted to play it he wasn't going to push the matter. For now, he would stay back, give her room, wait, watch, listen. Sami liked being in charge of her own life. That was fine by him. *Play it her way ....*

"When do you practice, Ray?" she asked.

"I don't," said Dylan, "Not anymore. I used to practice a lot. Not so much these days." He gave a half shrug. "Looks like it stuck with me."

"What, it's like riding a bicycle to you?" She gave him a flat look from above the edge of her shooter's glasses. "Once you know how you never forget?" As she spoke she started reloading the Sig's magazine.

"Something like that," Dylan said, watching her.

She saw a slight darkness come and go on his brow. Not much, just a trace, and only for a second. Then it was gone. She shook her head a little and adjusted the shooter's glasses up on the bridge of her nose as she worked pressing fresh rounds into the gun's magazine.

"Sometimes I don't know about you, Ray," she said.

Dylan smiled back.

(HAPTER SIX

Just before dark, Sami Bloom awakened to the sound of the doorbell. She had heard the bell on its first ring and stood up from the bed where she'd lay dozing after a long day at the firing range. The bell rang again, and continued to ring insistently as she stooped and pulled the Macy's bag from under her bed and gave a quick look inside. She stood and took a deep breath and walked from the bedroom through the house.

All right, I'm coming .... But the bell continued its monotonous *ding-dong*. "Okay, *okay* ...," she whispered. She stopped at the front door and gave a quick look through the peephole. Okay, it was the two of them, just as she'd suspected. They stood looking oval and penguin-like, distorted through the small rounded glass. The tall swarthy white man stood nearest the door, his dyed black hair stiff with mousse and spiked straight up atop a long bony face.

Sidney's brother ...? Christ there was nothing there that reminded her of Sidney Augio. *Nothing in any way* ....

Beside Aaron Augio a big black man stepped forward. His face grew more huge, more rounded as he tried staring back at her through the peephole. As his face blocked out any light, his big knuckles rapped on the storm door frame. It sounded like he would break the door down any second and simply walk on in through a tangle of twisted aluminum and broken wood.

"I know you're in there, Sa-*mantha*," the white man said in a mock tone. "We saw your shadow."

Of course she was in here. Where else would she be …? She wasn't trying to hide. She'd been expecting them any day now. She wanted to get this over with. She turned the deadbolt and knob and opened the door a few inches, no intention of letting them inside. Yet, before she could stop them, the big black man had stepped around her and stood looking all around the room, checking it, the same as he'd done on their first visit the week before. Aaron Augio stepped inside, pushed a pair of knockoff sunglasses up over his forehead and closed the door behind himself.

"See, K," he said smiling; he reached back and locked the deadbolt. "I told you this lady wouldn't disappoint us." He glanced at the Macy's bag. He said to Sami, "You remember my accountant *slash* bodyguard, Kireem, from last week?"

Of course she remembered the big powerful-looking black man. She remembered how he'd stood too close to her. How he'd towered over her, gave her a threatening look when she'd demanded them to leave her house. She didn't reply; instead she gestured toward the bag she'd laid on the chair.

"There it is, twenty thousand dollars. Half in

hundreds, the rest in twenties and fifties, just like you said."

"Excellent," said Augio. "Count it, K." He nodded at the Macy's bag.

"Count it?" K just looked at him, not seeming to like the idea.

"*Yes*, count it," Augio repeated.

Kireem gave him a sour look. But he took a step forward, pointed a thick finger down at the bag and said, "One …."

The two stared at each other for a second. Sometimes Augio couldn't tell if Kireem was serious or just getting over on him for the hell of it.

"Damn it, K," he said after a second, "I meant, count the money. Take it out of the bag and count it."

"Oh," K said, with the same flat stare.

"It's all there," Sami cut in. "It would be stupid to try and short you. What would it solve?"

"That's right, it would be stupid," Augio said, the amiable smile gone from his face. He watched Kireem pick up the Macy's bag and look down into it and run a hand down inside. "It would also be stupid for you to think I'm going to settle for twenty thousand dollars when I have it on solid sources that ole Brother Sidney left you *so much*."

"But you gave me your word this twenty thousand would square things—*straighten you out*, as you said," Sami replied, not really surprised that he was reneging now that he'd gotten a taste of the money.

"This does *straighten me out*, Samantha," he grinned. "But something's come up. I need money fast. We're going to have to call this a get-acquainted offer." He looked at the big black man tallying up the money in the shopping bag. Seeing Kireem engrossed in his efforts, he looked back at Sami, stepped in closer. "You and me being family of sorts, I've got a proposition for you. A sweet deal I'm cutting you in on."

Family of sorts. A sweet deal ...?

Sami stood tensed, listening. She thought about the Sig Sauer, in its box, in a closet, in her bedroom. *Forget that,* she told herself.

"I've got a thing I'm working on," Augio continued, "call it a short term *high-yield* investment opportunity." He looked down at her, lifted her chin on his finger. "Look at me, *Samantha*."

She stared up at him.

"You're going to go draw out a hundred and fifty bucks and lend it to me. Ten days later I'm going to pay it back, plus I'm going to give you ... let's say, an extra *fifty bucks* for your trouble." He grinned.

Sami looked confused.

"A hundred and fifty bucks?" she said. "What you mean is—"

"*Thousands*, sweetheart," Augio said, making sure she understood. He bobbed her head a little on his fingertip.

"Hunh-uh." she said, jerking her chin from his finger. "I don't have that kind of money! I barely had this much money available." She gestured toward the shopping bag, Kireem still rooting through the cash.

"Key word there is *available*, sweetheart," Augio said.

He'd gone from Samantha to sweetheart; Sami didn't like that at all. She knew the steps, knew where he was headed.

"I know that kind of money's not laying somewhere in a deposit box," he said. "Sidney would roll over in his grave. I figure he set that money up, put it to work *legally* somewhere, mutual funds, money market." He smiled close in, tapped a finger on the center of her breast bone. "That's why you've got seven days to free it up and get it to me."

She looked down at his finger on her chest. That was twice now he'd touched her. *Forced familiarity* .... She wasn't letting him go there. She shoved his finger away, stepped in the other direction and glared at him.

"Keep your hands off me," she said coldly. Then she said in the same tone, "It *legally* takes *ten days*. Whoever gives you your information should have told you that."

Augio paused, took a patient breath, his finger poised, suspended for a moment. Okay, she could get a little fiery—he didn't mind, he kind of liked it. He could see why Sidney kept this one warming on the sideboard. *She had some mileage,* he told himself, *but she carried it well.* He'd noted that the first time he'd seen her.

"Okay ... I'm giving you ten days then," he said, "what's three more days among family?" Again the smile. She got it. He was after money, but this tough talk was tuning him up—push a woman around a little, force her without actually forcing her. *What a son of a bitch.*

Sami stared, studying him. She decided she had gained herself some footing for shoving him away like that, giving him a cold shoulder. She needed to play on it, see what else she might gain.

"Let me get this straight ...," she said, the tone not as cold now, just chilled, critical. "You extort me out of twenty thousand dollars—twenty *bucks* as you call it. Now you want to '*borrow*' a hundred and fifty thousand?"

"See how fast you caught onto that," Augio said. *The smile.* "I'm thinking, once we get this deal done, you see the kind of partner I am, maybe I cut you in on some other things I've got going."

Partners now ....

Sami stared at him. She'd stood her ground for the time being. But nothing was ever going to be enough for this man. As far as him ever paying her back a cent of this *loan*, she could forget it. She looked at the big black man as he looked up from the shopping bag.

"So? Are we good there, K?" Augio asked.

"Yeah, we're good," said Kireem. He folded the bag down and handed it to him. Augio took it and clamped it up under his arm. He looked at Sami, pointed a finger at her as he moved back toward the door.

"Ten days, sweetheart," he said.

Back to sweetheart ....

Sami only stared, gave a short nod, and watched Kireem also back away and follow Augio out the door. When the door shut behind them, she leaped forward, locked it and set the safety chain.

Oh my God ...!

She turned around and sank back against the door. Her heart raced.

In the grainy evening light, Dylan watched the two men walk out the front door, down past the two queen palms standing on either side of Sami's driveway. They looked out of place among the plush breezy landscape, the thick rich carpet of Saint Augustine grass. They gave Dylan an image of hungry wolves prowling a public playground. No matter the motive, no good could come from their being here.

So, what was this ...? he asked himself, watching from a half block away. He'd slipped his Buick into a spot that allowed him to see Sami's front door without being seen himself. And what about the folded bag up under the white guy's arm? The bag hadn't been there going in. He watched the white guy look back and forth and swing the door open on the passenger side of a maroon Cadillac parked at the bottom of Sami's driveway. He watched the two of them duck down inside and close the car doors.

As the black man backed the car out onto the street, Dylan noted the Quebec license plate. Not unusual for this part of Florida, this time of year. *But snowbirds? These two?* Hunh-uh, the white guy wearing his hair spiked up, shades up above his forehead. The black guy looked like two hundred and thirty pounds of gen-pop chin ups, dead lifts and crunches. Dylan jotted the license number onto a piece of paper and stuck it down into the console, just in case. Starting his car, he gave the Cadillac an extra half a block lead before swinging away from the curb and following it.

He didn't like doing this, he told himself, nosing around, spying on Sami this way. But something was wrong, he knew it. Something had happened while he'd been in Chicago. He'd come back after a week, all of a sudden Sami's got a gun? Wants to learn how to shoot? Oh yeah, something was wrong here, and she wasn't giving it up. So what was he supposed to do?

Inside the Cadillac, Kireem Mateem Murabi, aka Big K, and in a former life also known as Cornell Mayes, glanced up into the rearview mirror and saw the same silver-gray Buick that had fallen in behind them leaving the woman's driveway. He sniffed his nose and closed the plastic bag of blow lying on the console. He folded the bag over and stuffed it into his trouser pocket. He sniffed again and drummed his fingers on his knee.

"We're being followed," he said sidelong, keeping his eyes alternately on the street ahead and the rear mirror overhead.

"*Followed* ...?" Augio said. "We just pulled out." He looked into the mirror outside his window. On the floor between his feet a leather brief case lay open. He quickly finished laying the twenty thousand inside it, shut it and latched it. He flattened the empty shopping bag and stuck it in onto the back floor.

"I can't help we just pulled out," said Kireem. "We're being followed." He arched his back, reached behind him and pulled out a large 10mm semiautomatic, shoved it down between his legs.

"What the hell, K?" said Augio. "I told you, *no guns* on this thing with the woman."

"I know you did," Kireem said. "But this ain't about the thing with the woman." He turned loose of the steering wheel long enough to rack the slide and set the gun on safety. "This is for *just in case* somebody comes following us—like now." He gave Augio a look.

Augio started to say more, but Kireem cut him off.

"Besides, *you're* packing," he said.

Augio just looked at him. Behind them the silver-gray Buick lagged back a ways.

"Yeah, I'm packing. But this is my gig," he said. "I set it up. I hired you to watch my back, remember?" The big man had been referred to him by a Detroit ex-con, Willie Hopps, *Psycho Willie* now living in Tampa Bay. Augio had found himself needing a backup man right away. Hopps had hooked the two up.

"Yeah, I remember," said Kireem, "that's why I'm packing, so's I *can* watch your back."

Augio stared at him. They'd have to talk about this later. He wasn't going to let hired muscle second guess him. *But not now,* he told himself. He cut a glance at the Buick in his side view mirror.

"You sure about this?" he said to Kireem. He wished he'd taken another cut from the bag of coke before Kireem put it away.

"Am I *sure*?" Kireem gave him a sharper sidelong look. "What're you paying me for?" he said.

"All right, check him out," said Augio, "hang a couple of rights and lefts. See if he stays with us."

"I *checked* him out," said Kireem, both hands on the wheel, "he's *following us,* I don't need to see it in writing." A right turn lay fifty feet ahead. "Want me to get rid of him?"

"All right, get rid of him," said Augio. "Just be cool—"

His words cut short; Kireem plunged the gas pedal to the floor, the thrust of it pressing Augio back into his leather seat. His shades flew back off his spiked hair. Tires squalled beneath them ....

A block behind them Dylan's Buick came to a dead stop. He sat watching the big sedan curve away around the corner, screaming in a cloud of smoke and rubber. *Jesus* .... The Cadillac dipped heavily on its right two wheels, then leveled and straightened and shot forward two hundred feet and made another scorching right turn.

Dylan sat listening as the big car roared out of sight. A few seconds passed; he heard tires screeching again, around another turn, the sound growing distant now. In a driveway he saw a woman and her Toy Poodle standing beside a mailbox in a waft of black rubber smoke. The little dog bounced straight up and down on its leash in a barking frenzy.

Okay ..., Dylan thought, not feeling so bad now about coming over here, cruising the neighborhood some. He had no idea what was going on here with Sami, but after what he'd just seen he was going to find out. He backed the Buick into the nearest driveway, turned around and headed back to Sami's. First things first, make sure she's all right. Besides, these guys saw he was tailing them. He didn't know why they'd taken off like maniacs. But he wasn't about to go chasing them through the neighborhood. Glancing into the rearview mirror he saw the woman with the bouncing poodle eyeing him as he drove away.

(HADTER SEVEN

As soon as Sami had managed to collect herself and stop shaking, she hurried from the locked front door to the bedroom, snapped opened the gun box and picked up the .380 and slid the clip up into its handle. She tried to rack a bullet into the barrel but her hands were oddly numbed with fear—too numb and weak to rack the slide the same way she'd done it so easily all day at the firing range.

This isn't like you, her inner voice told her. *Calm down* ....

On the third attempt she concentrated on steadying her hands, gripping the top of the gun in her fingertips and sliding it back. It worked. The inner mechanism picked up a bullet from atop a stack of five other bullets and like some living thing plunged it forward into the barrel. A smooth satiny click and, *There* .... She breathed deeper. Yet she knew that everything she was doing right now was all *after-the-fact.*

No matter what the two men had subjected her to only moments ago, the unloaded gun, in the other room in its hard plastic case, would have done nothing to stop them. Still, she gripped the loaded pistol in her hand, feeling safer just holding it. From now on the gun went where she went.

No sooner than she'd drawn an easier breath and let herself unwind, the ring of the doorbell coursed up her spine like a low voltage shock.

Jesus ...! She caught herself with a jolt and turned toward the door and froze for a moment, gun in hand. She waited for the second ring before approaching the door peeping out onto the porch.

Seeing Ray Dylan standing there in the motion activated porch light, she gave a sigh of relief and unlocked the door and swung it open. Dylan saw the gun she held down her side; he made no mention of it. He noted how she'd only glanced at him, then gazed out past his shoulder, up and down the empty street-lighted asphalt.

"Ray," she said, thinking her voice sounded steady enough, "what brings you back?"

He held the carton of .380 bullets out on his palm.

"I was almost home," he said, "I realized you'd left these in the car, thought I should bring them by." He shrugged. "I suppose I should have waited ... sorry."

"No, come in, please," she said, opening the door wider. She fluffed her hair as he walked inside. She was glad he'd come back. She didn't want to be alone. "I lied down and fell asleep when you dropped me off." She smiled, shied her eyes from him. "Don't look at me."

"Too late, I looked," he said. He nodded at the gun down her side, "Didn't get enough at the range?"

She raised the gun a little and looked at it as if surprised to see it there. Dylan saw the slightest tremor in her hand.

"Just getting used to having it around," she said. She noted the safety was off and clicked it on with her thumb.

Dylan noticed it too but said nothing. He watched her close and lock the door, and he followed her across the room to the kitchen. He laid the box of bullets on the table. Sami laid the gun beside it.

"I saw a strange thing just now," Dylan said, gesturing back toward the street. "Right up the street, two guys burning rubber in a maroon Cadillac—did you hear it?"

"No, I didn't," she said, "I must've really been dozing." She motioned him to a chair. "How about some coffee?"

She was lying, not realizing he'd been watching her house, had seen them leave here, had even followed them. He felt a slight stab of betrayal.

"Sure, if you're having some," he said.

She stopped and looked at him for a moment, considering something.

"Better still," she said, "how about some wine?"

"Even better," Ray said, aware of a whole change of agenda from an offer of coffee to an offer of wine. Whatever was going on with her would have to wait. Whatever it was, she'd just made it clear she'd rather lie to him than talk about it. *Okay, sit tight, it was coming. Until it got here, relax and enjoy the scenery*, he told himself. He watched her walk to the counter and take down a bottle from the wine rack. "Let me open that for us," he said.

"Thank you, Ray." She gave him the bottle; he picked up a cork screw. He liked the change in her voice and demeanor, the suggestive softness that came over her around this time of night.

"So, you didn't hear any of that …?" he ventured, making one more attempt as he peeled the neckband from the bottle.

She turned and leaned back against the counter beside him, watching him uncork a bottle of Ruffino. She gazed into his eyes when he looked up from the bottle as if still waiting for her answer.

"No, Ray," she said coolly, "I didn't hear anything outside. I must've been still half dreaming." She smiled and pushed her hair back and gave him a sultry look. "Want to know what I was dreaming?"

"If you want to tell me," he said, liking this mood she had slipped into.

"I was dreaming I opened my door and found a handsome man standing on my porch … bringing me a box of bullets." Her voice turned lower, softer as she spoke. They leaned and kissed, the wine bottle and two glasses standing close at hand.

God, he liked the feel of her close up like this. Whatever was going on with her could wait—would in fact *have to wait*, he told himself. If she thought *this right here* was more important, who was he to argue.

Darkness had set in by the time Kireem drove the Cadillac off the blacktop onto a sandy trail winding back into the Palms and Pines Mobile Home Park. He followed the worn potholed path back through acres of overgrowth and blackened trailers. At the rear of the nearly abandoned community he pulled into a weeded parking place alongside an ancient Airstream. The trailer sat on cinder blocks, thickly surrounded by cabbage palms and unkempt Saw Palmetto. A pair of red eyes glinted in the headlight beam and darted away into the surrounding bracken and marshlands.

"Man, this is some sorry shit right here," Kireem said looking all around the place. He turned the engine off.

"I told you it was just until I scored this cash," said Augio, the briefcase lying against his left leg. "Five minutes we're out of here." He swung open the door, took a last draw on a cigarette and flipped the butt away. "I'll grab my stuff." He picked up the briefcase and stood up out of the car.

Grab his stuff ....

Kireem watched him walk to the front door of the trailer through a circle of yellowy security light. Above, a thick swarm of insects circled the dim light, their shadows spinning on the windshield, the wide car hood.

"So, here we are …," he said under his breath. He reached around and retrieved a twelve pack sitting in the back floor beside a bottle of scotch they'd picked up over on Commercial Way coming here. Kireem sat the pack on the seat beside him, pulled out a cold sweaty can, opened it and took a long drink. He settled back, watching the trailer. A light clicked on inside. *All right* .... He sank back into the leather seat and leaned his head back and relaxed. But within a few seconds he straightened upright, hearing a tapping sound on his window. Looking around, he saw a man holding a short rifle pointed at his face through the glass.

Damn ..., Kireem said to himself.

"Out of the car," the man said, opening the

unlocked door halfway as he spoke. "Keep your hands in sight."

Damn ...! Kireem said again. He held his hands in sight, turning slowly, holding his can of beer.

"A robbery, hunh?" he stepped up out of the Cadillac, looked at the short rifle.

"Shut up, get going inside," the man said, gesturing toward the trailer with the short rifle barrel.

Kireem looked the man up and down and started walking slowly toward a rickety porch leaning against the front of the trailer.

"Who're you, Lucas McCain, the *Rifleman*?" he said over his shoulder.

"That's funny, shine," the man said. "Start running your mouth, I'll cap you right here." Even with the tough talk, Kireem thought the man sounded a little jittery.

Shine ....

Kireem shut up and walked on.

When he stepped inside the trailer, the man with the rifle right behind him, he saw Augio standing in a small dirty kitchen area. A man stood in front of Augio with a small caliber pistol in hand, a silencer attached to its barrel by a wrapping of silver duct tape.

"Over there," the man with the rifle said, giving Kireem a nudge with the gun barrel, ushering him toward the kitchen area. Kireem walked forward, eyeing the briefcase of cash lying open on a battered table with rusty chrome legs.

The man holding the silenced pistol looked at them, then back at Augio. He reached out and closed the briefcase.

"We're taking this for our trouble," he said. He

wore his long greasy hair pulled back, tied into a short tail hanging down the back of his neck.

Kireem crossed the dirty floor and stood beside Augio. The man with the pistol looked him up and down and said to his cohort holding the short rifle, "You checked the car out?"

"No, not yet," the man said. "I figured I'd get him in here first."

"There's nothing in the car," Augio offered.

"We'll take it apart and see," the man with the pistol said.

"Hey, that's my car," Kireem said. "You don't want to be taking it apart. You think there's something in it, we'll check it out together—"

"Shut up," said the pistol man. He said to the man holding the rifle, "If he says anything else crack his head."

"You got it," said the man with the rifle. "This one's a wiseass anyway." He held the rifle more intently toward Kireem with both hands.

Kireem glared at him through red dilated eyes, started to say something but stopped when Augio warned him.

"Easy K," Augio said. "They're not fooling around." He raised his hands a little. His eyes were equally red and dilated from the coke they'd snorted throughout the day.

"That's right," the man with the pistol said, "we're not fooling around. Give us the five keys of blow back and we're out of here."

"Five keys of *blow*?" said Kireem. "What are you talking about?"

"Shut up, K, I mean it," Augio said cutting him

off. "This is nothing to do with you. This is about some blow I bought from them to take back to Toronto—"

"Some blow you *ripped off* from us," the man with the duct taped pistol cut in. "What? You think Marty wouldn't send us out to kill you for five keys of blow?" He wagged his pistol at Kireem. "The spade too,for that matter?"

"*Whoa*," said Kireem, deciding to test these two a little, see how bad of a spot he was on. "What's all this *name-calling*?" He glared at the pistol man. "That's some racial shit."

"Crack him," the pistol man said.

The man drew his rifle back for a swipe at Kireem's head. He stopped short when Kireem didn't flinch, didn't back, just stood glaring at him.

"What about I just shoot him if he won't shut up, Sonny?" the man with the rifle said. He eased the rifle back down in front of him. Kireem watched, listened. A lot of people he dealt with would have already shot him, they wouldn't be asking somebody if they *could.*

"All right, shoot him then," said the man with the duct-taped silencer. He returned Kireem's hard stare.

These two weren't so bad—*dope running, swamp crackers* ....

Kireem looked all around the small kitchen area, getting the lay of the place. The man with the rifle stayed tensed, rifle aimed and ready.

"Now where's our blow, Auggie," the one with the pistol said to Augio in a mocking tone.

"It was stolen, Sonny. You were there same as I was," said Augio. "They stole your dope when they stole my money. We both lost out."

"I don't think so," said the pistol man, Sonny French. "I think you had some Tampa monkey boys bust in and do it." He gave a dark grin. "You thought Marty AM would fall for that old hustle?"

"You're wrong, Sonny," said Augio. "I had nothing to do with it."

"I'm not wrong," said Sonny. "Now give it up, it's the last time I'm telling you."

The name *Marty AM* clicked for Kireem. Marty AM … short for Marty Ambrose. Instead of saying a word, Kireem raised a thick finger, getting the gunman's attention. Sonny French turned his eyes to him.

"What?" he said.

Kireem made a show of reaching into his loose trouser pocket and slowly raising the rolled up bag that had started out at daylight as a quarter kilo of cocaine. He and Augio had been running lines from it all day. He reached over and plopped the bag onto the kitchen table. Then he stared at Sonny French.

Sonny gave the man holding the rifle a look.

"You didn't search him out there?" he said. "I told you to search him."

"Yeah, you told me to, but I didn't," The man said. "You want me to search him now?"

"Why search him now?" French said in a critical tone. He looked at Kireem and said, "All right, talk."

The man holding the pointed rifle stood at ease, but kept his hands poised on the grip and front stock.

"That's a quarter note we've been hitting on," Kireem said coolly. "Is that the blow you cowpokes looking for?"

French stepped in, turned the plastic bag over

and looked at an identifying blue line along the zip-top bag.

"That's the dope," he said, "street cut and ready for the market." He pulled the bag open and stuck a long pinky nail inside it, twice. Each time he dipped out a generous mound of white silky powder on his upturned nail and snorted the dope full throttle up his nose. "Oh yeah …," he said with satisfaction. He sucked his fingertip clean, sniffed and wiped his nose between his thumb and fingers. His eyes misted and widened. He said to Augio, "There's one bag. Where's the rest?"

Augio looked a little worried.

"Okay, this bag come from the product, before they all got stolen," he said to French. "I palmed it up under my shirt when they came busting in to rob us. Think about it," he added, "how many quarter bags did you see the thieves grab?"

French only considered it for a second. He shrugged.

"I didn't count," he said.

"*What?*" Kireem cut in. "You're a *big dope runner,* you don't even know how many bags of blow they was robbing from you?"

"It don't really matter now," said French, the coke kicking in. "I'm going to shoot you both anyway."

"It does matter," Kireem cut in. "You going back to Marty Ambrose and give him this weak-ass, half gone bag of blow, tell him that's all you got back?"

Hearing the name Marty Ambrose gave Sonny tense pause for a moment. Then he collected himself.

"I never said Marty *Ambrose,*" he replied, trying to play it down. "I just said Marty *AM.*"

"Oh, *my bad*," said Kireem. "How many Marty AMs you think there are, running dope all up this coastline?"

"You're a wiseass," said French. He turned the small pistol from Augio to Kireem. "What's your play in this anyway?"

"He's working for me," Augio cut in. He looked at Kireem and said, "Jesus, K. Why'd you pull that bag out?"

"Because I'm supposed to have your back," Kireem replied. "He was going to shoot you."

"You mean like he's getting ready to do now?" said Augio, his red eyes still looking worried.

"Dope runners don't act like this!" Kireem said; he shook his head in disgust.

"Both of you shut the fuck up," shouted Sonny French. He wagged the gun at a chair and said to Kireem, "You, sit down!" His eyes were now as shiny and wild as theirs.

The man with the rifle watched, ready for anything.

"All right, *I'm down*," Kireem said. He sat his beer can down hard onto the tabletop and raked out a chair with his foot. He turned the chair facing the man with the pointed rifle. But instead of sitting down he made a fast move for an iron skillet atop the stove, grabbed it by the handle. In a full powerful swing he planted the skillet flat against the rifleman's forehead.

The skillet gave off a dull ring; the rifle flew from the man's hands. His eyes rolled upward. With another solid swing Kireem laid the flat cooking utensil against the man's lower belly, the hard round edge of it striking the pubic arch mantling the man's crotch. The skillet rang again; the man jackknifed at the waist and slammed down onto the table. His weight caused one of the chrome legs to buckle under.

Both man and table crashed to the floor. One end of the table went down, the other end stuck up in the air. A roach fled for its life. The man lay limp, face down. An ashtray of cigarette butts, the twelve pack and the bag of dope all slid down the high tilted table and gathered around his shoulders.

Jesus ...!

"Fucked him up," Kireem said, staring down at the man, then at the skillet still hanging in his hand.

Sonny stood stunned; so did Augio. But Augio snapped out of it an instant quicker. He grabbed the .22 pistol from Sonny's hand and held it out at him, ready to fire.

"Now *you're dead*, Sonny!" he shouted. He started pulling the trigger. The first shot spat out of the silencer with a sharp little crack. Sonny, five feet away, grasped his chest and let out a dog-like yelp.

"Wait!" shouted Kireem.

But Augio ignored him. He squeezed the trigger again and again, four times in all. The second shot sent the silencer and scraps of duct tape flying in the air. The small hot bullet bored into the palm of Sonny's upraised hand and stuck there, smoking. Sonny shrieked and flapped his hand wildly. The third shot, without benefit of the silencer sounded much louder. Sonny twisted and fell backwards, both hands digging at his ribs. A fourth pull on the trigger, the gun only made a little metallic click.

"What the hell ...?" Augio shook the gun as if

a good shaking was all it needed. He tried to fire again; the gun wouldn't work for him. Sonny lay on the floor writhing in pain.

"Forget that gun," said Kireem, "You've got to stick it against his head to kill him." He moved in, tossing the skillet down onto a chair. He picked up the short rifle while Augio still tried to shake the small pistol's problems away. Augio cursed and finally tossed the gun aside. He kicked the silencer and a wad of smoking duct tape across the trailer floor.

"Give me the rifle, K, I'll finish him off," he said to Kireem.

"Don't shoot me again, Auggie, please," Sonny begged, his mocking tone gone. He pushed himself onto his knees.

"Fuck you, Sonny, you're dead," said Augio. "Give me the rifle, K."

"Wait a minute," Kireem said, "Don't you want to ask him something first?"

"Ask him what?" Augio said. His red eyes followed Kireem to the floor as Kireem bent down and picked up the bag of blow and the twelve pack. The knocked out gunman groaned, tried to lift his head but couldn't do it. Kireem looked at the swelling purple forehead turned toward him, then stood and laid the twelve pack and dope atop the stove.

"I was you, I'd ask him how he knows about the missing product being cut, *ready for the street,* like he said." Kireem gave Augio a curious look. "How long you been moving product?"

"Long *enough*," Augio said, getting agitated. "Now give me the rifle."

"Hold on, my man," said Kireem. He kept the rifle in hand. "I want to know even if you don't. We been hitting this blow all day. If it was pure high-grade, it would have torn our heads off."

Augio stared at him considering it. Then he sniffed his raw nose between his thumb and fingers and looked at Sonny.

"Yeah, Sonny," he said. "How did you know the dope was already stepped on, ready to sell?"

Sonny looked worried; he held his bloody hands chest high.

"Hey, come on man," he said, jittery. "I *didn't* know. I just said it, that's all."

Kireem leveled the short rifle at Sonny's bloody chest.

"We're not going to ask again," Kireem said. "I'm going to count to *one,* then I'm going to start popping caps." He gave him a flat smile and laid his big finger over the trigger. "You ready? Let's go then." He clenched the rifle, ready to fire.

"Wait, please, *hold it!*" said French, blood trickling from three shallow bullet wounds. "I'll lay it all out for you, everything, okay?"

"We're listening," said Kireem, stepping in, taking charge, the rifle hanging in his hand.

(HAPTER EIGHT

The four sat in rusted chrome-back kitchen chairs around the wobbly table that Sonny French and Augio had propped back up onto its straightened leg. The gunman, Hal Decampo, who Kireem had nailed with the iron skillet, had regained consciousness. He sat in pain with a tall can of cold beer against his forehead and a tray of ice from the refrigerator wrapped in a dish towel lying on his sore crotch. His short rifle lay on the table pointing at him, the rear grip resting near Kireem's right hand. Beside Kireem, Aaron Augio sat with his own pistol out now, lying beside his glass of scotch.

Sonny sat beside Decampo; both had a can of beer standing in front of them. Sonny held an ice cube wrapped in a paper towel in his wounded palm. He'd stuffed waded paper towels inside his shirt, against his chest where he'd scraped out a bullet with his fingers, and against his side where a bullet still stuck in his ribs.

"And there's the whole story," he said, when he'd finished telling them the history of the open quarter bag of coke laying in the middle of the table. He took a long pull on a cigarette and let go a stream of smoke. "I set up the deal with you on my own. Marty AM doesn't know anything about it."

"Let me get this straight," Augio said. "The blow was supposed to go to street dealers—which is why it's already been stepped-on and ready to sell." He looked from Sonny to Kireem, who nodded, listening.

"Yeah," Sonny said. "It would have played out good, except we got robbed. We figured it was you behind it."

"You were wrong," said Augio. "I lost a buck and a half, money that belongs to some backers of mine. Now I'm on the hook for it. I figured it was you who set up the robbery." He looked at Sonny and Hal both. "I'm still not convinced. But I wasn't sticking around to argue." His hand crawled over his pistol and laid there. "I've been out scoring cash every way I can to make this thing right with my backers."

"It wasn't us, I swear to God," Sonny said.

Augio picked up the pistol and turned in back and forth in his hand.

"Okay," Kireem cut in, "let's not start all over here." He gestured a nod at Augio's gun. Augio laid it down easy but kept his hand over it. He looked at Sonny.

"You cowboys got to get Marty AM's product back before he misses it," said Kireem. "He'll send you on an airboat ride."

"Yeah, we *know that,*" Sonny said, agitated, red-eyed, "What do you think I've been saying here?"

Kireem ignored him and turned to Augio.

"How cool are your backers?" he asked.

"How cool do you think?" Augio said. "They

fronted me a hundred and fifty thousand to score product for them—the money and the dope are both gone. Soon as they find out about it, I'm dead."

"Us too," said Sonny. "I've seen what Marty AM does to people who lose his dope."

Augio just looked at him.

"So you were going to hang it all on me?"

Sonny returned his cold stare.

"Okay, focus here, both of you," said Kireem, drawing their attention to him. "I know a brother in Tampa—Ybor City. He knows everybody who's into ripping off product. I go to him, he tells me who's got *your* dope, and *your* money." He looked at each of them in turn.

Sonny and Augio looked at each other again, this time with a little less malice. Augio turned to Kireem.

"Suppose he does know?" he said. "How fast can we move on this?"

"Fast as you want to move," Kireem said. "Like *right now*," he said. "Soon as I find out who's got it, we go get it back." He looked at Sonny and Decampo. "What do you say, *cowpokes,* you down for it?"

Sonny French gave him a suspicious look. Decampo just sat with his head lowered, the cold can against it.

"Why are you doing this?" Sonny asked.

"For ten percent, that's why," Kireem said. "It's not social work." He said to Augio, "Ten percent of your hundred and fifty thousand." He said to Sonny, "Ten percent of the dope's value, which is the same amount, I figure." He shrugged. "So … fifteen thousand each." He looked back and forth. "Take yourselves *half a second* to think about it. You want to do it, we do it. You don't, I'm done here." He looked at Augio and said. "You still pay me for being your backup."

Augio considered it, but only for a moment.

"Yeah, sure, why not?" he said. "If I don't get straightened out I'm a dead man and you won't get anything."

"I'll get you straightened out," Kireem said. "Florida's my turf. I know every dog on the track. My boys have been scheming, smuggling all up and down these coastlines since Columbus landed in Miami. You just got to do like I say, you'll be all right—"

"Holy shit, check it out!" Decampo butted in, rising half up from his chair. He stared past Kireem, out the front window where flames licked high, raging up from the underbrush, twisting and braiding up the namesake palms and pines all around the trailer. In the distance a shrill siren screamed.

"My car," said Kireem, looking around, seeing the fire rage outside the small trailer window. He sprang up from the table, grabbing the short rifle. "Let's get out of here." Without waiting for anyone he ran out the front door. Augio grabbed the briefcase, the dope and the half bottle of scotch. He wagged the other two out with his pistol and ran out behind them. Sonny carried the remainder of the twelve pack in his good hand. Decampo staggered forward unsteadily, still holding the beer can against his forehead.

The three caught up with Kireem at the open door of the Cadillac. Fire crackled on the pine trunks and the dried fronds of cabbage palms. Smoke pressed low and hot all around the car.

"Hurry up, get in," shouted Kireem, starting the engine. He pulled the shift lever into drive and stabbed the gas pedal down as Sonny and Augio pulled Decampo into the back seat and slammed the door behind him.

At the blacktop, a fire truck slowed enough to make the turn into the trailer park. The firemen saw the maroon Cadillac fishtail off the sand onto the asphalt and speed away in the darkness. Inside the car, Sonny jerked upright when they saw and heard a dazzling ball of fire erupt up out of the tree line.

"There goes your truck, Hal," he said to Decampo.

"Yeah, Hal. Tough break," Augio said, lacking empathy. He sat in the seat beside Kireem, hiked around, loosely keeping his gun on Sonny and Decampo. Kireem just gave him a look and sped toward the main highway.

PART II

(HAPTER NINE

Ray Dylan knew early on that Sami Bloom was not a woman to be taken for granted. She was not to be misjudged, misled, or mishandled, and he liked that about her—her classiness. To the outside world it might appear odd that he saw something bothering her and refused to bring it up, even found it more suitable to slip around and watch her house like some half-a-stalker than to confront her with it. But he realized that one sure way to watch Sami's taillights speed away would be to stick his nose into her personal business, uninvited. The two of them were a lot alike in that regard.

They were each private people who held their past as well as their present lives closely guarded. Dylan was comfortable with that. He liked the cool confidence of privacy, the certainty of it, even though with it at times came a sort of sadness that exacted its own price on the spirit. He accepted that whatever knowledge, wisdom or certainty of self he might have gleaned in this inimitable profession he'd chosen, it had come to him hard-earned, with a built-in occupational demand for solitude. For reasons he might never know he sensed the same need in Sami Bloom, and regardless of those reasons, he was okay with that too. He felt at peace considering this place the two of them had made for each other. He smiled to himself and pressed the gas pedal on the Buick when the light changed.

The hitter and his mermaid ....

They'd spent much of last night making love, sipping wine to soft jazz on the FM station out of Clearwater. In the morning they had eaten Egg Beaters with wheat toast and fresh sliced tomatoes out on the lanai while they watched the news—the lead story, a landmark trailer park burning to the ground in a wild brush fire. Dylan had noted a sad downturn in her voice watching the reporter talk to the owner of the Palms and Pines Mobile Home Park community. The owner spoke of the park once being the pride of the central Gulf Coast. Now, he didn't know what the future held for the park, no insurance, a bad economy, fallen rental income ....

Sami had shaken her head, listening.

"You think you have everything and then, one day, just like that, it's all gone," she'd remarked.

Dylan had only looked at her. She'd looked troubled by something more than a news story, he thought. Another thing, while they drank their coffee, out of nowhere she asked him, "Ray, suppose I actually had to shoot someone. Would I only have to shoot them once, or would it take several shots before I stopped them?"

Dylan sipped his coffee. He treated the question as purely hypothetical, gave a little shrug.

"It depends on the person's size, body density, factors like that," he said. "Also depends on where you shoot him, or how much dope he's on."

She looked at him questioningly.

"If it's some heavy weight, or some blown out crackhead," he said. "It could take two, three, four body shots or more before he goes down."

"Unless, of course, I hit him in the head?" she countered.

"Yes," Dylan said. "But aiming for the head is not always a good idea in a life or death situation. Any shooter will tell you, go for the largest target. Aim for the body and start shooting, hope you hit the heart and lungs."

Her expression soured a little. Dylan saw her forcing herself to continue the conversation.

"It's not a pleasant topic, but it is something you should know if you're going to be armed," he reminded her.

"Yes, I understand," she'd said. "I asked for it. I brought it up …."

At that point Dylan had watched her emotionally excuse herself from the conversation. *Strange*, he thought, *since she'd brought it up in the first place.*

He gave his left turn signal and swung off the highway into a gas station.

He paid cash inside, and went back to the pump and filled his tank. When he'd finished, he slipped back into the driver's seat, started the Buick and eased across the station lot back toward the highway. But instead of emerging out into the traffic, he glanced across the wide street and did a quick double take. There, turning out of the traffic was the maroon Cadillac. He watched it turn off of the highway into a self-service car wash—pulled right inside an empty bay.

All right ....

Dylan veered the Buick over off of the station's driveway and hit the brakes. He grabbed the pair of small binoculars from his console and raised them to his eyes in time to see the black man step out of the Cadillac and look the car over. Tightening the focus in close on the man, then moving down the rear of the car, he saw that the Canadian plates were gone. In their place was a newer looking plate from the state of Michigan.

Nice try, Dylan told himself, *but this is the same car, no question about it.* Except for the shiny red plate, the rest of the car looked streaked with smoke. Smudges and flecks of soot covered the rear window. From the passenger side, the man with the spiked hair stepped out and straightened. His eyes were hidden behind a pair of sunglasses; his face looked drawn and pale. Dylan saw him adjust the butt of a gun sticking up from his waist behind his shirt. From the back seat two haggard, bloodstained men climbed out and limped over to a curbing beside a row of commercial auto-vacuums. One held a beer can against his forehead. He plopped down and leaned back onto a strip of grass. The one standing peeled off his shirt, wadded it and tossed it into a trash can. Dylan saw clean white bandages on his side and chest.

What a crew ..., he said to himself. He tried to come up with any possible reason why these two had been at Sami's house. He drew a blank. As he gazed through the small binoculars, a car horn bellowed out behind him. This was no slight reminder tap; this was a *get-the-hell-out-of-my-way* blast that turned heads from every direction. Even the black man across the street turned and looked toward the sound. He continued staring long and hard at the Buick as Dylan lowered the binoculars and eased the car forward out onto the street.

Dylan drove away in the traffic without looking back to see if he was still being watched. At this point he had to assume he'd been made.

"You see that?" Kireem said to Augio, the two of them staring as the silver-gray Buick sped off along the highway. "It's that same car."

"I see it," said Augio. "You really think it's the same?"

"What'd I say?" Kireem said. "You've got heat on you?" He asked as he stared after the Buick, even after it moved out of sight. He stepped over to a coin machine to make change. At the curbing Sonny French and Hal Decampo stood up and walked over closer, listening.

"Heat on *me?* Hunh-uh, I don't think so, K," said Augio. He also stared after the Buick. "Only people interested in me are my backers. If that was them we wouldn't have seen them." He looked at Sonny and Decampo. "What about you two?" he asked them.

"No," said Sonny, "we're cool."

Kireem looked the two up and down.

"You *think?*" he said.

"Yeah, *I think,*" Sonny said, feeling a little better, getting some attitude back now that he'd gotten his shallow wounds bandaged with supplies from a CVS store. He stood staring at Kireem, bare-chested. "What about you? Maybe there's heat on you."

Kireem just gave him a look.

83

"Yeah, right," he chuffed. He looked Sonny up and down. "Get you a shirt out of the trunk," he said to him. "You can't be walking around Tampa, no shirt on, bullet wounds showing." He pitched the trunk keys to Augio. "Show him where stuff's at back there."

The three went through a pile of loose clothes in the trunk while Kireem soaped down the front of the smudged Cadillac and rinsed it off with a high pressure wand.

"Hey, these clothes are all dirty … they stink," Sonny called out, holding up a silky wrinkled shirt with scenes of parrots drinking Margaritas on it.

Kireem only shook his head, washing the car.

"Look down under the dirty clothes," said Augio, "there's some folded tee shirts there." As he spoke, Augio took out the bag of dope and unrolled it under the shelter of the raised trunk lid. As Sonny went deeper through the dirty clothes and pulled up a folded tee shirt, Augio dipped into the cocaine with a small plastic spoon he found lying among the clothes and debris. He snorted a mound and handed spoon and bag to Decampo.

Kireem saw what the two were doing as he moved to the driver side with the wand and rinsed it down. He shook his head; he couldn't believe these guys.

When the car was washed and the four were back inside, a new cold twelve pack of beer sitting on the rear floor, Kireem drove the Cadillac out onto the highway and headed north to Cortez Boulevard. At Cortez he took a right and drove on, headed east, passing a succession of car dealers, chain restaurants and strip malls until he reached the Suncoast Parkway and headed south toward Tampa. He kept a sharp eye on his rearview mirror, yet even so, he failed to see Dylan's silver-gray Buick lagging back, managing to keep a car or truck between them, tailing the Cadillac from a safe distance away.

A forty-five minute drive later, Kireem guided the big Cadillac down off the Suncoast onto the steamy asphalt tentacles of the city where streets narrowed between rows of boarded up buildings and weedy lots. Off the main street of Tampa's old cigar producing section, Ybor City, he pulled the car into a narrow one way brick alley and parked.

"Everybody hang here," he said, turning off the engine.

"I should go with you," said Augio. "What if there's trouble?"

"If you go with me there *will* be," Kireem said. He stood up from the driver's seat in the open door and adjusted his 10mm into the waist of his loose-fitting trousers. The three watched as he closed the door, looked all around and walked across an ancient sidewalk into a door with a sign that read: Cano-Randley Imports Inc.

"This is not cool," Sonny French said. "We should both be with him. How do we know what he's doing in there? All of a sudden he's in charge?" He sounded nervous.

"Chill," said Augio. "We agreed for him to do this for us."

"Did you just tell me to *chill?*" Sonny gave him a look.

Augio played it off. He reached around between the front seats and pitched the rolled up bag of dope onto Sonny's lap. The three bowed over the white powder as if gathering in prayer ….

Ray Dylan had parked his Buick out on the

street. Wearing dark shades and a straw Panama he'd taken from the trunk, he moved into the alley on foot and slowed to a halt when he spotted the three men waiting in the Cadillac. He browsed the renovated buildings like a tourist, yet he was familiar with this area. By people in his circle the alley was called *Smuggler's Roost* or *Contraband Cove*. Many of the chic storefronts lining the narrow alley were thin facades for illegal drug and gun running operations.

Jesus, Sami .... The deeper he probed, the less he liked his findings.

By the time Kireem came back to the car fifteen minutes later, Dylan had retreated from the alleyway and walked back to where he'd parked his Buick. Circling the block he'd parked in front of a wide delivery truck twenty yards from where the one way alley emptied back onto a through street. Unseen from either the alley or the traffic coming up behind him, he took off the straw Panama and dropped it onto the passenger seat beside him. He waited. They had to come this way.

"What'd you find out?" Sonny French asked Kireem.

"Plenty," Kireem said, sliding in behind the steering wheel. "Put the blow away." He motioned toward the open bag of dope as he started the car, half turned in his seat and dropped the shifter into *reverse*.

"What are you doing?" Sonny asked, looking back as the Cadillac traveled in reverse.

"I'm backing us out of here," Kireem said, looking over his shoulder. Beside him, Augio grabbed the bag of dope, closed it and put it away.

"Why?" said Sonny, looking all around.

"Why …?" The Cadillac gave a little screech of rubber as Kireem backed out and around onto the street. He stopped, dropped the shifter into *drive* and put the car forward. He gave a sly little grin into the rearview mirror. "Because sometime it's good to do what nobody expects. That's *why*," he said, running his hand inside his shirt. "Here, my friend said Merry Christmas." He tossed a rolled bag of reefer onto Augio's lap."

Sonny and Decampo craned forward for a look.

"Cool," Augio said, hefting the bag on his palm. He eyed a pack of Zig-Zag papers rolled up into the bag.

"Yeah, cool, but what about our dope and the money?" Sonny asked. He caught the bag of reefer Augio pitched to him.

"I got good news and bad," Kireem said, driving to the corner and taking a left. "I found out who ripped you off. It's three gangsters working on their own—nobody protecting them. I even know the place they're laid up." At the next corner he took another left. Cruised right past the Buick, didn't notice it. "Good news is they know me. They'll let me in when I come to deal."

"Good. I say let's go nail them," Sonny cut it. He handed the bag to Decampo, who opened it, smelled it, and took out the pack of papers.

"Bad news is," Kireem continued, "once I do this, they'll be after me from now on."

"What about masks?" said Sonny.

"Listen to you," Kireem said. He glared at Sonny in the rearview. "How we going to get through the door wearing masks?"

Sonny fell silent.

Kireem said to Augio, and to Sonny in the rearview. "After you get your money and Marty AM's product back you're gone. I'll be watching my back for these Tampa boys from now on."

"So what are you saying?" Augio asked Kireem. "We agreed on your cut."

"I get more for going in," Kireem said, "Call it a *bonus*." He rubbed his thumb and fingertip together in the sign for greed.

"No way," Sonny said. "We made the deal, you agreed to fifteen percent—"

Before Sonny could finish, Augio cut him off.

"Five thousand *bonus* from each of us when we're done," he said to Kireem, getting impatient. "Where are they, and when are we doing this?"

"We do it as soon as I pick us up an AK from a friend and we get ourselves a job car. The rippers are moving product out of a motel room over in Hudson Beach."

"You mean today, right now?" Sonny said, holding the joint Hal had just rolled and handed to him.

"We don't get there soon your dope will all be gone." He looked at Sonny in the rearview. "Then you'll paying Marty AM for his dope at street price."

Sonny nodded and stuck the joint up behind his ear.

"Take us to a mall," he said. "Hal will get us a car."

(HAPTER TEN

Instead of the Cadillac coming out of the alley onto the
through street, Ray Dylan saw it drive past him where he
sat watching for it from the cover of the delivery truck.
As soon as he saw it he started the Buick and moved
out into the afternoon traffic, keeping the big Cadillac in
sight from a safe distance back. It had been a long time
since he'd tailed a car on busy city streets. Luckily he
hadn't lost his touch.

At the end of a short drive through a trashed-out
area of Tampa's downtown perimeter, he watched the car
pull over and park in a rundown rental complex where a
half-hairless dog stood licking at something on the edge
of the sidewalk. Easing the Buick over to a curb a quarter
of a block back Dylan watched as the big man left the
Caddy and walked into a ground floor unit. While he sat
watching it he reminded himself that he'd been tailing
these four most of the afternoon. But that was okay. He'd
wanted to find out more about them; he was certainly
doing that.

Watching this crew was like a witnessing an

oncoming crash—he could see it coming. He couldn't stop it; yet, he couldn't turn his eyes away. He'd seen enough, but there seemed to be no good place for him to break it off and go home. As he considered how he was going to approach Sami with all this, he saw the black man come out of the apartment door and walk back to the trunk of the car carrying a beach towel wrapped around what had to be a firearm.

Dylan watched him open the trunk, deposit the wrapped item and close the lid behind it. In a moment the man was back in the driver's seat. He started the Caddy and swung out onto the street.

Jesus Sami .... Dylan said again. He shook his head, gave the Caddy some lead-way, then swung back out behind it. They were getting ready for something, no doubt about it.

He followed and watched.

As he drove he fished a hand over into the console and found a well-seasoned unopened granola snack bar. Wasting no time, he opened it with one hand and his teeth and devoured it. He washed the dry granola down with tepid coffee from a McDonald cup that had sat in the drink holder all day. He wasn't about to stop now ....

A grainy darkness had set in when the Caddy pulled off the highway again and prowled the outer edges of a sprawling mall parking lot. Dylan nosed the Buick into a herringbone parking space and watched the Cadillac stop long enough to let one of the men step out from the back seat. The man looked back and forth without raising his face, and walked away into a line of parked cars.

Okay ..., Dylan knew what was coming next.

He sat with the Buick's engine running, lights off, the AC set on Low against a mild cloak of winter humidity. He wasn't surprised a moment later as he watched a charcoal-black Ford Taurus ease out, blink its lights and follow the Cadillac away. No stopping now …. Whatever was happening it appeared to be going down tonight, *right now ...*, he told himself. He let the two cars roll a good ways past him before turning on the headlights and following them.

Out of the bug-circled security lights of the Gulf Breeze Motel parking lot, Kireem killed the Taurus's headlights and slowed it to halt behind the cover of a Ligustrum hedge. The four watched a young man wearing dark baggy street clothes walk out the last battered door in a row of neglected units. He climbed into a parked Chevy Trailblazer and drove away. The room door closed. Behind the screen of a half open window a pair of drapes parted an inch then fell back in place. Kireem nodded at the door.

"There's your product, and your cash, what's left of it," he said to Sonny and Augio.

The four waited for a silent moment. Small fruit bats careened in and out of the overhead security light. At the other end of the row of closed doors an overweight man wearing untied construction boots walked out, looked all around, and climbed into a pickup truck. The lot sat empty, the rooms all dark now except for the one on the end. Kireem looked in the rearview at Sonny and Decampo through a wafting cloud of reefer smoke.

"You cowboys ready to *swing up?*" He asked.

"Let's do it," said Sonny.

Hal Decampo turned up the last drink from a can of beer, mashed the can in the middle, folded it double and dropped it on the floor. Sonny stubbed out a joint and dropped the roach in the ashtray. He picked up the AK-47 leaning against the seat beside him.

Kireem looked at Augio.

"Ready?" he said.

Augio nodded and pulled his sunglasses down over his eyes, least the thieves recognize him as one of the men they'd robbed. He held up a two-tone 9mm Bersa, racked its slide and shoved the gun down in his waist. He smoothed his shirt down. For extra assurance he picked up a black beret he'd taken from the trunk of the Caddy and adjusted it down onto his forehead.

"My man …," Kireem said under his breath. He said over his shoulder to Sonny who held the AK across his chest, "Hang back until the door opens and make sure we've got it blocked—"

"I know, I know," said Sonny, sounding jazzed. "Then we come in fast." Looking at Decampo, he reached for the door handle. "Me and Hal's got this."

Kireem started the Taurus as he and Augio watched the two step out of the car and close the doors behind them. They both took cover against the tall hedge.

"What's to keep us from killing those two punks and keeping the dope *and* the money?" Augio asked.

"You want to kill them, you should have said so before I stuck the AK in Sonny's hands," Kireem said.

"Just a thought," Augio said, letting it go.

Kireem backed the Taurus, turned it around the end of the tall hedges and drove into the motel lot, right up to the concrete parking bump in front of the door. As the two stepped out, Kireem saw the window drape once again pull back an inch, then fall back in place. He heard voices whisper on the other side of the window screen.

"*Jamal*, it's me, open up," Kireem called out loud enough to evoke a quick response from inside. He pounded a fist on the metal door facing.

"*Ahh man, shit!*" said a voice inside. "He's shouting my name out! Get that fool in here! Shut him up!"

A safety chain hastily fell and rubbed back and forth against the inside of the door. A deadbolt turned quickly.

"Man, what is *wrong* with you?" said a voice as the door opened a crack; a black face peered out and looked back and forth warily.

"We come to buy some blow, Jamal," Kireem said in the same raised tone of voice. He pushed the door open a little more and made sure he stood blocking it from being closed.

"Mutha*fucka!*" said the nervous voice. "Get my name out of your mouth!" A black hand wearing a large silver ring pulled the door open more.

Kireem laughed aloud and stepped inside far enough to keep the door open. He moved a little to the side to allow Augio in beside him.

"We're both high here," he said. "There's nobody out there listening anyway, *Jamal.*"

The thin black man, Jamal Bachman shook his head and gave a thin nervous grin; he stepped back and tugged at a strip of a goatee.

"That shit ain't funny, man," he said. "Get in here, shut the door!"

Standing off to the side a stocky young white man named Neil Baker stood holding a sawed-off shotgun. He wore a long shaggy ponytail under a Yankee's baseball cap. He watched and listened in silence.

"Wait a minute," said Kireem, blocking the open door, "we got one more coming. His shoe fell off."

"Fuck his shoe, shut the door!" Jamal shouted. When Kireem only looked outside over his shoulder, Jamal demanded, "Shut the door! Shut the door! Shut the door!"

The white man with the Yankee's cap looked tensed, getting nervous.

"Here he is now," Kireem said coolly, moving a step closer to Jamal.

Sonny French thundered into the room, the AK at his shoulder, pointed and ready, aimed at the man with the shotgun. Behind Sonny, Decampo stepped in and moved to the side, the short rifle back in his hands.

Kireem snatched up his 10mm and aimed it at Jamal's head. Augio brought up his two-tone Bersa and aimed it at the shotgun wielder.

"Drop it, Baker!" Kireem shouted at the man with the shotgun. He saw the man keep the shotgun steady, clenching it in both hands. "*Now!* Or I'll burn him up!" Kireem shouted.

Baker still held firm; he looked at Jamal who stood frozen with Kireem's gun jammed to the side of his head.

"Toss it, Neil," Jamal said, "this muthafucka go crazy you don't do what he say."

"Better listen to him, boy," Kireem warned Baker.

Baker turned slightly and pitched the shotgun down onto one the room's sagging double beds.

"When did you start ripping dope, big boy?" Jamal asked.

"Shut up," said Kireem. With the big 10mm still against Jamal's head, he studied the closed door to the bathroom for a moment, then called out, "Benny, don't even think about it in there. I'll bust Jamal's head wide open."

"Come on out, Benny," Jamal said. "They got over on us this time." He looked at Kireem. "If he told you Marty AM is going to give you a sweet roll for this, he's lying." He nodded toward Sonny who stood ready to fire the AK at any second.

Kireem nudged the tip of the gun barrel against the side of his head.

"I got my own *sweet roll*. I'm not working for Marty AM," said Kireem. The door to the bathroom opened. A young Asian-American, Benny Wu, stepped out, one hand in the air, the other holding up his unbuttoned trousers.

"Then who you working for?" Jamal asked Kireem. "You ain't just stepping out on your own, robbing dealers."

"Why not?" said Kireem. "You boys doing pretty good at it."

"He's working for me," Augio said. He shoved the sunglasses up revealing his face. "That was my cash you ripped off."

"The Canadian cracker," Jamal said flatly. He gave a slight shrug and said to Kireem, "It's all in the shower—Benny watching about it." He gestured at the open bathroom door. Benny Wu stood staring, holding his baggy pants up at the waist.

Augio took a step forward, getting curious.

"How did you know I'm Canadian?" he looked Jamal up and down.

Jamal gave a tight little chuckle.

"*Shiit*," he said. He looked sidelong at Kireem. "Didn't you tell him how things work down here, big boy?"

"We're all through catching up, Jamal," said Kireem. He gave the thin man a shove toward the bathroom door. The others watched Kireem guide him through the door, then back into the room a moment later. Jamal carried an Adidas bag against his chest and pitched it down on the bed beside Baker's shotgun.

Sonny and Decampo held the AK and the short rifle aimed and ready, watching Baker and glancing at Augio as he spread the bag open on the bed and rummaged through it.

"Well? How do we look?" Sonny asked. He saw the angry glare on Augio's face.

"Not so good," Augio said in a low even tone. He held up a quarter bag of blow, two short stacks of cash; he let some loose bills fall from his hand. "Where's the rest of it?" he asked Jamal.

Jamal managed a sly little grin. Instead of addressing Augio he looked at Kireem and said, "Don't this fool know I got expenses? Help a nigga out. Tell him how this works—"

"Look at me, *Jamal*," Augio said, cutting him off.

"Look at you for what, *muthafucka?*" Jamal said, getting strong attitude in spite of the gun pointed at him.

Augio didn't reply; the Bersa bucked three times in rapid succession. Two bullets nailed Jamal in his chest.

The third streaked through his right eye and out the back of his head. Blood misted; fragments of brain matter splattered the wall. Kireem jumped back from Jamal. Sonny saw Baker ready to make a move for the shotgun on the bed. He braced the AK to his shoulder and pulled back on the trigger for a full-auto spray of bullets. But the rifle only snapped once, on an empty chamber.

Decampo fired the short rifle. The shot flung Baker over the bed onto the floor. He lay shrieking in pain, his hands squeezing the bullet hole in his side.

"Ah, *man* ...," Kireem said with regret. He turned his 10mm to Benny Wu as Benny reached for something behind his back. "Don't do it, Benny," he warned. "You're coming with us."

Benny Wu's hands raised in front of him. Kireem stepped over to him, turned him around and jerked a large revolver from the back of his waist.

"You gave me this fucking thing *unloaded?*" Sonny shouted at Kireem in disbelief, shaking the AK in the air. "A fucking unloaded gun?"

"My bad, I forgot," Kireem said coolly, turning his 10mm toward Sonny.

Sonny saw Augio's Bersa 9mm also aimed at him. He looked back and forth between them, red-eyed and enraged, half stalled on all the coke, reefer and beer he'd ingested.

"Come on, get the stuff, Sonny," said Decampo, jogging him back into motion, seeing no good coming from Sonny pushing his issue right then.

Augio waited until he saw Sonny lower the empty rifle and start gathering the money and dope into the gym bag. Then he stepped around between the two beds and stared down at Neil Baker who lay silent, writhing in pain.

"Look at you," Augio said down to him. "Bet you wanted us to forget you're here, eh?" He held the Bersa aimed down at Baker's sweaty grimacing face.

"Don't … shoot me," Baker managed to say in a halting voice. "I won't … say nothing. I swear."

Augio gave a little shrug and a half-grin.

"Well, okay then," he said affably. But he pulled the trigger anyway, twice, put both bullets into Baker's face. Then he stepped back, giving Sonny and Decampo a strange bemused look.

"Let's go, Benny," Kireem said.

Shoving Wu along in front of him, Kireem led the others out of the biting odor of carbide toward the parked Taurus.

"Whoa, look at this," said Augio, gesturing the Bersa toward the silver-gray Buick backed off the street into a weed-grown alleyway facing the motel.

Kireem opened the Taurus's rear door; Benny Wu sat down into the backseat.

"Stay cool, Benny Wu," he warned the young Asian.

Wu only nodded up at him. He sat buttoning and zipping his baggy trousers.

Kireem grabbed Decampo's arm as Decampo started to slide in the back seat on one side of Wu, Sonny sliding in on the other side.

"Make sure you cowpokes don't shoot him, you hear me?" Kireem said.

Decampo nodded and Kireem turned him loose.

"What about this guy?" Augio said, staring hard

across the dark street at the Buick.

"He's not the law," said Kireem, "or he'd already be lighting us up." He stared at the Buick, seeing only a darkened silhouette on the driver's side.

"I don't like leaving a witness here," Augio put in, the Bersa hanging in his hand.

Kireem eyed him closely.

"Shoot him then," he said.

Augio stepped forward raising the gun out at arm's length.

"No, man!" Kireem said, grabbing the back of his shirt just in time. "I'm fucking with you." He gave a dark little chuckle. "Get in the car, let's go. He follows us, we *will* kill him." He looked toward the Buick and saw it back up fast, spinning sand, its lights off. The two hurried into the front seat of the Taurus as the Buick turned a half circle out of the sandy lot and sped away in the night.

CHAPTER
ELEVEN

Ray Dylan had gone to bed late, yet before dawn he'd gotten up, dressed and sat at his kitchen counter sipping his second cup of black coffee. Last night as the blare of sirens finally resounded in the distance, he'd made his way back from Hudson Beach using several back roads and side streets into Spring Hill. He'd kept an eye on the road behind him, made a few unneeded turns to make sure he wasn't being followed before turning into his driveway and pulling the Buick into the garage for the night.

Safe enough.

But he'd decided to get the Buick farther out of sight before sunup. He also wanted to pick up another vehicle for himself, one that last night's dopers wouldn't recognize. He referred to them as *dopers,* but he'd seen enough to know they shouldn't be taken lightly. They were dangerous, enough so that he knew he'd have to go to Sami and tell her what he'd seen. He wasn't going to put it off any longer. If she didn't like the fact that he'd followed them, spied on them on her behalf, so be it, he told himself. It had to be done.

Finishing his coffee, he turned off the coffeemaker, picked up his keys and the .45 semiautomatic he'd brought in from the car last night. He'd cleaned, oiled and inspected the big gun on a cloth spread on the kitchen table. He kept the big powerful street gun in the console for emergencies over the years, hoping he would never again have need for it. Looking down at the semiautomatic, hefting it on his palm, he slipped it into its slim leather holster on his way out the kitchen door into the garage. He found something strangely reminiscent about the weight and the feel of the big gun—memories of the *bad-ole-days,* he told himself. Before getting into the Buick he pushed the garage door button on the wall and stood in the shadows, gun in hand as the door clattered slightly and rose overhead.

He walked to the edge of the open door and looked back and forth into the grainy morning darkness. Then he walked back, got in the Buick and started the engine. Gun at his side, he backed the car out onto the empty street and drove it half a block before turning on the headlights. He was sharply aware that every precaution he'd just taken for his safety would have meant nothing had some seasoned shooter like himself followed him home and been waiting here to kill him.

As he drove, his thoughts traveled back to a time on a gray early morning like this when he'd stood on the outside of a large suburban home waiting as a garage door rolled upward in its track. That day he'd waited crouched between the house's brick front wall and an ornamental evergreen slightly taller than himself. When the door finished opening, a Lincoln Town Car backed out slow and easy, the man inside watching the driveway behind him in the rearview mirror.

Dylan stood so close to the side of the backing car, he'd only had to raise the gun up from his side, arm's length. He pulled the trigger with the tip of the silencer only inches from the closed window. Four .38 special shots spat out the end of a six inch silencer making noise, but nothing like the noise of high grain bullets—more like an anemic weed trimmer backfiring. The side glass had cobwebbed on that first shot. The next three shots had blown out much of the clinging safety glass and exposed the man's fatal head wounds.

Unscrewing the silencer from the threaded gun barrel, Dylan watched the car continue to roll backwards on its own, as if in slow motion. A few feet down the driveway the car crept over against a short creek-rock wall and died there. The man fell over into his seat. Dylan slipped the gun into his right coat pocket, the silencer into his left, and walked away in the gray morning gloom.

And that was that. Must've been twenty ... twenty-five years ago, he told himself ....

He put the memory away and drove south along Commercial Way to a sprawling storage complex where he kept two twenty-by-thirty foot storage units leased under another name. His units stood back to back with a heavy metal fold-up door dividing them. Dylan kept the center divider raised, creating a *sixty*-foot stretch of garage and storage with a wide drive-through door on either end. It worked out perfect for him.

The double unit housed a plain white Windstar van facing what had become the rear overhead door. Dylan kept the van clean and serviced, ready to drive anywhere any time, if called upon. Now that the Buick had been spotted in last night's shooting it was a good time to switch rides, get the Buick out of sight for a while. Behind the van a vintage Porsche 911 project car sat shrouded beneath a soft tan car cover.

Someday ..., he promised himself, tossing a glance at the covered Porsche.

Stepping out of the Buick he shoved the .45 down behind his belt and walked to a wide metal tool cabinet standing beside a work bench against the wall. A key stuck in the lock on the cabinet's left double door, but it only hung there for show. To open the cabinet Dylan clicked on a small TV sitting on the work bench. As the screen lit up, electricity from the TV cord sent power to a switch hidden beneath the bench top. He reached under the bench, pressed the switch and heard a metallic click as the cabinet doors unlocked.

Using both hands he pulled the false insides of the cabinet open from the middle. Shelving, power tools and all swung forward, revealing a secretive row of select weaponry and ammunition—*tools of the trade*—he'd acquired for himself over the years. Nothing he needed right now, he reminded himself—hopefully nothing he would need again *period*. But his inventory was here if he needed it—a long range sniper rifle, a pump shotgun, a Colt M2, all standing in a row like old friends ready to make his issues their own. On the cabinet's back wall above the rifles and shotgun, a row of both revolver and semiautomatic pistols hung on S hooks by their trigger guards. Shelves on either side held an assortment of ammunition boxes, stacks of loaded 30 round clips for the M2.

Dylan took a cheap pocket size .22 caliber toss

away revolver from its peg—a gun he'd customized for himself, removing any bothersome serial number. With it he picked up a stubby black pill-bottle silencer of his own creation from its place on a shelf. He took out low grain ammunition for the .22 and loaded it. Then he shut the inside compartment and closed the cabinet's metal doors. He turned to the TV on the workbench and saw a young news reporter standing out front of the Gulf Breeze Motel. In the background he saw yellow plastic tape strung the length of the parking lot.

"... *two bodies found in what Pasco County and Florida State Police consider may have been a drug-related incident ...,*" the announcer said into his microphone.

Dylan stood watching for a moment, then seeing nothing he hadn't seen firsthand the night before, he clicked off the TV, picked up the guns, silencer and ammo, and walked to the Windstar. Inside the van he opened the console lid and raised a false bottom and laid the .45 and the silencer and extra ammo for the .22 down under it. He shoved the loaded .22 revolver down into his right pocket. Closing the false bottom he laid a Florida map inside the console and shut the lid. All done, he clicked open the rear overhead door, drove out and clicked the door down behind him. The sun was well on the rise now and mantling a clear blue Florida sky. Palms swayed on a mild eastwardly breeze.

Another day in paradise ....

He took a deep breath and looked at the anonymous storage units lined row upon row in his rearview mirror. He had a feeling he'd be coming back soon.

Hernando Beach Florida:
78 degrees, balmy

Sunlight glistened on the calmly lapping water of the canal and the endless gulf it widened into. Overhead the squawk and chatter of looping seagulls resounded on the warming breeze. On a dock post a pelican stood with its wings spread, drying in the sun after its morning feed. On her way from the screened pool enclosure to an unfinished guest building in the rear corner of her yard, Sami Bloom returned a wave from two neighbors cruising along the canal behind her house on a small canopy-covered pontoon. The small craft idled and bobbed along easily on the last few yards of restricted no wake zone.

Sami carried an empty black travel bag under her arm.

Inside the empty stucco building, she turned on the light and pulled down a set of wooden folding stairs that reached up into the attic. Climbing the steps, she immediately felt the gravity of stale heated air close around her. Sweat beaded on her forehead. *Okay, no fooling around up here. Get done, get out.*

She pulled on a light chain and walked stoop-shouldered beneath the slant of the roof and its cross-framing to a stack of boxes which she scooted aside to reveal a stacked wall of barrack-style footlockers. When she had the boxes moved out of the way she took down a locker from atop the stack, opened it on the floor and stooped down in front of it.

Working quick, she unsnapped the front latches on the footlocker and raised the lid. Neat stacks of US dollar bills stared up at her. As always the sight of so much money in one place took her aback for a moment. But she took a breath of stale air collecting herself, and wiped a hand across her forehead and opened the travel bag lying at her knees and went to work. *Got to do this,* she told herself.

Keeping a tight count of the ten-thousand dollar stacks of cash she passed one hand to the other and into the bag, she didn't hear the white van pull into her driveway and stop; she didn't hear its door open and close ….

Out front on the porch, Dylan rang the bell again—the third time, he reminded himself, looking around the street, the rows of plush green front yards on either side. He knew Sami was a morning walker, but usually it was earlier than this. What then, the pool?

All right ….

He walked down from the porch and around the corner of the house. As he started back toward the pool area he noticed the door to the outbuilding standing ajar. The sight of it put his senses on higher alert. He glanced all around as he walked to the partly opened door and pushed it open a little more. He looked into the shadowy building and stepped inside, his right hand going down into his pocket to the 9mm.

Having never been inside the building before, at times sensing that Sami didn't want him in here, Dylan looked around for anything out of place, not knowing exactly what *out-of-place* looked like. He eyed a stack of folding chairs, a restored Cushman Eagle motor scooter sitting under a canvas cover, folding stairs that stretched from the attic to the floor. Realizing that no one he ever knew left attic stairs hanging down except when they were in use, he looked up at a dim light glowing in the shadowy darkness. Listening, he heard the slightest movement up there. He started to call out Sami's name. But he stopped short when the travel bag sailed out of the overhead space and landed on the concrete near his feet. Dust billowed. His hand clenched instinctively around the pocket gun. He heard footsteps moving back across the attic's plywood floor.

"Sami, are you up there?" he called out, poised for anything after the events of last night.

Dead silence. Even the footsteps came to sudden halt.

"Sami? It's Ray, are you up there?" he called out. Another short silence.

"Oh, Ray?" she called down in surprise. "I—I wasn't expecting you, *was* I …?" She hurried to the locker. Looking down at all the money still left inside, she shut the lid, latched the top and hefted the locker back in place. She started stacking the boxes back in front of the lockers.

"Are you all right?" Dylan asked disregarding her question; he moved over and looked up the stairs, seeing only the dim light.

"I'm fine, Ray," Sami called down in a tight voice. "I'll be right down?" She hurried, grabbing the boxes one after the other with a little grunt and restacking them.

Dylan listened curiously to the short grunts and groans and the thump on the plywood floor each time she dropped a box in place.

"Are you having sex up there?" he asked, just to check her voice, her response.

A short pause.

"Yes," she said coolly, "of course I am. What else would I be doing up here?"

Dylan gave a slight smile.

"Would you like my help?" he asked.

"Thank you, no," Sami replied. "I'm doing fine on my own. It's terribly hot up here."

"Then come down," Dylan said. As he spoke he looked at the travel bag near his feet, the uncoupled zipper having spread open upon landing on the concrete floor. He saw the rows of money inside. One stack had flipped up and stuck halfway out through the open zipper. Dylan stooped down and looked closer as he heard Sami's footsteps coming closer to the ladder.

Jesus .... What's she up to?

He shoved the exposed stack of money back down into the bag and pressed the top closed just in time. Sami reached a leg down into sight and descended the steps.

"Ray, you startled me," she said, taking her time coming down. Ray took her hand as she stepped off the stairs onto the floor. "Look at me, I'm soaking wet, and I was only up there a few minutes." She looked at the travel bag and stooped and zipped it shut. She stood up, picking the bag up with her.

"Here, let me get that for you." Dylan reached out offering to take the bag; Sami drew it away from him.

"Thanks, I've got it," she said. "Anyway, it's got wheels if I need them. See?" She gestured at the set of small wheels on the bag's bottom edge.

"Looks heavy," Dylan said, checking her expression.

She just looked at him.

"What brings you by this morning, Ray?" she said, turning to the open door. She was working against a nervous undercurrent Dylan found barely perceptible in her voice. He stepped out the door behind her, watched her lock it, and followed her across the yard to the lanai. He'd already decided to wait a few minutes before bringing up what he'd seen last night, how he'd first seen two of the men involved leaving her house. Seeing the money in the bag was raising a red flag—time to reevaluate.

"Thought we might go for breakfast," he said stepping in front and opening the lanai door for her.

"Breakfast …?" She stepped inside the lanai and sat the bag down on a white wicker table. "I'm afraid I wouldn't be very good company today." She gave a sigh and turned to him. He saw the troubled look on her face.

"Next time I'll call first, I promise," he said. "It wasn't a good idea dropping by—"

"Forget it, that's okay, Ray," she said. "Actually I'm glad you're here." She stepped over to a coffeemaker on the kitchen counter, took down two cups and began filling them instinctively. "I'm in a mess. I don't know how I'll ever get out of it."

"Oh …?" Dylan saw the distress in her eyes. "Here, Sami, sit down." As he spoke he ushered her to the table and pulled out a chair for her. "You know you can talk to me, if you think it might help."

She studied his eyes for moment as if considering his offer. Then she appeared to make up her mind.

"Yes, Ray." She sounded relieved. "I certainly *do* need to talk to someone." She watched as Dylan brought their coffee cups over and placed them on the table. He pulled out a chair for himself, scooted it over closer to her and sat down. He wasn't going to mention what he'd witnessed last night, not until he first heard what she had to say. He had a feeling this would all connect at some point—the shootout at the Gulf Breeze, the money in the travel bag. He knew he could cut in at any point and tell her what he'd seen. For now, though, this seemed like a good time to keep quiet and listen.

CHAPTER TWELVE

Sami told Dylan about the late Sidney Augio's brother, Aaron Augio, his *accountant slash bodyguard,* Kireem, and the twenty thousand dollars Aaron Augio had extorted from her. She explained how the twenty thousand had only seemed to encourage him to grab for more. Now he was coming back, pressuring her out of another two hundred thousand under the ruse of it being a loan. Dylan let her talk, get it all out before asking any questions. When she'd finished, she shook her head and looked a little embarrassed.

"I know how naïve it sounds, thinking twenty thousand dollars would get rid of him. I should have stopped right there and called the police."

The police ....

Dylan arched his eyes up a little from his coffee cup and looked at her. He sat with his hands spread on either side of his cup.

Sami said, "Maybe I still should? I don't know how else I'll ever get rid of him. He has *implied* some things, if you know what I mean." She gave him a look.

Dylan only nodded, not giving her a glimpse of what was going through his mind. She was right, it had been naïve of her, thinking a person demanding money was going to stop once they saw their plan was working. But he didn't need to say that. She felt foolish enough about it without hearing it from him. Instead he went to the question of calling the police.

"Sami," he said, "calling the police might not be the best thing to do."

"Then what should I do, Ray?" She gestured at the travel bag on the edge of the table. "There's the money. I took it from my deposit box yesterday," she said, lying. "I was nervous having it here, so I was hiding it in the guesthouse."

"When will he be coming for it?" Dylan asked, glancing at the bag.

"Soon. I didn't tell him it was in a safety deposit box," she said.

"Good thinking," Dylan said.

"I told him I'd have to draw if from a mutual fund account. He knew it would take ten days to clear." She paused a second, doing the math. "Ten days will be Wednesday. He'll be here with his hand out, him and his 'accountant.'" She paused again, this time breaking down a little. "Oh, Ray, What on earth am I going to do?"

"First things first," Dylan said, reaching a hand over, cupping it atop hers. "We take the money back to the bank, today, because there is no way you should give this punk that kind of money—"

"Of course, you're right," Sami said. "But I'll take it back."

"Are you sure?" Dylan said. "That's a lot of cash. I don't mind going along—"

"I brought the bag here alone, I can take it back alone." Sami said. "I'm not some inept feather-headed—"

"You're right, I'm sorry," Dylan cut in. He saw she was reclaiming whatever self-assurance she might feel she'd lost in all of this.

"Listen to me going on like some hysterical ...." She let her words trail and caught herself. "I didn't mean to snap at you, Ray," she said. "See how shook-up all of this has been making me? I've been so afraid, I haven't been thinking straight lately."

Ray tilted his head curiously.

"Is this why you wanted to learn how to shoot a gun?" he said.

Sami looked a little sheepish.

"Yes, sort of," she said. "I haven't known what to do. He refers to me as 'family.' The way he says it makes my skin crawl."

Dylan gave a slight shrug.

"Okay, so the money is back at the bank where it belongs. Maybe you drive down to Clearwater for a few days, visit Millie, talk about when you were mermaids together. Leave me your door key. I'll get here early Wednesday morning. Instead of finding you here, they find me. I'll talk to them, let this Aaron Augio know there's nothing here for him." He laid his hand atop hers again and gave her a faint smile. "And I mean *absolutely nothing.*"

Sami thought about it and nodded.

"All right, I'll call Millie," she said. "She's been asking me to drive down the past month."

"There you are," Ray said.

"Thanks, Ray," she said, "it's good to know I can count on you." She considered the matter further; a look of misgiving came to her eyes. "Only ..., I'm not sure these are men you can talk to."

"I can be persuasive, Sami," Dylan said. "After all, I am in real estate." He smiled a little. "Anyway, most times guys like these are bullies and bluffs. This one thinks he has an edge because his brother and you used to be together. When he sees you're not alone, not a pushover, he'll fold his tent and move on. Go visit Millie. All right?"

Sami looked more uneasy.

"Are you sure calling the police is a bad idea—"

"Sami, look at me ...," Dylan said quietly. He took her hand more firmly. "The police are a reporting and referral agency. You call them, they'll make out a report and tell you who you should have called instead of them. They like to make you think you're wasting their time—time they could be out solving real crimes." He shrugged. "Whatever that means."

"Ray, that sounds so cynical," Sami said.

"Sorry," Dylan replied. "The thing is, you call the police, the next thing you know you're explaining to them why you've got this bag full of money. The police always have more questions than answers. Believe me."

"A referral agency. That's a new one ...." Sami pondered the idea.

"My point is," Dylan said, "leave the police out of this unless you want to let them into your personal business."

Sami shook her head.

"No," she said, "I don't want that."

"Good," said Dylan. He patted her hand. "I don't want you to worry about this. I've got it for you."

Kireem sat relaxed back in a chair, shoes off, facing the TV in the double suites Augio had rented at the Bayside Rental Suites north of Port Richey. Beneath the front window an AC unit roared against the pressing humidity. With the doors open between the adjoining suites he could hear vintage Allman Brothers blaring from the nightstand radio. He sipped scotch from a water glass and sucked on a grape popsicle he'd taken from an ice bucket on a small TV table beside him. He'd listened for an hour as Sonny French complained on and on about the amount of coke they had retrieved from Jamal at the Gulf Breeze.

"This is no small thing," Sonny said to Augio who sat with his head bowed over a line of coke on a kitchenette table. "If Marty doesn't get all his product back, or enough cash to make up for what's missing, Hal and I are headed for the swamp."

Aaron Augio gave a long deep snort along the line of blow. He raised his head, eyes red and bulging and caught his breath and rubbed the tip of his raw nose.

"Sad story," he said in a coke-strained voice, "but I've got my own problems. Your man is no tougher than my backers."

Kireem sat in his chair, watching, listening. Benny Wu lay on a bed with his eyes closed. Hal Decampo lay in one of the beds in the adjoining suite, smoking a thick joint, listening to Dickie Betts playing kick-ass lead guitar. Two popsicle sticks lay on the nightstand beside the bed. Earlier a man in the next unit pounded on the wall, but Decampo couldn't hear it.

French turned to Kireem.

"Come on, man," French said to Kireem. "You've got to front me enough cash to take care of Marty AM. I'm dead if you don't."

Kireem watched TV as if he hadn't heard a word, the popsicle stick inside his cheek.

"At least front me the fifteen bucks I owe you," French turned and pleaded with him. "That'll help me some."

Kireem gestured toward Augio.

"He's the man, I work for him," he said. "Talk to him about any *fronting* needs done. As far as my fifteen, it's going to be in my hand before you leave here."

Both the blow and the cash now lay in the Adidas bag on the table. The empty briefcase stood in a corner. Sonny glanced at the Adidas bag, then at Augio, then back to Kireem.

"How come he's the man now again all of a sudden? You've been calling all the shots. Tell him to front me for a while—"

"What's in it for me if I front you?" Augio cut in. Kireem looked back at the television. But he listened.

"Ten percent of everything I have to move to get your front money back," French said quickly, "—another ten percent for the whole amount when we settle up."

Augio looked at Kireem, who stayed with the TV but spoke to French without looking at him. The popsicle stick bobbed in his teeth.

"How you going to raise the front money without Marty AM seeing you moving his product around?" he asked.

"I won't be moving Marty's product," said French. "I know most every supplier along the Gulf. Marty don't have to know dick about it. I'll even put you in solid with these suppliers after we're done. You can keep the connections, keep right on dealing."

"I already know every supplier on the Gulf," Kireem gave a shrug.

"Not all of them you don't," said French. "But you will if you front me, let me get straightened out with Marty." He looked back and forth between them. "What do you say?"

Kireem gave Augio a look.

"*Can* you front the man, get him to stop crying?" he asked, knowing around how much money was in the bag with the product and how much was left of the twenty thousand.

Augio thought about it, knowing the money he needed to pay his backers would be in hand in another three days. He was picking up two hundred, but he'd only need a hundred and fifty thousand to clear himself with his backers. If fronting fifty thousand would get him ten percent of every sale, ten percent of the total amount and leave him knowing French's connections—*not too bad,* he told himself. With his own suppliers, nothing like this would ever happen to him again.

"How much front money are you talking about?" he asked French.

French perked up.

"Forty thousand," he said, "maybe forty and change?" He looked back and forth at them again. "I get Marty's blow back to him tomorrow, make up the difference in cash and tell him I got lucky, caught Jamal with all of it still on hand."

"I can front it," Augio said to Kireem. "Let me hold off on paying you for a couple more days, I can come up with it."

Kireem thought about it. He took the popsicle stick from his mouth and bit off the remaining grape-colored ice.

"All right," he said, knowing Augio had the money coming from the woman in Hernando Beach. He looked at French. "Who do you know on the coast that I don't already know?"

French breathed easier and gave a sly little grin, seeing that he had a deal going.

"You'll see," he said. "I know some heavyweights. We get this done, you might want to make me a partner."

"What about *Lucas McCain* in there?" Kireem said nodding toward the sound of the music. "Want us to make the *Rifleman* a partner too?"

"Hal's got no head for this business," French said. "He's a good gunslinger if I need one."

"He didn't show me much," said Kireem, "letting me hang a skillet on him." He grinned. "Thought he was headed to the last roundup."

"He should have been paying more attention," French said, "But he will from now on. He's been with me a long time."

"I understand if you cowpokes want to stick together," Kireem said. "But if you keep him around, you've got to take care of him on your end."

"I've got him," French said.

Kireem emptied his scotch, stood up and walked over to the table in his sock feet. He picked up the .22

with white sticky from duct tape still on its barrel. A small roll of pink and yellow duct tape with smiley faces on it that Kireem bought earlier at the convenience store lay beside the gun. So did the silencer. Sonny French and Augio watched him pick up the gun and unload it and examine a bullet between his finger and thumb.

"Look at this," Kireem said, holding the bullet out toward French. "Ten dollars says these bullets are half loads—hitter's bullets. That's why they didn't kill you the other day."

French took the bullet, looked at it and laid in on the table.

"So …?" He shrugged. "Lucky me, hunh."

"Hold this," Kireem said. He put the small gun in French's hand.

"Why?" said French, but he held the gun anyway.

Kireem put the silencer against the barrel and placed his popsicle stick up underneath, like a splint. "Steady now," he said, and he picked up the duct tape and wrapped it around and around, taping the barrel, the pistol, and the silencer all together, good and straight. "That's how you do it," he said.

French looked away with disinterest.

Kireem stood loading the bullets back into the gun.

"Is this firearm *inconjunctable?*" he asked in mock legalese.

French shrugged.

"It's clean if that's what you're asking. I got it from one of Marty's men. They check shit out real good."

"They better," said Kireem. "See … these little guns are only good for one thing, whacking a man up close, nice and quiet-like. Use them once, throw them away."

"I know all that," French said. Double band aids crisscrossed his shallow bullet wounds.

"Yeah? Did you know all this?" Kireem picked up a thin pillow from beside Benny Wu and stepped over to French. "You put a pillow, a towel, whatever, right here."

"Hey, watch it," said French, trying to duck away.

But Kireem crooked a big arm around his head, held the pillow against the other side, drew him close and put the tip of the silencer to his temple. He held his thumb on the gun hammer and looked at Augio.

"I could put two in your boy's head, the bullets wouldn't even come out the other side—they did, I'd catch them in the pillow. These half loads you get no noise, no mess, no nothing." He leaned close to French's ear. "They just dig deep, make scrambled eggs out'n your brains."

"Get the fuck off of me!" French shouted, trying to push Kireem away. But Kireem held firm for a moment longer, wearing a flat grin.

"*Pop pop,* real quiet like," he said, keeping his voice low. Then he turned French loose, stepped back and tossed the pillow on the bed beside Benny Wu. He spun the silenced pistol on his finger. Pink and yellow smiley faces spun like a pinwheel. "That's how the bad boys do it. That's how I'm going to do it, I see you ain't playing straight with us."

"I'm playing straight, motherfucker. Don't put your hands on me again," French warned, rising from his chair.

Kireem just looked at him with a dark chuckle, the little gun twirling on his big finger.

French saw it was time to cool down. He took

a breath and ran his hands back along his hair. Hearing French's raised voice, Benny Wu rose on the bed and looked back and forth.

"Go back to sleep, Wu," Kireem said. Wu dropped back on the bed.

"Hal, get your shoes on, get over here," French called out to the other room. He stood straightening his over-sized shirt, returning Kireem's stare.

Decampo walked into the room.

"Why, where we going, Sonny?" he said, the half-smoked joint in his fingers. His shoes hung in his hand.

"*No*-where, *Lucas,*" Kireem cut in before French could answer. To French he said, "Nobody's leaving here tonight."

"There's a tit bar up the highway," French said. We're walking there. I'm sick of looking at you ugly fuckers. I want to find some cush."

"Yeah, and I could use something to eat," said Decampo.

"Have another popsicle," Kireem said, "Nobody's leaving here tonight. You want cush, order it in. Call in some pizza, some fried chicken while you're at it. You hungry, Player?" he said looking at Augio. Augio gave him a silent nod.

Kireem looked at Benny Wu on the bed.

"You hungry, Wu?"

"I could eat," said Benny, without sitting up again.

"Order Wu some fried dog and rice," he said.

"Real funny," Benny said.

"Go back to sleep, Wu," said Kireem. "We'll wake you when the food and cush gets here."

CHAPTER THIRTEEN

In the afternoon when Ray Dylan arrived back at his house, he played a phone message he'd received from Chicago while he was out. The caller hadn't identified himself, but he didn't have to. Dylan recognized the gravelly voice, as well as a few key words delivered in a way to let him know the call was legitimate. He returned the call, left a message himself and waited for a call back. So it went with these guys, he reminded himself—always a few defensive moves being made before anybody said anything. He poured himself a cup of coffee and sat waiting by the phone. When the return call came he caught it on the first ring.

"Hello," he said, and he waited. A couple of seconds passed.

"It's me," Phil Rodell said finally, without mentioning Ray's name.

"Yeah?" Dylan said.

"You feeling all right?" Rodell asked.

"I'm good, thanks," Dylan said. He waited again.

"Okay …," Rodell came back after another pause.

"There's a problem, that thing you did. It's nothing big, but I thought I should bring it to you up front."

"What's that," Dylan said.

"The client says there was a person on the jobsite, wasn't supposed to be there. You know about it?"

The woman, Jill Markley ..., Dylan reminded himself, picturing her there that morning, sprawled naked on the bed.

"No," he lied. "I didn't see anybody."

"Did you look the jobsite over?" Rodell asked.

"Hunh-uh," said Dylan, "I was told the inspectors had already been through, everything was done."

"It wasn't though," said Rodell. "Now the client is making a thing of it. Says he ain't paying the help."

"See, this causes me concern," said Dylan, already shifting the responsibility to where it belonged. "What else wasn't the way it was supposed to be? I was told things were taken care of. I shouldn't had to check things. I'm told it was *set up.*"

Rodell got it. He knew Dylan was talking about any and all security cameras being turned off before he got there. Now he was glad he'd gone in wearing the goofy disguise. It never hurt to underestimate these guys.

"Everything else was good," said Rodell. "If it wasn't, we would have heard something before now. This person who was there got out before the whistle blew, which is a good thing."

"So, what about this person," Dylan asked. "How do we know it's even true?"

"The person who was there said something to a friend—mentioned some things. The friend told another

123

friend. Pretty soon it got around to the client. Now the client's getting an attitude, doesn't want to pay."

Dylan considered it.

"Think it's buyer's remorse setting in?" he asked.

"Maybe, we'll see," said Rodell. "Like I said, I wanted you to know about it now instead of later."

"If it is buyer's remorse?" Dylan asked.

"Then you might have to come up, convince the client it was the right decision."

Dylan knew what that meant. He didn't have to ask.

"Thanks for telling me. I'll keep my calendar clear," he said. Again he thought about the woman. In spite of this news he still felt he'd done the right thing, getting out of there, leaving it to look like natural causes.

"We're okay?" Rodell asked.

"We're okay," Dylan answered.

"Everything else good there?"

"Everything's good," said Dylan. Then he said, "There is something, just out of curiosity ...."

"Yeah? About the jobsite?" Rodell asked.

"No, something else." Dylan said. "It concerns your friend here."

"The one with the legs?" Rodell asked.

"Yeah, that one." Dylan gave himself a little smile. "I've got a question."

Rodell fell silent.

"Her friend the Canadian," Dylan said. "What can you tell me about his brother?"

"Sidney's brother, Aaron," said Rodell. "What about him?"

Jesus ....

It caught Dylan by surprise, Rodell using names that way, both Sidney Augio's and his brother's.

"It's okay," Rodell said with a little chuckle, as if knowing Dylan would be taken aback. "The dead don't worry about wiretaps."

"That's Sidney," Dylan said. "What about Aaron Augio?"

"Him too," Rodell said.

"Hold it," said Dylan. "You're saying *Aaron* Augio is dead, too?"

"Dead as last week's race tip," Rodell said. "So, how much you want to know?"

"Whatever you feel right telling me," said Dylan.

"This *Aaron* was nothing like his brother, Sidney. He was a real head case. The Augios wanted nothing to do with him. He spent most of his adult life in Canadian gated communities. A lot of it *max-sec* for a string of murders—sick *psycho* shit. Canadian court decided to see how his brain worked, sent him to *Philippe Pinel* Institute. He didn't like the view, so he hung himself. Must've figured what-the-fuck, after they seen how his brain worked, he was never coming out." He paused, then said, "End of story."

"Phillipe Pinel Institute for the criminally insane?" Dylan asked.

"Yeah, that's what they used to call the place. But *criminally insane* don't cut it these days—it could injure a lunatic's self-esteem." He paused then said, "What? You're surprised he's dead? I didn't know you knew him."

"I didn't," Dylan said. "I only heard of him lately, through your friend here."

"Yeah …?" Rodell's tone took on a change. "Why's my friend talking about him?"

"No reason," Dylan said, pulling back instinctively. "His name came up. I was curious, like I said."

A pause, then Rodell said, "The Augios are good people. Even the best families pop out a maniac now and then. He shoulda got a good citizen award for hanging himself."

Dylan listened until Rodell stopped.

"You still curious?" Rodell asked.

"No, that does it for me," Dylan said. "Thanks."

"Any time," Rodell said. The line clicked and went silent.

Dylan cradled the phone and looked at the floor for a few seconds as if a jigsaw puzzle lay scattered there, waiting for him to fit the pieces into place. Finally, he let out a breath, picked up the phone and dialed a friend up in Maryland.

"It's me …," he said, recognizing the voice that answered on the second ring. He waited a beat and said, "How're you feeling?"

A slight pause ensued.

"I'm good, thanks." the voice replied, then waited.

"I've got a name for you," Dylan said. "A Canadian, from a wealthy family. You ready?"

"Shoot," the voice said.

"Aaron Augio." Dylan spelled out both names. "I'll tell you what I already know, you fill in the rest. I'm just verifying some information I got from a friend of mine."

"A second opinion. You got it," the voice said.

"How about tomorrow?" Dylan asked. "I really need it."

"No problem," the voice said. "In fact I should have in before that. My sources move fast. You want me to call you sooner if I get something on it tonight?"

"Yes, any time, day or night. Thanks," Dylan said, and he hung up. He sat a moment longer sipping his coffee and looking down at the floor. Finally, he took a breath and straightened in his chair and looked around his empty house.

Here's where you are, he told himself ... *and this is what you've got to do ....*

Darkness had fallen as the guests of two Bayside Rental Suites carried baggage to their cars, loaded the bags and suitcases into their trunks and drove away. A pizza delivery car on its way into the lot passed the irate guests in transit. Kireem straightened up from changing the license plates on the Cadillac. Screwdriver in hand he waved the delivery car in, waited as the driver stepped out, then ushered him into one of the suites with his armload of flat boxes and white paper bags.

The pizza man looked around the room.

"What are you looking at?" Sonny French growled, standing shirtless in the open bathroom door. He weaved in place and held onto the door jamb.

The deliveryman didn't answer. In a cloud of reefer smoke, he laid the stack of flat boxes and bulging white paper bags on the kitchenette table and turned to Kireem with the bill in hand. Kireem motioned him to Augio who sat at the table with cash sticking out of his shirt pocket.

A hard beat of rap music blared from the adjoining

127

suite as Augio lifted the folded cash from his pocket and handed it over. On his way to the door the deliveryman glanced around at three women who lounged on the two double beds. Benny Wu sat cross-legged in one of the beds rolling joints, the bag of reefer spread open in front of him. The women, in tight toss-away mini shorts—one black, one white and one Latino—had sauntered in single file moments earlier off the highway on the other side of a buffering hammock of shrubbery, hedging and palms. They'd emerged from the asphalt and darkness in long silhouette, on tall heels, wearing black net stockings and carrying large purses. The music had drawn them like predators from some netherworld to the scent of warm flesh.

Following the pizza man outside, Kireem stood watching in speculation as the taillights streaked off the parking lot. As he saw the car go out of sight behind the palms and hedging, a Pakistani night manager, Dawood Davi, walked up to him from the office. This was Davi's third attempt to eradicate the noise from the two adjoining suites.

"We're running low on ice, *Davie Dagwood?*" Kireem said without looking at the man.

"Is not Davie Dagwood," the fuming manager replied. "Is Dawood Davi."

"Whatever," Kireem said, still gazing away, the screwdriver in his big hand. "We still running low on ice."

"I am not here about the ice," the manager said. "I am here to tell you *again,* this music has to stop. Other guests complain to me. Some have left!"

Still looking off, Kireem said, "I understand,

Dagwood. Tell me who's complaining, I'll go talk to them."

"No, no, is not what I want!" the manager said, quaking with fear and anger.

"What do you want then?" Kireem said. He turned facing Davi, his eyes shiny, wide and red on coke, reefer and scotch. "You don't want to take a bad fall, crack your egg open on the con-crete, do you?"

Davi stared at him, too stunned to reply as Kireem placed a hand, screwdriver and all on his narrow shoulder, his big thumb resting right there against his carotid artery.

With his other hand, Kireem produced a folded hundred dollar bill and shoved it down into the manager's shirt pocket. He patted the shirt pocket and said, "See, you need to go back to your office, sit down and decide how you'd like to see your night end." He gestured a nod down the long row of units toward a metal sign reading ICE. "Me ... I want to end my night not killing you—*if I can.*" Behind them inside the suites, music rolled and thumped, the front of the unit seeming to throb on the hard pulsing rhythm.

(HADTER
FOURTEEN

At midnight a charcoal-gray Explorer eased into a parking lot across street from the Bayside and sat for almost a half hour, watching in the darkness. Finally the three occupants straightened in their seats as Sonny French walked into the doorway, shirtless, one hand holding up his sagging unbuckled jeans. Upon recognizing French, a black Tampa gunman, Curtis *Smoke* Duvall laid a hand on the 9mm under his shirt tails.

"There's one of the muthafuckas!" he said. "Pizza-boy was right."

Behind the wheel a rough-faced white gunman named Kenny Sails reached for the door handle. Without a word he checked the gun behind his belt as he stepped out of the car. From the back seat a third gunman, Danny Udall stepped out and quietly shut the rear door. The three spread out and started walking.

"Don't forget, Marty wants them alive," Sails reminded the other two as they walked on ….

In the doorway, Sonny French saw the Explorer's interior lights turn on and off as the car doors across street opened and closed. Stoned to a stupor, he saw it but missed the meaning. In the room behind him, Kireem also caught the lights blink on and off. Without mentioning it to anyone, he nodded Augio toward the open bathroom door, picked up the travel bag of cocaine and cash from the table, and walked into the bathroom. Closing the door, he opened the small bathroom window and stuffed himself through it, his 10mm out of his belt and in his hand.

In the open front door, Sonny French stood watching the gunmen walk closer across the lot towards him, but his mind and senses were too addled to tell him to run. By the time the danger warning registered, the three were upon him. When he finally tried to turn and get away, Curtis Duvall grabbed him by his long hair, yanked him around, and held him in place facing him. He put his 9mm to French's head.

"Well hello, mutha-*fucka!*" he said as Sonny gave up resistance and stood with his hands half raised. From the next suite, Hal Decampo heard Duvall's voice and ran out front. Misjudging how close the men stood to the open door, Decampo ran into their arms; a hard swipe of Sails' gun barrel against the side of his face sent him to the ground. Sails and Udall grabbed him and pulled him to his feet.

"Hey man," Sonny said in a half-slurred voice, "I don't know who you think we are—"

"Shut up, fool," said Duvall, shaking him. "We know who you are. You so high you can't see it's us?"

French batted his eyes and tried to clear his mind.

"Smoke?" he said, as if it were only a guess.

"Yeh, muthafucka," Smoke grinned, his 9mm still

against French's head. "Now you're getting somewhere." He shook French by his long hair. "Pay attention," he demanded, seeing French's eyes wander to Sails and Udall. "Marty AM sent us to find the product you and this cracker can't seem to find." He gestured a nod toward Decampo who stood with his head bowed, blood dripping from a long welt on his cheek bone.

"No, Smoke, man, we found it, we've got it!" said French, coming out of his stupor a little. "We're going to bring it to Marty tomorrow—next day at the most."

"Next day at the most?" Duvall gave a wide grin. "Listen to you." Keeping a grip on the long hair, Smoke lowered his gun barrel from French's head and tapped it on his bare chest. "Buckle your pants, fool. We taking you and your boyfriend to Marty AM—give him his product, maybe he won't kill you, I don't know."

"I can't give him his blow tonight," Sonny French said. "I ain't got it."

Smoke looked at him.

"You said you got it," he said. "Was you lying to me?"

"I mean I've got it," said French, "But not *all of it*. I'll have it all tomorrow—"

"*Next day at the most* …?" Smoke said, finishing his words for him. He gestured at the bandaids on French's bare chest, his side, the palm of his upturned hand. "What is this?" he asked.

"A dude shot me with that little gun, the one Marty AM's hitters gave me."

"Nigga, what?" said Smoke. "Somebody took your gun away from you? Shot you with it?"

"It's a whole long thing," said French.

"I bet," Smoke said.

"I've never liked these weak cracker pricks," Sails cut in with disgust. "Cap him, Smoke. I'll cap this one, tell Marty they threw down on us."

"It's the truth, we've got Marty's blow—some cash too!" French said. "Just not all of it. Yet!"

Standing between Sails and Udall on wobbly legs, Decampo struggled against his captors, saying, "Wait! Turn me loose! He's not lying! I'll go in, get the product for you."

"Yeah, I think you *had best* do that," Smoke said. He raised his gun barrel and tweaked the tip of the barrel on French's nose. "Why don't we all go in?"

"Wait!" French said, not wanting to spark a gun fight inside the close quarters. But it was too late. Smoke shoved him inside with the tight grip still holding onto his hair. The other two led Decampo in between them. They all stood inside looking around in the cloud of smoke, the blaring music.

"Turn that shit down," Smoke shouted. One of the women jumped to her feet at the sight of the guns. She hurried into the adjoining room and turned the radio down. Instead of fleeing out the other door while she had the opportunity, she walked back in and stood staring, red-eyed.

Sitting crossed-legged on the bed, Benny Wu looked up from licking his tongue along a newly rolled joint.

"Who's this muthafucka?" Smoke asked, waving the 9mm at Wu.

"Man, it's Benny Wu," French said, his head

twisted to one side in Smoke's grip. "Don't you know Benny Wu?" As he spoke, he and Decampo both looked all around, surprised at not seeing Augio or Kireem.

"Hunh-uh, I don't know Benny Wu," Smoke said. He shoved French down into a chair at the table. "Where's the shit?" He looked all around the smoky room.

Decampo and French both noted that the Adidas bag was gone from atop the table.

"*Aww*-man!" said French. "It's gone! So's the Canadian!"

"Who's the Canadian?" Smoke asked.

"The dude me and Hal met with to buy the product," said French.

"I thought he got ripped off too," Smoke said.

"He did," said French, "but we hooked up to find the ones who ripped us. That's how we got the product back. Only now it's gone, so's he." He looked around again frantically as if the 'Canadian' Augio might appear. He didn't.

Smoke eyed the briefcase standing in the corner and stepped over to it. The women watched, wasted on reefer and coke. Smoke flipped open the empty briefcase, looked inside it, let out a breath and walked back to French.

"*Damn* ...." He shook his head. "The more I talk to you the more I do want to cap your ass." He looked around at the women who stood staring, and at Benny Wu who continued rolling, licking and laying joints aside. "All you-all bitches get on up out'n here." He flagged the woman toward the adjoining room. "Take this slit-eyed dope rolling muthafucka with you."

Decampo and French watched the women and Wu move off into the other room.

"Wha— what are you going to do?" French stammered.

"What does it look like I'm going to do, muthafucka?" Smoke said.

"Cap him, Smoke, I got this one," said Sails, raising his gun to Decampo's head. Decampo struggled. It took both gunmen to hold him still.

Smoke grabbed French by his hair again, twisted it in his hand, held the 9mm aimed at his face.

"You hear Kenny say cap you?" he said. "I've been trying hard not to, but I'm thinking he's right."

"Man, don't do it, Smoke!" French pleaded.

"Cap him, Smoke!" Sails put in.

"Yeah, cap him," said Udall.

"Take your hand off my nigga, *nigga*," Kireem's voice called out from the front doorway. He stepped inside and jammed his gun barrel in Sails' back. He jammed a stiff finger in Udall's back.

"Who the fuck are you?" Smoke said. But he loosened his grip on French's hair and stood staring at Kireem as if in disbelief. He tossed Sails and Udall a hard look for not making a move.

"I can't," Sails said, interpreting Smoke's order, "He's got a gun in my back."

"Mine too," said Udall.

"Pitch the guns over on the bed," Kireem said to the two. They did. He said to Smoke, "Now you get on away from my boy and drop your gun. You and me are going to talk." He took his gun from Sails' back and held it pointed at Smoke.

"Talk …?" Smoke stood his ground, his gun back pointed at French's face. "Hunh-uh, negro, you and me ain't talking, not with your gun aimed at me." He grinned, stayed cool. "Tell me how this sounds. You drop *your* gun, or I burn your boy here before you can pull the trigger."

Before Kireem could speak, he and the other gunmen stiffened, seeing Augio walk in quick and straight from the other room with a pillow in his left hand. Before Smoke could turn and stop him, Augio grabbed him from behind in a standing headlock. He pressed the pillow against the side of Smoke's head—the way he'd watched Kireem illustrate it earlier on French—and popped two silent bullets into his skull.

"Holy *shit!*" said Sails, him and Udall watching Smoke crumble to the floor as if his legs suddenly forgot how to stand. French and Decampo both winced at the sight, French still holding his trousers up with one hand.

"Damn, Player, look at you," said Kireem to Augio with the slightest smile. "I only was going to shoot him in the leg. Make him take us to Marty AM and straighten all this out."

Udall bolted, fearing he and Sails would be next. Before he could get out the door, Augio leaped over behind him and shot him in the back of his head. Udall fell to the floor jerking and twitching; Augio stooped and put two more silent shots in his head—almost the same spot.

Kireem grabbed Sails by his shirt. He turned to Augio as if protecting Sails from him. French and Decampo only stared. A thin wisp of smoke curled up from the duct taped silencer. "Are you through, Player?" Kireem calmly asked Augio.

Augio stared hard at Kenny Sails, the smiley-faced silencer hanging in his hand, pink and yellow smiley faces staring happily unmoved by the violence around them.

"Don't shoot, man, please," Sails said.

"Shut up," said Kireem, shaking him. He looked at Augio. "We need one of them alive to take us to Marty AM."

"I'll— I'll take you to Marty AM," Sails said in rattled halting voice. "Just don't kill me."

"See?" Kireem said to Augio, "He'll take us to Marty AM. Reload little *smiley face* and put it away." He looked at French and Decampo who stood together staring. "All right, cowpokes, boots and saddles." he said, looking the two of them up and down. "Get these bodies out of here and clean up the blood. We're going to vacate this *domicile*, take this party some other place."

"I have for you a cookie factory," said the young white woman, a Russian-Czech named Zlata Bepa Veaky. She stepped forward on long slender legs and clear plastic heels.

"I bet you do, sugar," Kireem said, "But not now, okay?" As he spoke, he looked around at her, Benny Wu, and the other two women lurking in the adjoining doorway.

"No, no," said the girl in a waning accent, "I mean, I have a place for us to go—a closed cookie factory where I live, near the water. Also is carnival rides there, too."

"Sure enough?" Kireem stopped and looked closer at her. So did Augio. "What's your name, sugar?" Kireem asked.

"Zlata," the woman said, "but you can call me Zee, or Blonde, I don't mind."

"Can't the maid clean up this blood?" Decampo cut in. "That's her job."

Kireem and Augio turned from the woman and just stared at Decampo.

"Jesus, Hal, straighten up," said French. "We can't leave blood on the floor here. Cops will be all over the place."

"Aw, yeah," Decampo said, finally getting it.

"Throw some water on your face, *Rifleman*," Kireem said to Decampo. To French he said, "And you, buckle your pants up and get a shirt on, cracker-boy, we ain't in South Beach." Turning back to the woman he said, "So, tell me, Blonde. Will we have to shoot your pimp when he shows up at your cookie factory?"

"My pimp is Johnny Moscow," the woman said. "He has disappeared and is perhaps dead." She shrugged.

"Can we get rid of our *friends* there?" Kireem gestured toward the two bodies on the floor.

"Oh yes," said Zlata. "There are so many dead buried behind the cookie factory, I am afraid to plant tomatoes. There is even a gator hole back in the woods."

Kireem and Augio gave a dark little chuckle.

Sails stood listening, tight-lipped, knowing the bad spot he was on. Once he took them to Marty AM he'd be lying dead somewhere himself—the cookie factory, the swamp. He was sure of it.

Augio looked Sails in the eyes with a creepy grin as he spoke to the woman.

"Sounds like a wonderful place," he said.

"Perfect," said Kireem.

An hour later the Explorer followed the maroon Cadillac down a narrow sand trail off the county road, leading to the water south of the artist community of Aripeka. Upon seeing the oncoming beams and orbs of bright headlights bounce over sand dips and potholes, red eyes blinked in the bracken and darkness and skipped away deeper into the swampy marchlands. Large water birds batted upward from their perches and sailed off, shrieking in outrage.

"Not so much farther now," Zlata said, sitting in the front seat of the Cadillac close to Kireem's side. She pointed at the moonlit darkness ahead with a joint glowing between her fingers.

As the two vehicles rounded a turn through a stand of ragged cabbage palms, a thin bearded man in a shredded Army field jacket stood up beside a meager fire and watched them pass. The broken stub of a shovel handle hung from his hand; an ancient-looking dog with silvery-gray flews rose stiffly and stood at his side. Behind the man and dog stood a dim lantern, a dirty cardboard lean-to and three freshly killed egrets hanging upside down from a rope line.

"You have *so* much money," Zlata said, referring to the bag of cash and drugs on the floor at their feet. She tilted her head almost onto Kireem's shoulder; her left hand lay loosely on his crotch.

Kireem grinned.

"Yeah, sweet ain't it?" he said.

"Is it all *party* money?" Zlata asked.

"What other kind of money is there?" Kireem said, going along with her ….

The Cadillac braked to halt on a crumbled

weed-grown asphalt apron facing an abandoned factory building. Kireem stepped out, the Russian-Czech woman right behind him. The other two women got out of the back seat, Benny Wu with them. Driving the gray Explorer, Aaron Augio swung the big SUV around and slid it to a stop beside the Cadillac. French and Decampo climbed out and looked the place over. Everyone stood staring in the darkness at the tall silhouette of a Ferris Wheel standing in the moonlight above the roof of the dilapidated factory.

"That's some trippy shit," Decampo said to French, passing him the glowing joint. The two stood staring up at the shadowy round framework.

"Is that what I think it is?" Kireem asked Zlata.

"It *is*," Zlata said. "There are all kinds of carnival rides back there. Come, I will show you."

"In a minute," Kireem said. He looked over at French and Decampo and gestured them to the back of the Explorer. "Get them out," he said to the two.

In the rear of the Explorer the bodies of Danny Udall and Curtis *Smoke* Duvall lay piled on the floor. Udall's arm flopped out when Decampo stepped over raised the rear door. Stepping back to the trunk of the Cadillac, Kireem opened the lid.

"Roll out, Sails," he said. Kenny Sails rose stiffly and climbed out of the trunk. Kireem said to French and Decampo, "Take Wu and this one and get these stiffs buried." He looked at Zlata and said, "You bring your tricks here, sugar?"

"No, is too far from the highway," said Zlata, moving in closer to him. "Besides I do not want for you to be a trick—"

"But you do have a pair of handcuffs, no doubt," Kireem said cutting her off.

"I *do*, right here," said Sarita Centos, the Latino woman, already searching through a large faux leopard-skin purse. She fished up a pair of pink handcuffs with the key in them and jiggled them on her finger."

"*Pink!*" Kireem grinned. He took the cuffs and pitched them to Augio.

"Here, Player," he said to Augio, "Take Sails inside, cuff him to something solid. He gives you any atti-tude, crack his nut for him."

"The electricity is still on. The switchbox is on the wall inside the door," Zlata said to Augio as he gave Sails a shove toward the factory building.

"Player will find it," Kireem said. "Come on, Blonde, let's go to the circus."

(HAPTER FIFTEEN

The phone call from Dylan's friend in Maryland came in the middle of the night. He awakened on the first ring and collected himself. The second ring stopped short as he raised the receiver to his ear.

"Hello," he said, in an almost guarded tone. He waited.

"It's me …," said the voice on the other end, recognizing Dylan's voice. "How're you feeling?" he asked.

A slight pause ensued.

"I'm good, thanks." Dylan said, completing the ritual. He waited.

"You said call anytime day or night," the voice said.

"That's right, no problem," Dylan said.

"Okay, here's what I learned," the voice said, getting straight to business. "Some of it you already know."

Dylan listened as his friend sketched out Aaron Augio's life down to his height, build, color of eyes and hair, and a small mole above his right upper lip.

"Is that your guy?" he asked Dylan.

"No, not even close," Dylan said.

"You want me to go on, then?" the voice asked.

"Yes, go on," Dylan said. Even though nothing in the physical description came close to fitting the man he'd seen leaving Sami's porch, Dylan's antenna was up for something more than appearance. As he considered the information, six foot three, two hundred thirty pounds, sandy hair, ruddy complexion, he realized the description was spot on for Sidney Augio as best he could recall Sidney from memory—or from the framed photo Sami had kept sitting out on a table until only recently.

"Okay," the voice said, "I'll fast forward to the fun stuff. Aaron Augio came from a solid family, normal upbringing. He was diagnosed in his twenties as mentally incompetent. By then he'd became a frequent-flyer in the Canadian correction system. When the family caught on to his state of mind they committed him to a laughing academy in Ontario. He burned it down—never proven. When the Augios realized how dangerous he'd become, they pulled back, fed him to the head hunters and washed their hands of him." He paused and asked, "Any of this helping you?"

"Not yet," Dylan said. "I'm still listening."

"He came forward on his own and admitted to seven murders during his residence at Philippe Pinel Institute," the voice said. "Some of the confessions were questionable, but he gave some unreleased police details, so he got to wear them. He'd settled into a life of psychotic drugs and game-shows, but then he flipped out for good when his lover at Phileppe Pinel institute gained a release. Augio hung himself in a utility cellar, or so the death report said. An inside source of mine tells me the staff didn't believe it."

"His lover?" Dylan asked.

"Yes," the voice said. "His lover's name is Carson Betto. The RCMP looked for him for questioning after Augio's death. They noted how many other residents had hung themselves during Betto's stay there. But those Mounties never found Betto—still haven't. Suicides and murders both fell off after Betto left."

Dylan was curious.

"Have you got anything else on this Carson Betto?" he asked.

"I do," the voice said. "I figured you might ask."

"Thanks," Dylan nodded.

"Carson Betto," the voice said. "Age forty six— younger than Augio. Six foot one, a hundred and eighty pounds. Medium dark hair. Medium blue eyes."

Bingo ..., Dylan said to himself, comparing the description to the man with the spiked hair who had stood staring at him out front of the motel the other night.

"I like this one," Dylan said.

"Good, then you'll like this too," the voice said. "Betto has what some of the pros call *emulation syndrome.* You need me to explain what it is?"

"I can hardly wait," Dylan said. "I'm going to guess it's something like a copycat?"

"Good guess, but more than that," said the voice. "Betto is schizophrenic ... a casebook sociopath with a penchant for violence. But his condition is impossible to detect if he's emulating someone else's behavior. He becomes whatever personality he's emulating. Like some crazy human chameleon." He paused then said, "These kind are sharp as a tack—conmen out of this world. They convince themselves that what they're doing is real. Watch out if you cross them, or do anything to shatter the role they've taken on."

"I've known guys like that," Dylan said.

"We all have to some degree," the voice said. "But take the ones you known and multiply their craziness by ten, maybe more. What you come up with is Carson Betto."

Dylan considered it.

"Your sources figure this Betto killed Aaron Augio?" he asked.

"That's the consensus," the voice said. "Aaron Augio and Carson Betto were a couple of crazies. They were lovers. The timing and the atmosphere was right. I go with my sources. Augio didn't hang himself. Carson Betto hung him, made it look like suicide. But for good measure he left him hanging somewhere where his body wouldn't be found until he was long gone."

"Sounds plausible," Dylan said.

"Here's something else plausible," the voice said. "It's a good bet that wherever Carson Betto is right now, he's convinced himself that he *is* Aaron Augio. Killing Augio would have completed a circle for Betto—made his picture on himself complete."

"Meaning?" said Dylan.

"Meaning, for what it's worth," said the voice, "that Betto is probably somewhere right now *being* Aaron Augio."

The old man and the aged dog that the two vehicle caravan drove past on the way in, stood watching the bonfire blaze outside the old cookie factory. The two, former Army Sergeant James Edmunds and his dog Rebel, observed from the cover of swamp bracken, palmetto and palm fronds, like forward scouts on patrol. They shied back a step as the few working bulbs in a string of colored lights came to life and glowed above a weed-grown storage lot where faded carnival rides sat turning to rust and ruin.

"Switch it on," a voice shouted from among the rides.

Rebel growled low under his breath as a voice called out in the darkness above the sound of classic Led Zeppelin blaring from an ancient boom box inside the factory walls. The old man lowered a hand and rested it on the dog's head, silencing him. The two watched as a grinding screeching metallic sound rose above the low factory roof and the Ferris Wheel begin a slow laboring turn.

"Hush, Reb," Edmunds whispered. He and the dog had followed and watched as the men dragged the two bodies out into the overgrowth beyond the factory perimeters to a secluded gator pond Zlata had directed them to. He'd watched a swirl of tails and eyes in water as the bodies tumbled down a short slick bank. *Yes, these were dangerous people ....*

Back at the weed-grown asphalt lot, the old man watched as Hal Decampo shouted, "No-*fucking*-way!" in stoned disbelief. He stood weaving and laughing in a cloud of reefer smoke and gazed overhead as the big wheel creaked to life and turned on its stiff rusty axels. A large bird rose from one the higher up seats and batted out across the purple darkness.

"I want to *ride!*" Sarita Centos squealed with delight. She jumped up and down on bare feet, the tall heels of her shoes stuck down into the back waist of her shorts. She held a lit joint between her long gold and black striped nails.

"You is crazy, girl. I'm not riding *none* of it," the young black woman, Tisha Lavelle, said. She raised a baby spoon up beneath her nose and snorted a mound of coke from it.

Having seen enough, Edmunds and the dog backed away into the jungle of fronds and palmetto. They faded into the greater darkness and moved away like shadowy ghosts. Led Zeppelin's *Battle of Evermore* followed them all the way back to their campsite ....

Aaron Augio stood up beside the fire, took a deep snort of coke from a line on the back of his hand and walked away into the palms and palmettos. He only stopped long enough to look back and see Hal Decampo and Sonny French pushing and pulling on the controls and brake handle of the large Ferris Wheel. Then he walked on, following the path the old man and his dog had taken.

Between them, Decampo and French figured how to draw the rusted Ferris Wheel to a rough and uneven stop. To the side Benny Wu sat smoking one of the handful of joints he'd stuck into his shirt pocket. He drew circles in the darkness with the glow of the joint while his head bobbed in rhythm to the music.

"Don't forget we're supposed to be watching him," French said to Decampo, the two of them standing at the Ferris Wheel controls.

"I'm *watching* him," said Decampo a little defensive, "he ain't doing nothing."

"Smoking a lot of dope," French put in with grin, looking over at Wu, Wu's joint looping in the air like a firefly. "Think he's worried that Marty AM will kill him when we turn him over?"

"I don't know," Decampo said. "I should walk over right now and cap him while he's high."

"You heard Kireem," said French, "he wants him alive." He took a draw on a joint and passed it to Decampo.

"I know that," said Decampo, taking the joint between his finger and thumb. "I didn't say I was going to, I just said *I should*." He took a draw on the joint, held it back and said in a strained voice, "Who the hell put this *shine* in charge anyway? We work for Marty AM, not him."

French gave him a flat stare for a second.

"We put him in charge, Hal, remember?" he said. "We agreed to pay him to find out who ripped us—get this thing straight. So far he's done that. We've got the money, we've got the product, most of it anyway, the rest with the Canadian fronting us. You got a problem with it? Rather face Marty AM and tell him we're short?"

"Naw, I'm good with it," Decampo said grudgingly, letting out the smoke. "I just lost it there."

"Stay focused, *Hal!*" French said, giving him a rough shove on his shoulder. The two laughed and smoked.

"Are we ready to ride?" Sarita called out, hurrying over on bare feet, excited.

"Yeah, hop on," Hal said, gesturing her to a grimly dusty cracked vinyl seat.

"Hunh-uh girl, don't you get on that," Tisha called out.

"It's safe," Hal said, "we checked it out good."

"They didn't check nothing out—they crazy, Sarita! Stay back off that thing."

But Tisha's warning went unheeded. Sarita climbed into the empty seat as it rocked back and forth making a rusty creaking sound. Hal tried to fasten a safety bar across the seat but the bar came off in his hand. He laid it across Sarita's lap and grinned, undeterred.

"Just keep it laying right here, you'll be all right," he instructed.

Sarita held the loose bar with both hands, squirming with excitement. Hearing Sarita's squeal of delight, and Tisha's cries of warning, Wu looked over through bleary eyes as the big rusty Ferris Wheel began making a bumpy move forward, then halted and began moving quicker more smoothly counterclockwise.

"I'm going backwards!" Sarita squealed out as she drifted back up and away.

"So what, you're riding ain't you," Hal called out, trotting alongside her until the big wheel lifted her up overhead in a long backward arch. Sarita laughed and shrieked and soared, turning her eyes to the purple moonlit heavens.

(HADTER SIXTEEN

Inside the vacant factory, standing naked at a dirty window, Zlata watched the Ferris Wheel turn and creak in a cloud of rust and dried bird droppings. Each time the wheel reached its apex in the purple moonlight Sarita shrieked with laughter, in fear and ecstasy. Behind Zlata, Kireem sat on the edge of a large water mattress, his trousers open, his shoes and shirt off. He looked all around the candlelit room—a former executive's office it appeared to him. A small nightlight glowed from a wall socket.

"Who pays the electric here?" he asked, the bag of coke lying on the mattress beside him.

"What electric?" Zlata asked. As she asked she heard the rusty Ferris Wheel turning faster, gaining speed.

"This, that …," Kireem said, gesturing to the nightlight, to the string of lights outside the windows. "Somebody pays for it," he added.

"Oh that …," Zlata said, she only pondered it for a second and gave a shrug. "I don't know … somebody, maybe?"

"For sure, somebody," Kireem said. He chuckled and picked up the bag of coke and took a small plastic spoon from inside it. "Somebody always pays for something." He spooned a little mound of the coke up and held it ready to snort. "You got running water here too?"

"Yes, I have the water," Zlata said. "I have also a shower and a toilet." She looked around at him with a hand on her hip. "So there," she smiled victoriously. "I even have a swim-pool at the other end of the building."

"A cookie factory with a swimming pool. That's living," Kireem mused.

"But I can't use it. There is dead deer and a skeleton in it. Everyone lives good in America, eh?" Outside the Ferris Wheel moved ever quicker, the creaking louder, steadier, overpowering the music.

"You have a deer skeleton in your pool?" Kireem said.

"No, it is a *dead* deer. It is a *people* skeleton." Zlata corrected him.

"A *human* skeleton …," Kireem said. He shook his head and smiled to himself. "Nothing like living on the outside—off the beaten path."

"Do you want to see it—the skeleton," she offered, "or the deer?"

"Not really," Kireem said. He paused then asked, "Mind if I take a shower, wash up some in your *fa-cility?*"

"Help for yourself. I join you, and wash your back?" Zlata walked over to the mattress and bent and held her nose out toward the spoonful of coke. Outside the creaking of the Ferris Wheel had become louder. As it turned faster, a terrible bumping sound emitted at some point in every revolution.

As Zlata snorted the coke and straightened up, rubbing her nose, a longer than usual scream came from up in the air, beyond the window. Another scream accompanied from on the ground outside.

"What the—?" Kireem sprang up from the mattress. Closing the bag of dope, he walked to the window, Zlata beside him. Outside they saw Decampo and French struggling with the Ferris Wheel controls and the long brake handle.

"*Jesus H—!*" said Kireem, seeing the large rusty mechanism turning quicker than any carnival ride he'd ever seen. He quickly buckled his belt, hearing the screams of both the women, the cursing shouting of French and Decampo.

Instead of going out the office door and down the hall to the side exit, Kireem raised the window in its stiff frame and climbed out and jumped the six feet to the ground.

"Hurry, hurry!" Zlata shouted, jumping down naked behind him.

The two ran to the Ferris Wheel, seeing Sarita streak past French and Decampo, going backwards, her hair whipping out on either side of her face like blinders. She held the safety bar across her chest with both hands. The car rocked dangerously as the Wheel bumped and shivered and groaned under its own speed and weight.

Running naked behind Kireem, Zlata and he both slid to a sudden halt as the large wheel began throwing metal on metal sparks and screaming in a monster's voice that only tortured steel can make. Decampo and French, thinking the whole thing had caught fire, leaped away from the controls and ran back twenty feet and stopped and stood transfixed. Sarita made one last pass, shrieking as she began another backwards climb into the purple moonlight. The bumping of the wheel turned more violent as it tried to slow itself. Sarita bounced up and down out-of-control in the open rocking car, the safety bar hugged against her.

"Holy shit ...!" said Decampo; French stood frozen. Tisha screamed loud and long beside them. As Sarita's car reached the peak of its turn, the whole wheel slammed to a terrible screeching halt. The impact launched Sarita, car, safety bar and all, forward, out across the tops of palms, scrub oaks and palmetto. As the stricken assembly watched, gravity pulled the weight of the heavy car from beneath the helpless woman and left her flying on her own, the safety bar stirring above her head, like the lance of some warring angel.

"Oh my-lord, my-lord!" Tisha cried out, wincing as the empty car ripped and thudded and bounced down through the treetops, followed by an abruptly ending scream and the softer sound of the woman landing farther out in the spiky up-reaching arms of the tropical canopy.

"Do you think she is alive?" Zlata asked, standing bedside Kireem. French and Decampo came running to them. Tisha fell to her knees, her hands over her face.

"I don't know, get some clothes on," Kireem replied. "Bring my shoes and socks." He looked all around for Augio and Benny Wu, seeing neither. "Come on," he said to French and Decampo, "spread out and find her."

Spread out and find her ...?

French and Decampo looked at each other.

"Fuck this," said Decampo. But rising beside them, Tisha shoved them toward the harsh surrounding terrain.

"You heard what he said," she said with tearful eyes. "Find that poor girl, she might be alive."

"Yeah, right." French chuffed as the two walked on.

Sami Bloom's sleep had been restless and sporadic, troubled, and she knew why. Today was Tuesday. She knew what tomorrow held in store. Finally, realizing that she'd gotten all the rest she was going to, she got out of bed and looked east out her window as the first ray of sunlight spread along the flat horizon. She started to take the gun from behind the radio on the nightstand where she'd kept it overnight and put it back in its box, but it slipped her mind as she breathed deep and tried to relax. She would worry about tomorrow when it arrived, she decided. Until then she needed to put it out of her mind. She had a plan ….

When she'd put on her long sweats and walking shoes, she strolled the sleeping neighborhood for a half hour and stopped at her usual place a quarter of a mile from her house and jogged her way home. Back inside her kitchen she'd poured herself a cup of coffee from the coffeemaker she'd turned on before she left. She set the cup aside to let it simmer and cool a little, while she showered.

When she'd enjoyed a warm steamy shower, she stepped out without picking up her terrycloth robe and stood in front of the steam-covered vanity mirror, as had been her custom since her days at Weeki Wachee. The saying in those days among the mermaids, or *mermaidens*, as their handler Bernice Steward referred to them, was that *a girl who doesn't watch her figure will soon see it's gone.*

Vain? Of course it was ..., she smiled and reminded herself, taking a hand towel from the rack on the wall. She folded the towel and wiped the layer of steam from the full length on the bathroom door. She turned back and forth in the mirror, posing a bit, even a little sensually but what of it? Then she reached over above the basin and began wiping steam from the half-length mirror. But she froze and gasped aloud as the second swipe of the towel revealed Aaron Augio leaning against the wall behind her, leering with menacing red-rimmed eyes.

"Oh no!" she half-shrieked, as if to ward off what horrible fate she knew was being cast upon her. She saw the front of his trousers bulged from watching her; she snatched a bath towel from the rack and tried to cover herself. But Augio stepped forward, leering up and down her body, and snatched the towel away.

"Oh yes!" he said, his eyes piercing, a white smear of coke powder on his upper lip. He reached out and grabbed her shoulders. But still wet from her shower, she was too slippery to hold. She turned away quickly, reached for the door and swung it open.

"Get out of here!" she screamed, not knowing if her words were directed at him or herself.

"Take it easy, pretty lady," Augio said, his voice thick with reefer and coke. He shot his hands out at her again.

She screamed. She rushed out the door as his hand grasped at her wet hips. Still she slipped away. She made a dash for the front door, mindless of going out into the street naked. She didn't care. Being naked, screaming in the street would end this. But as she ran on wet feet on the hall tiles, she found no traction. Her feet went from under her as if on ice. She didn't scream, this time she sobbed, loud. She scrambled, sliding, slipping along, getting nowhere, as if trapped inside some terrible nightmare.

"Right here then, *Sa-mantha,*" Augio said, breathing heavy. He walked forward, following her down the hallway, taking his time, his hand cupping the standing erection pushing in his trousers. "I've been doing this to you all night."

Oh God, oh God! Why couldn't she move, crawl, get away, get somewhere! She only gained inches for all her effort on the slick tiles. But she felt her hand grip an edge of carpeting in the threshold of her bedroom and dragged herself forward. *Her bedroom! Oh no!* Yet it was her only option, her only source of traction. Then it came to her—*the gun! Right there, behind the radio!* She had to get to it.

But Augio was upon her as she pulled herself forward on the carpet, halfway into her bedroom. He grabbed her by her hips, pulled her backwards half onto the hall tiles and turned her over and stooped down astraddle of her. He held her pinned there as his free hand fumbled, pulled his zipper down and freed himself.

"Oh yes, here we are, here we go," he said with surging, bated breath, gripping himself.

She tried to scratch his face as she struggled and squirmed beneath him. Augio clamped her to the floor with one hand. He turned loose of himself and slapped her hard across her face.

"You like rough stuff, hunh?" he shouted in her face, so close she smelled sour scotch on his breath. "Keep fighting me, you'll get plenty of it." He grabbed himself again and spread her legs apart.

The hard slap ring in her head; she felt her senses go weak. She batted her eyes to keep from passing out. She wasn't going to take a beating from this man, or worse. She forced herself to stop resisting him—she was losing anyway.

"Wait, no, I don't like it rough. *Please, Aaron, no!"* she begged. "Not like this. I'll do whatever you say. But not here, not like this. On the bed—on the bed, please. I want to do this for you."

As she spoke she ran her hand down between them and closed it around him, gentle but firmly. She stroked her hand back and forth on him, "It's just right over there," she whispered, coaxing, gaining control of herself. "Let's go there." She moved from beneath him without waiting for a reply, her hand steadily stroking, pumping.

"Oh yeah …," he moaned, standing up with her, being led into the room by her. "This is good," he said, imagining that this was what he might say if he were Kireem being led by her instead of himself. "So good, sugar …," he said, his voice dropping in pitch.

She laid him down on her bed and bent down over him, all the while stroking, feeling him grow larger, harder in her hand. She swallowed back a bitter sick taste in her mouth from what she was doing—from what she'd forced herself to do. But all right, she was doing this, she told herself, toughening her attitude, her determination. She wasn't going to take a beating from this man—not if she could help it. She had no doubt this man would've killed her if she'd continued to resist.

Lying back, he opened his belt and spread his trousers open more. She saw what he expected of her.

"Is this like you did Sidney?" he asked, breathing heavy. For some reason the question stunned her. She knew Sidney would have never discussed the two of them in this manner. But she collected herself.

"Yes, exactly like this," she said. She continued what she was doing and with her free hand reached to the travel bag sticking an inch out from under the bed. She pulled it out and raised it and laid it beside him. "Look, I have your money, the whole two hundred thousand."

"That's tomorrow," he said with singular purpose. "Do me." He moved his hips in rhythm to her hand.

"I was mistaken," she said. "It came through yesterday." As she spoke she unzipped the bag with her free hand, She glanced at the radio on the nightstand, knowing what lay behind it.

"That's good," Augio said. He only glanced at the bag, then he dragged it to him, tucked it against his side. "Do me." He arched his back and thrust himself up at her.

The money hadn't worked. But she wasn't going to give up. She glanced again at the radio.

"I will, I'm going to," she said. She tried to sound sensual, accommodating, not easy under the circumstances. "Let's take our time, Aaron," she cooed. "We've got all day, don't we?"

Augio relaxed a little. But he was insistent on his desires.

"Yes, all day," he said. He chuckled under his

breath. "First you're going to do me." He reached his hand toward her head. She couldn't let him take charge. She lowered her head before he could grab her.

"How's this?" She cupped his testicles with her free hand, kneading them, stroking them at the same rhythm.

"Oh, you're good, baby girl. You're fine," he said, visualizing how Kireem might say the same thing if he were him, somehow. Yet his hand still reached for the back of her head. She lowered her face down over him. She blew a stream of warm breath on him. Her eyes cut to the radio, gauging the distance; gauging her move. She heard him moan; felt him stiffen and harden more.

"Oh, do me, baby," he said. "I'm going to cum. I'm going to cum." His hands went away from her. He gripped the mattress sheet on either side of him.

"That's good, that's good, cum for me," Sami whispered, sounding filled with passion herself. "Cum for me, Aaron." She gripped him more firmly, but leaned up away for him. She saw him close his eyes as he cried out and stiffened his back for his orgasm. *Now ...!*

She turned him loose, hurled herself toward the radio, knocked it aside and grabbed the gun. At the same time she sprang up from the bedside and turned, the gun out at arm's length, aimed at his chest.

Augio caught on quick; the sight of the gun widened his red-rimmed eyes. He sprang up onto the side of the bed and stood up grabbing his blared open trousers.

"You lousy old bitch," he said in a low menacing tone. "Guns don't scare me. I'll stick it down your throat!" He took a step toward her, trying to gather himself inside his trousers and fasten his belt. "Go on, shoot! I *dare* you to."

"Get out of *my house!*" Sami screamed, the gun cocked ready to fire, but trembling in her hands. "There's the money! Take it and get out!" She heard her voice turning to a sob and she stopped herself. She wouldn't allow it. She forced her hands to stop shaking—she wasn't having that either.

Augio stopped. Mentioning the money registered with him, she could tell. He looked down sidelong at the travel bag seeing the top open, the money showing inside it. He leaned and picked it up.

"I'm not going anywhere," he said. "You won't shoot me, you worn-out old sow—"

The shot rang out, cutting his words short. He flinched, feeling the draft of the bullet screaming past his ear, so close that he raised a hand to make certain he wasn't hit. Sami stood staring, the gun steady and level and ready to fire again. Her face was unreadable. She hadn't been able to shoot him. At the last second she'd realized she couldn't shoot somebody. She had pulled her shot away. But he didn't know that, and she wouldn't dare let him see it in her eyes.

"I won't miss this time," she said with determination.

Augio stared at her and let out a breath.

"I'll leave, but I'll be back. You're the only family I've got here," he said with a slight shrug. "If you don't shoot, I'll take it as an invitation." He grinned slyly. "Next time, I won't settle for a hand job."

She saw the wet spot of semen on his trousers, smaller wet spots on her bed. She wanted to pull the trigger again. *It's a mistake not killing him*, she warned herself. He would be back. She knew it. But killing a man was more difficult than she had imagined. Look at what he'd done to her—what he'd made her do. Still she was stepping away, letting him slip past her on his way to the living room.

She followed, grabbing the discarded towel up from the hall floor on her way, holding it against her. She held the gun out at arm's length until she watched him wink at her.

"Thanks for *everything*," he said. He jiggled the travel bag, stepped out the front door and closed it behind him. He stopped for a moment on the porch, getting himself together. Okay, he had his backer's money. His first move was to get the one hundred fifty thousand to his backer's local contact here—the Free Bird Bail Bonds office on Spring Hill Drive. Then back to the cookie factory, let everybody know he could front the money they needed to straighten out Marty AM and get their own deal going. He smiled and walked off the porch to the Explorer ....

Inside the house, Sami watched him leave through a parted window curtain. Her stomach knotted and churned as she sprang forward, locked the door, and watched the Explorer awaken with a rumble and roll away done the street.

Lousy old bitch ... worn out old sow ...?

The surge in her throat came up so fast, so violent, she had to turn and race to the bathroom, hoping she could make it there before the sickness spewed from her clenched lips and spilled on the floor.

(HAPTER SEVENTEEN

At dawn Kireem had made it back to the cookie factory and collapsed onto the water mattress and managed to close his eyes. He had found Sarita, or parts of her lying on the ground. He'd located a loose eye, a large patch of facial skin and scalp stuck to the tree trunk higher up at the bottom of a long smear of blood. The young woman had landed some sixty feet up in the tangled interwoven tops of pine and turkey oak. In the broken moonlight he and Zlata had seen her bare leg sticking out among the limbs and leaves, as if she were now a part of the tree canopy itself. But they both decided to keep their discovery to themselves, seeing no way their drug-dazed group might retrieve the body ….

Now, as mid-morning sunlight shone through the dirty window, Kireem turned over and opened his eyes and pushed himself up from the mattress. He had not been asleep, only lying as still as he could for as long as he could with the coke still aboil deep inside him.

"Aw-man …," he said, looking all around. Picking up his 10mm, he checked it and shoved it down into his waist. The bag of coke sat blared open on the floor beside the mattress. He followed a sound of water running down a long hallway and walked into an employee locker room. Inside a long tiled shower room, he found Zlata standing, leaning against the wall with water pouring down her.

She looked around at him as he turned on the shower head beside her and undressed standing under the fall of water. He pushed his trousers and gun aside with his foot and leaned forward against the wall on both palms and closed his eyes.

Zlata stepped over closer and ran a hand down his broad hard shoulders and started to move her lips in near his throat.

"Get out," he whispered in low half growl.

She pulled her hand back from him as if to save all of her fingers. But she stayed in close.

"I thought we would perhaps—"

"It's laying by the bed," he said, cutting her off, still in the low, half-menacing tone. "Get out."

She backed away, looked at him and started to stoop down for the big gun.

"Leave it be," he said without opening his eyes or turning toward her.

"It—it will get wet?" she stammered in surprise. She stopped short and watched him intently.

"You women were never there," he said. "Nobody knows nothing."

She straightened and turned and walked away from the gun to where a faded rose towel hung from a tile hook by the mouth of the shower. She took the towel down, wrapped it around her and left ….

Letting the cool water run down over him, Kireem ran the tangled surrealistic visions of last night through his mind. The coke was starting to slowly burn off; the depression was edging in. He wanted to leave here as quick as his wheels would take him. But he knew he couldn't … not just yet. He washed himself down, soapless, with his hands, turned off the shower and picked up his trousers and gun.

He walked back down the hall, through the room holding his wadded up trousers and gun in front of him. Zlata sat on the mattress edge in her towel, the plastic spoon under her nose and watched him walk past her and step out the open window naked, still wet from the shower. She stood up and rubbed her raw nostrils.

"Where do you go, honey?" she asked in a flat mechanical voice.

Kireem only heard her as he jumped down, his bare feet touching the spiky sandy ground beneath the open window. He walked across a stretch of dried grass to where he'd parked the Cadillac. Passing the blackened fire site, he saw a large skillet with a lid over it. Cans of beer lay half submerged in an open cooler of tepid water. He saw French, Decampo and Tisha lying half-entwined on a thin blanket in varied stages of undress.

The young black woman laid topless, her underwear down around an ankle, her toss-off shorts on the ground nearby. Her breasts stood firm and round in the sunlight; her eyes were closed—not asleep. A tall clear heel was still on one foot. The other heel lay discarded halfway between the blanket and the shorts. Sonny French and Hal Decampo lay on either side, sandwiching her, their eyes closed, their faces near her breasts like young sucking pigs.

"Get up," Kireem said down to the two. He walked on as the pair stirred, neither of them sleeping, and sat up on the blanket. They stood up and watched and straightened their underwear as he reached the trunk of the Cadillac and opened it and bent out of sight. Tisha sat too. She looked around and began gathering what she could find to cover herself.

"Where's *Player?*" Kireem called out as he rummaged through wrinkled clean clothes in his trunk. He pulled up some clean boxer shorts and put them on. "Where's Benny Wu?"

French and Decampo winced.

"Hey, *bro*, I meant to tell you," French said, speaking to the open trunk lid, "Benny Wu is gone. So is the Canadian."

"*Bro ...?*" Kireem stepped into a pair of wrinkled khakis and buttoned the waist. He closed the trunk lid firmly and stood glaring at the two from above it. A wrinkled polo shirt hung over his wet shoulder. "You was supposed to be watching about Benny Wu."

"Yeah, I know," French said, "but with all goings on and that, he must've just saw a chance and bugged out." He shrugged. "Want us to look for him?"

Kireem pulled the shirt on and shook his wet lowered head.

"Forget it," he said, "we don't need him any. He won't say nothing." He looked around. "What about Player?" As he spoke he saw Zlata had jumped down from the office window and walked toward them, straightening out a tight cotton dress she'd pulled on. She carried Kireem's loafers in her hand.

"He left before daylight," said Decampo. "Brought us some birds to cook. Then he took off in the Explorer." He grinned and nodded toward the skillet sitting by the blackened campfire. "You want some Florida chicken?"

Kireem just stared at the two of them.

"And you cowpokes didn't even tell anybody he left?" he said in a low even tone.

"Tell anybody what?" said Decampo. "Nobody told me he couldn't leave."

"He'll be back," French said. "Sure you don't want some Florida chicken. It's pretty damn good."

"I don't eat egret," Kireem said, sounding a little testy.

"Why not?" said French with a stupid goading grin. "I was raised on it. It's *good.*"

Kireem stared at him harder.

"I *said* I don't *eat egret,* cracker-boy. How far you going with this?"

"*Whoa,* be cool," said French holding up his hands, "your boy Player brought them to us, already plucked and gutted."

"Yeah," said Kireem. He gave a troubled look off into the overgrowth, along the sandy trail. "I know where he got them."

"And I cooked them," Hal volunteered.

"Good for your ass," Kireem said, getting more and more irritated, the coke wearing away, leaving a jagged edge through his frontal brain lobes.

Just in time, Zlata walked up and held the plastic spoon out to him.

"For to open your eyes with?" she said. She dropped his loafers at his feet.

Tisha stepped in and stood beside Kireem as if lining up at a free gifts counter.

Kireem brushed off the soles on his feet and stepped into his loafers sockless. He took a wakeup snort and stepped back, hearing a vehicle coming in the sandy road. As he wiped his nostrils he saw the Explorer bob into sight through saw grass and palmetto and slide down to a halt beside his Cadillac. Augio swung the door open on the Explorer and stepped down, an extra large bucket of Popeye's chicken in one arm, a travel bag in the other. He walked straight to Kireem who stood half glaring at him.

"Player, where the fuck you been?" Kireem said.

"Here's the front money for Marty AM," Augio said, shoving the travel bag out to him. French and Decampo perked right up. Kireem took the bag, unzipped it and looked inside. His sour expression changed instantly, seeing the front money they needed, five packs of crisp new hundred dollar bills—ten thousand to a pack—lying there. Augio wasn't going to mention the hundred and fifty thousand he'd delivered to a bail bondsman's office on his way back.

"My *man!*" he said with a wide grin. "You are always on the stick." He held the open bag out French and Decampo to see, then zipped it and clamped it under his arm. He gestured for Decampo to take the chicken bucket. Decampo quickly took the chicken bucket from Augio and walked to the blanket and sat it down and opened it. He took out a leg and bit into it.

"Everybody get winged up," Kireem said to his recovering partiers. "Let's go see Marty AM."

As the four fell upon the chicken bucket, Kireem

and Augio moved away and stood by the Cadillac. Kireem still held the loosely loaded travel bag.

"This come from the woman in Hernando Beach?" he asked.

"It did," Augio said.

"You wasn't supposed to get this money until tomorrow," Kireem said. "I hope you didn't hurt that pretty lady."

"No, I didn't," said Augio. "She was mistaken on the days. I dropped by on a social call." He smiled slyly. "I got the urge last night. Something told me it was time to go visit family." He leaned a little closer and said, "She already had it … gave it right up without me asking."

"Yeah?" Kireem eyed him. "What else she give up?"

"Everything I wanted," said Augio, a little boastfully. "What's family for?"

"I hear you." Kireem nodded toward the skillet sitting beside the blackened campsite. "Did you go take that old man's egrets?" he asked.

"Yes, I did," said Augio. "He came snooping around, him and his dog. I followed them back to their camp."

Kireem's voice lowered.

"You kill that old man, Player?" he asked.

"I killed him and his dog," Augio offered. "Why, is that a problem?"

Kireem looked over at the chicken feast and shrugged, considering it. He stepped over and took a tepid can of beer from the cooler French had carried in closer and sat down beside the blanket.

"Not so long as you made sure they were dead," Kireem said. The beer spewed a little as he popped the top. "We don't want to leave nobody alive out here."

"I knew that," Augio said. He followed suit, picked up a beer and popped its top. He looked disappointed when his can didn't spew the way Kireem's did.

Kireem looked him up and down, smiled and bumped fists with him. "You're all right, Player," he said. "We'll check out the man and his dog on our way out."

"We don't need to check them out, they're dead," Augio said firmly.

"Get you some chicken, Player," Kireem said. "Give Decampo the key to Sails' cuffs." He looked at Decampo and French and raised his voice and said, "When you finished eating, take some water and some egret to our prisoner. See will he eat it."

Decampo grinned.

"I bet Sails will eat an egret while it's still trying to fly. I would."

"We know *you* would, cracker-boy," said Kireem. "Run Sails through the shower, get him some clean clothes and bring him on out here. We got lots to do today." He looked at Zlata. "Can we drop you ladies back off at the highway …?"

An hour later, when the chicken barrel sat empty and Sails had showered and breakfasted on pan-seared egret, the two vehicles rolled away slowly along the sandy trail and stopped at the campsite where the bodies of both Edmunds and his dog Rebel lay half hidden in weeds. Overhead a pair of vultures circled high as if waiting opening time of an all-day buffet.

The two women, in the Cadillac with Augio and Kireem, stared grimly as Kireem got out, walked over and stood looking down at the old man. As if to justify checking on Augio's handiwork, Kireem took his 10mm from his waist and aimed it down and fired two rounds at the old man's head. The woman flinched at the loud explosions. Augio only stared. They watched Kireem drag the body farther into the weeds and walk back toward the car, shoving his gun down behind his long polo shirt.

Sitting beside Sails in the Explorer, Decampo tweaked the handcuffed man's ear with the tip of his short rifle barrel. Sails had to drag his eyes away from Kireem standing over the body in the weeds and look around at Decampo's grinning face.

"Just think, Kenny *bro,"* Decampo said, "that could be you laying out there catching bullets with your teeth." He still had a welt on his face where Sails had smacked him with a gun barrel. He hadn't forgotten it.

"Fuck you, Hal," said Sails.

"*Uh uh,* be nice now," Decampo warned him, tapping the rifle barrel on his chin. "Don't forget we both work for Marty AM ... just in different job capacities."

"Yeah, I'm one of his enforcers," Sails said. "You're just one of his street punks. You can't even get in to see him. That's why I'm here. Once we're in Marty's office, you'll have to turn me loose. Don't think I'll forget how I've been treated."

"You wasn't treated bad, you fucking sissy," Decampo said.

"Really?" said Sails. "I was handcuffed all night, had to piss down my leg."

"So? Don't you always?" Decampo cackled with laughter.

Sails bristled.

"Had to eat a damn swamp bird." He grew more angry as he spoke.

"It's good for you," Decampo said, "I grew up on pan fried egret. I considered it eating a *delicacy.*"

"Sure you did," said Sails, "along with eating your sister."

Decampo fell dead silent and just stared at him.

Behind the wheel, French looked sidelong at them.

"Take it easy, both of you," he said. "Hal, why don't you fire us up a number."

"Yeah, *Hal,* why don't you. I could burn one myself," Sails said, eyeing Decampo as he spoke.

PART III

CHAPTER EIGHTEEN

At noon, Ray Dylan walked around the corner of Sami Bloom's attached garage and took a quick peek in the side window. Through the slightest crack along the edge of closed venetian blinds he saw Sami's Impala sitting in its usual spot. What was this? He stepped back and looked around. She was supposed to leave early in the morning, drive down to Clearwater. Ray had brought along tape, plastic drop covers, two single sized heavy-duty mattress covers. Everything he'd need—all right there in the van.

Good thing he hadn't let himself in carrying any of that ..., he told himself. Had she changed her mind about Clearwater? Was she just running late ...?

At the front door he slid the key in the lock, intending to enter as planned without tipping her off that he'd checked and seen her car in the garage. But the door stopped short on the end of the safety chain. *Okay* .... He reached over and pushed the doorbell as he looked inside through the narrow opening.

"Sami? Are you home?" he called out. He saw

175

her come into sight around the hall corner, dressed and fastening an earring as she walked. *All right, running late ...,* he told himself.

"Hi, Ray," she said. She closed the door enough to slide open the safety chain, then she opened the door for him.

"Hello, Sami," Dylan said, "I was expecting you to leave early this morning." He lightly kissed her cheek. Did he feel her pull back a little? *Barely noticeable ... but just a little?*

"I know, but I got a late start," she said, turning, dismissing the matter. "Come in, get yourself a cup of coffee. What brings you by today?"

"I'm in the area, I've got a key. Figured why not check on the place while I'm here," Ray said. "Real estate guys lose our self-worth if we're not checking on a property *somewhere.*"

"Oh ...? I never knew that," she said mechanically over her shoulder. He watched her go into the hall and toward her bedroom. Was there a slight stiffness in her walk? He saw her hand brush along the wall as if to steady herself.

"Sami, are you all right?" Dylan said. Never mind the coffee, he walked behind her and caught up to her at her bedroom door as she paused for a moment. From the hallway leading to the garage he could hear the washer running, the dryer too, he thought.

"Yes, I'm fine, Ray," she said. "I must've slept wrong last night. I hate when that happens," She wise-cracked and smiled at him when he reached her side and took her by her arm. Even then he felt her shy from his touch as if she were protecting a sensitive spot on her arm.

"Are you sure?" Dylan asked. He had to turn loose of her arm, knowing his hand was unwelcome there.

"Sure, I'm sure. Ray, stop it." She kept her smile but with her face turned slightly from him. She stepped into the bedroom. Dylan followed her. "I told you I slept wrong. I had a bad night. I suppose all this Aaron Augio thing has upset me more than I realized." She patted his arm and stepped over to her dresser. "You're a dear. Thanks for your concern."

Dylan had already glanced around the room. Something wasn't right; he knew it. He couldn't decide what, but something. He noted the bed had been stripped to the mattress. Not unusual for a person going on a trip, but on a two or three day jaunt to Clearwater? Then he saw the radio on the floor, not sitting there, but looking to have fallen, or to have been thrown?

"What? You didn't like the music?" he said, gesturing toward the radio. When he realized she saw no humor in the remark, he studied her face closer and saw puffiness on her left cheek. A touch of makeup had not done its job hiding it. Seeing his eyes scrutinizing her, she turned away. "Wait, Sami, what happened to your face?"

"What is this, Ray? Why all the questions?" she asked.

He gave a little shrug, knowing something was wrong, but seeing he'd pressed too far. He drew it back.

"Nothing," he said, "Maybe I'm a little rattled over this Augio business myself. I'll be glad when it's over tomorrow. I'm not a tough guy at heart." He offered a smile but he knew it wasn't working.

Sami saw he realized something was amiss here. She wasn't going to be able to keep it from him. She knew he was watching as she stepped over and picked up the radio and sat it back on the nightstand. She knew her move was a giveaway that the radio had been knocked down, or thrown. She turned back to him.

"Aaron Augio isn't coming here *tomorrow*, Ray," she said.

Dylan looked at her, curious.

"He was here this morning," she said.

"This morning? They've already been here?" he said.

"Not them, just Aaron by himself," she said, ready to let it all go now. "Yes, he was here …." She let her words trail as if to let him make of it as he would.

Dylan stared, a little stunned, But his mind began to click, putting pieces together. The bare mattress, the radio on the floor. The puffiness on her face, the guarded way she carried herself.

"Jesus, Sami, what's gone on here?" he said, moving to her, carefully looking her over.

"Nothing like you're thinking," she said. She didn't appear open to him taking her in his arms. "We—we had a fight, Ray. I fought him off."

"Look at me, Sami," Dylan said, raising her face gently with his fingertips. He tilted her cheek to him, seeing the imprint there. "Did he—?"

"No," she said, cutting him off. "He tried, but he didn't. He was drunk, high, something. I don't know …," she said. She shook her head. "I shot at him, Ray. I meant to kill him … but I couldn't make myself do it." She paused and looked down at the floor. He saw the tears start. "Oh, Ray I feel so weak and helpless. I—I couldn't even defend myself." She came forward into his arms. He held her against him carefully. "After learning to shoot, how to aim, everything I should do. The time came and I couldn't do it."

"Sami, you did good. Real good." He stroked a hand down the back of her hair. "Don't feel bad because you can't kill a person. Taking a life shouldn't be easy— not to any normal rational human being."

"You're normal," she said. She turned her face up to his with a questioning look.

"Yeah, I'm normal, Sami," he said, "I'm good with a gun, I know what to do. But if it came down to it, I don't know." He gave a slight shrug. "Maybe I couldn't pull that trigger either. Who can say about something like that unless they've faced the situation? Anybody might cave."

"That's a very honest thing for you to say. I wonder if most men could admit it," she said.

"I can't speak for most men, only myself," Dylan said.

"See, that's what I admire so much about you. You don't have to play the big strong macho role." She laid her head back against his chest.

Dylan felt a little guilty, but he let it pass.

"The main thing is you're here, Sami. You're *alive.* What better outcome can you have hoped for." If she knew what he now knew about this man, Carson Betto, posing as Aaron Augio, she'd realize the truth in what he was saying.

"Ray, you're so understanding," she said. She let out a breath and relaxed against his chest. "Sometimes I think you can't be real. I feel like you're someone I made up for myself, or some angel sent by some greater source to watch over me—"

"Shhh …," Dylan cut in, considering what she said. "I'm real, Sami," he said gently, "As real as I *can* be."

"I know," she whispered against his chest.

They stood silent for a moment, Ray feeling another slight twinge of guilt from which he once again recovered quickly. He wasn't proud of himself for lying to her, but what choice did he have. He had after all been sent by some greater source to watch over her. The angel part was giving him trouble.

"I think I should tell you, Ray," she said finally, "I gave him the money."

"You what?" Dylan stepped back from her.

"Yes, I gave him the money," she said. She also stepped back.

Sami, *why?"* Dylan said. "We had it all planned. It would have worked."

"But the plan wasn't working, Ray," she said. "Him coming here so early changed everything. I was desperate to get rid of him. I thought the money would distract him."

"But it didn't," Dylan said. He shook his head in regret. "Jesus, Sami, *two hundred thousand dollars!* That's a lot of money. Maybe I can find him. Get it back from him." She saw the wheels turning in his mind.

"No, stop it, Ray," she said. "The money's gone. I don't want you getting hurt—"

"Sami, I can't let this happen—"

"Yes, you can," she said cutting him off. "I don't want the money back, Good riddance to it. I'm glad it's gone."

Good riddance to it? Glad it's gone? Two hundred thousand dollars gone, just like that ...?

Dylan just stared at her.

"Sami, we talked about this. He'll be back. People like him never get enough."

"I know," Sami agreed. "He even said he'd be back. But I think he won't." She sounded almost sure of herself, Dylan thought. He wanted this man in his sights, and not just because of the money. He knew what a dangerous manic they were dealing with.

"*Why* do you think he won't?" Dylan asked.

She looked at him long and hard as if deciding whether or not to let him in. Then she let out a breath. "Because the money isn't real," she said. "It's fake ... bogus." She paused then seeing the look on his face, added, "It's counterfeit. He'll go to jail when he tries to spend it."

Dylan found himself staring again.

"You mean you had two hundred thousand dollars *counterfeit cash,* in your bank deposit box?"

"I have much more than that," Sami said, coming clean now that she'd let her secret out. "It was never in my deposit box. It was in the guesthouse—the attic is full of it."

Dylan stood speechless.

In the attic of the guesthouse, having scooted the boxes aside, the two stood looking at the wall of stacked footlockers. The center stack reached up into the point of the gable roof. Other stacks descended on either side with the roof's pitch.

"Jesus, Sami, you always amaze me," Dylan

said, speculating how much cash would be in these if every one of them were full—which she assured him they were.

She stood with a hand on her hip and shook her head slowly.

"Imagine how I felt when Sidney first showed them to me, and opened one just to make sure I believed it," she said. "I was absolutely flabbergasted! I'd never seen so much money in my life, real or otherwise …."

Dylan stepped forward only half-hearing her as she continued talking about the day she had stumbled onto the cash and had Sidney bring her out here and explain it to her. "Sidney didn't tell me where it came from," she went on, "simply that a friend had brought it to him, asked him to keep it for awhile."

Dylan stood taking it all in.

"At that time, several international businessmen had been kidnapped and held for ransom," Sami continued. "Sidney said if something like that happened to him, some associates of his would come here for the money to pay his abductors. He said this money is almost perfect—hard to distinguish from real cash …."

Never really told her where it came from …. Dylan almost smiled to himself.

Of course Sidney never said where so much counterfeit money came from, or how his friend happened into possession of it. But Dylan would not have had to ask her; he knew the history of the footlockers the minute he laid eyes on them. He'd seen them before, years ago. He'd helped move a few of them from Miami to Jacksonville.

"They're from Cuba," he said, cutting in as she spoke on.

"Cuba?" she said, stopping mid-sentence, watching as he kneeled and opened the locker on the floor. "I hope you're not going to tell me Sidney was doing anything illegal." She paused with an anxious look. "Are you, Ray?"

"No, Sami, nothing like that," Dylan said, raising the locker lid as he spoke. "Well, maybe a little," he corrected himself.

"A *little* illegal?" Sami queried.

Dylan picked up a stack of bills, riffled it and examined it. He even recognized the paper bands on the stacks of hundred dollar bills. They were faded now, but at one time the printing on the bands had been purple and gold. He smiled to himself, turning the stack in his hand. Sidney had been right, these bills were next to perfect. He laid the stack of bills back in its place and stood up.

"In the eighties," he said, "when the Berlin wall came down, Russia's KGB had orders to pull back on a lot of smuggling going on between Cuban agents and agents in Miami, Tampa, other shipping ports. Cuba and Russia had the best counterfeiters in the world producing US currency—*ghost bucks*, or *spook money* it was called."

He closed the lid on the locker.

"So, yes, it's illegal having possession of this stuff." He dusted his hands and tipped the lid closed with his foot. "But Sidney Augio would never be involved in passing bogus money—he had plenty of the real stuff."

"That's a relief," Sami said. "Then the story about ransom is true?"

"Yes, most likely," he said. "Good quality counterfeit sold on the underworld market for as much as twenty-five cents on the dollar in bulk—*or so I heard,"* he added quickly. "When the wall came down, Russia and Cuba wanted their people out of the business so bad, the cost of fake cash dropped like a rock. Got so cheap, people who would never have bought it before, started buying it like crazy. It must've made sense to businessmen like Sidney Augio to have some on hand, in case of an emergency."

"I never liked having it here," Sami said.

"But you never got rid of it," Dylan pointed out.

"I know I should have. But I felt like I sort of promised Sidney I'd keep it on hand. So I did," she said. "I was almost glad to get rid of it, some of it, at least. Now that I've put it in Aaron Augio's hands, I think I better do something with the rest of it in case he gets caught and points the finger at me." She paused, then said, "Don't you agree?"

"Oh yes, I do agree," Dylan said. "You need to get it out of here right away." He looked at her. "Were you still going to Millie's after everything that's happened here?"

"I can," Sami said. "She's still expecting me, unless I call and cancel."

"No, go ahead if you're up to it," Dylan said. "I'd feel better if you're out of here for awhile." He eyed the stack of footlockers as he said, "I'm going to load these and get them out of here. We need to talk about Aaron Augio while we're at it …."

In moments Dylan had backed the van around to the front porch of the guesthouse. As they loaded the footlockers into the rear door, he told her everything he'd learned about Aaron Augio. He told her how the miscreant psychotic brother of Sidney Augio had died in the Canadian mental facility; how his equally psychotic lover, Carson Betto had most likely murdered him, left him hanging, and taken on his identity—told her how Betto was a natural for taking on the personality of people he knew, especially those he admired.

"The ones he admired enough to kill," he said. "I figure he learned a lot from Aaron Augio," he went on. "The Augios were known from Canada all the way down here. Aaron used the family name to help himself. Betto figured on doing the same."

"But the Augios are all respected businessmen," Sami said. "I know Sidney would have no connections with anyone his brother Aaron or his psychotic boyfriend would have benefited from knowing." She stared at Dylan. "Am I right?"

"Yes, exactly," Dylan said. He wasn't going to say anything derogative about Sidney or the Augio family. What she didn't know about the Augios she'd have to learn for herself or figure out on her own. "Sometimes just dropping the right name at the right time is all it takes to open a couple of doors."

She started to say more as he sat the last locker in back of the van and got ready to close the door. But the she noticed the rolls of plastic drop covers and masking tape sitting to the side. She looked at Dylan.

"What's all this for?" she asked.

"Oh …." Her question caught him off guard for a moment, but he recovered, fast.

"All right, I'm busted," he said. He managed a little smile. "I thought you'd be gone when I got here. I was going to surprise you, paint your kitchen while you were away at Millie's. I heard you mention it a while back."

"Well, aren't you a sweetheart, Ray," she said. Looking around inside the cargo area, she asked, "Where's the paint?"

"I was going to pick it up today after I taped and covered everything—" He cut himself off and said amiably, "You sure ask a lot of questions, ma'am." Then he closed the van's rear door and walked her over to her car inside the open garage. He opened the driver's door on her Impala and ushered her in behind the wheel. "I'm going to follow you out of here a ways until I'm sure you're headed safe for Clearwater." He closed her door and stepped back.

Sami lowered her window halfway.

"We'll talk some more about this Carson Betto later," Dylan said. "The main thing is, you happen to see him anywhere, get away as fast as you can. Don't take chances with him, he's a killer." He gave her a serious look. "All right?"

She nodded. "All right." Then she asked in a lowered voice, "Are you sure the place where you're taking the money will be safe?"

"Yes, it'll be safe there," Dylan said. "But as soon as things are settled, we take it somewhere and burn it." He looked at her closely. "Is that a problem for you?"

"No, not at all," Sami said. "The sooner the better."

"Good," he said, "Then that's our plan." He watched her pull out the garage and stop, ready to drive away in front of the van when he brought it around. As he walked to the van he reminded himself that he wasn't about to burn the cash until he knew more about what he was dealing with. Some things were starting to click in his mind. He needed to check them out before letting anything happen to this money. In his world even phony money was worth something—*maybe a lot,* he thought, climbing into the van.

(HADTER NINETEEN

Tampa Florida:

Marty AM stood watching the five men on the security monitoring screen even though they were all less than twenty feet away on the other side of his closed office door. Three of the men standing out there worked for him. One of them, a gunman, Kenny Sails, had been sent along with two other gunmen to hunt for the two men now standing one on either side of him. *Interesting* .... Those two were Sonny French and Hal Decampo, two small time street punks he kept busy checking out new sources for him, new product, new deals. *Nothing big*, he reminded himself, watching them as his two door men approached them in the narrow hallway.

One of the other two men he'd never seen before. But he took him as the Canadian he'd been hearing about for the past month. A man with backers, down here looking to set up a pipeline to the high North. *All right, Canada, I'm listening ...,* Marty told himself. He rolled his cigar in his mouth. The black man he recognized from a photo and some scraps of information passed along to him by his man, a civilian employee in Hillsborough County Sheriff's Department. The black man's name, Kireem Mateen Murabi, *or some such shit*, he chuffed to himself. *Always with the names, these black guys.*

But everything he'd seen or heard about this *Kireem* had been good, he reminded himself. His civilian at Hillsborough County had checked him out. Said Psycho Willie Hopps spoke well of him. Said this Kireem was a promising up-and-comer, greedy but patient. Known by the right folks in Tampa as a solid man to deal with. Okay, let's hear your story, *Kireem Mateen Whatever.* He chuffed again, turned away from the monitor screen and walked around behind his desk. He opened the top right hand drawer, took out a big nickel plated .50 caliber Desert Eagle and laid in on his desk. *Just in case*, he told himself ….

In the monitored hallway, Kireem and Augio had walked up the stairs ahead of the others and stopped, letting the other three gather up around them. Kireem gazed up at the camera in the ceiling as he stepped forward real slow-like, making it known that while someone was watching him, he was staring right back at them.

"Hold it right there," said one of the two door guards walking toward him and his entourage. A long .45 in the guard's hand lay leveled at Kireem. Still, Kireem didn't stop right away. He took his time, sort of slowed to a halt.

"Hey, it's all right, Rudy," Sails said, stepping up beside Kireem. "I called ahead, Marty's expecting us."

The door guard, a tall light-skinned black man

named Rudy Turbo didn't like the way Kireem had slow-walked him. He stared hard at Kireem through green wolf eyes, and said to Sails, "Makes no damn difference, Kenny. I still gots to search everybody comes up. You know that." He eyed Sails up and down and said, "Raise your shirt. Mr. AM wants to see you first."

Sails raised his shirt and turned full circle. Looking at Sails' bare belly and back, Rudy gave him a shove toward a door at the end of the hall, then turned his stare back to Kireem.

Returning his stare Kireem eased the 10mm up from under his shirt tail and held it out. "All right, cowpokes, ya'll heard the *Marshall,"* he said to the others over his shoulder, "hand over your guns."

Both door guards took a tight stance when Augio, French and Decampo raised guns from under their shirts and held them out, barrels pointed down at the floor.

"Take they guns, Maurice, pat them down," Rudy Turbo said to Maurice Ison, the other guard.

As Maurice gathered guns, and turned and laid them on a table against the wall, Rudy Turbo turned back to Kireem whose 10mm still hung from his fingertips. "I still gots to search you," he said. As he spoke he reached out to take Kireem's big Glock.

"In that case I *gots* to search you too, negro," Kireem said, pulling his big Glock back from Rudy, righting it in his hand.

Maurice tensed, his gun pointed at Kireem; but Kireem's 10mm was only inches from Rudy's chest.

Rudy stood rigid. He looked at the big Glock 10mm, then back up at Kireem.

"Big *10,"* he said coolly. "That's an FBI gun."

"*Hunh-uh.* Used to be," Kireem replied, just as coolly. "They gave it up, said it hurt they hands too much."

Rudy stared more intently.

"How you know about the FBI, nigga?" he said with suspicion.

"How do *you* know about the FBI, nigga?" Kireem said, giving it right back to him.

They stood staring each other down.

"Boys, boys," Marty AM's gravelly voice said through a recessed speaker in the ceiling, "stop seeing whose dick's the biggest. Give me five minutes with Sails and bring them in, Rudy."

Rudy looked up at the ceiling camera as if it were a living thing.

"Don't want me to search him?" he said.

"Let him search you, *Kireem Mateen Mulorobbie*, or whatever the fuck your name is," said Marty AM. "Raise your shirt and turn around, slow."

Kireem gave the speaker a surprised look.

"It's *Murabi,*" he said. "It's Kenyan."

"Yeah? It sounds Muslim," AM said.

"Whatever," Kireem said. He handed Maurice his gun, raised his shirt tails with both hands and turned a slow full circle. Rudy and Maurice looked him over good; so did Marty AM, on the monitor. Augio and the others followed suit. "How you know my name?" Kireem asked the monitor.

"I know plenty about you, Kireem Mateen *Whatever,*" Marty AM said.

"Kireem will do." Dropping his shirttail. he turned to Rudy and said, "You through admiring my ass, nigga?"

"Let's go," Rudy said, wagging his gun. He and Maurice followed the group halfway down the hall and stopped and waited outside the closed office door.

Five minutes later:

Marty AM stood behind his desk, the large window behind him overlooking Tampa Bay at the mouth of the Hillsborough River. The four men filed in and stood on the other side of his desk, Augio and Kireem in front. Augio held the travel bag at his side. Behind them in the open doorway, Rudy Turbo and Maurice Ison waited until Marty AM waved them outside.

As the door closed behind the guards, Kenny Sails stepped to the side, having told his boss everything that happened. A blue-red imprint of Marty AM's hand covered the side of Sails' face. He wiped a waded tissue under his equally red nose.

"Before we talk about anything else," Marty AM said in a threatening tone, staring at Augio, "where's my blow, and why'd you killed my boys Smoke and Danny Udall?" He leaned on his palms, his right hand close to the big Desert Eagle.

"I killed your boys for being stupid," Augio said, not backing an inch. He held the travel bag at his side.

"Stupid, huh?" Marty said. "And you *are?*"

"I'm *Aaron Augio*, from Canada," Augio said, putting some emphasis on his name. He raised the travel bag of coke and cash and jiggled it a little in his hand. "I say they were stupid, or else they would be handing you this blow and this makeup money instead of me."

An Augio standing here wanting to do business? Okay, this'll work ....

Marty kept cool and played it off, looked at Decampo and French.

"It's true, Mr. AM," French said. "The four of us got your product back for you." He gestured at Sails. "Kenny and Smoke and Udall came around on the tail end of everything—started pushing everybody around."

Marty looked at Sails, then back at French.

"I pay them to *push everybody around,*" he said. "I sent you two looking for these two." He nodded from French and Decampo, to Augio and Kireem. "You never came back. I didn't tell anybody to kill you, but I could have—still might, so shut up." He gestured at the travel bag. "You giving me that bag, or what?" he said to Augio.

"Yes, I am," Augio said. "The ones who took it sold some of it off. But we got the cash from them—fifty thousand to be exact."

To be exact ....

Marty AM stared at him for a second. He picked up his cigar, rolled it around in his mouth and left it there, talking around it.

"Why you being so good to me, Canada?" he said. Kireem watched and listened.

"I want to do business with you," Augio said. "That's the only reason your boy Sails here is still alive. I wanted an introduction, meet you in person. I want to buy dope from you and bring it up North."

"You don't buy my dope from me, you got to buy it from guys like these," Marty AM said. He gestured his cigar toward French and Decampo.

"I tried that," Augio said. "We see how that

worked." He took a step forward, sat the travel bag on the large desk, unzipped it and pushed it slowly across. "So, let's start over, try again."

Marty didn't reply right away. He reached over and spread the bag open enough to look inside. He saw the blue-lined quarter bags of blow and the neat banded stacks of cash. *What's this ...?* He knew the street buyers didn't pay in large bills.

As if reading his thoughts, Augio said, "I cashed in the chump change so your boys wouldn't have to bother with it."

"So sweet of you, Canada," Marty AM grinned. He relaxed a little, moved the Desert Eagle from his desk, back into the drawer. He needed to stop calling the man *Canada* now that he knew he was an Augio. But he couldn't do it all at once, make himself look weak. He had to let it happen over the course of the conversation, like now.

"Let me ask you something, Augio." He took his hand back away from the bag. "What are you doing, moving around these streets with a gun in your hand. All your gunmen on strike up there?"

Augio smiled, easy-like, but didn't answer.

"My people wanted me to walk away when we got ripped-off, send you the bill," he said instead. "I told them *no,* shit happens. I figured I'd see this through, take the opportunity to see the *ground floor."*

Marty AM chuckled.

"Now you've seen it?" he said.

"I don't want to see it again," Augio said with a shrug.

Marty AM pushed a button on the inner edge of

his desk. The door opened; Rudy Turbo walked in, went around the desk and picked up the bag and left with it.

"I've got to say, you haven't done bad for a snowbird," Marty said to Augio as the money and the product left the room to be checked and counted. He looked at Kireem and said, "Where do you play into all this?"

"I work for Mr. Augio," Kireem said. "He wants to buy your dope, I back him up on it—if you want to sell it to him, that is." He shrugged.

"You're too modest, Kireem," Marty said. "I heard Rudy say you carry an FBI gun?"

"I do," Kireem said, not the least intimidated, "You rather see me carrying it, or them?"

"Sails also said he saw you put two bullets in a man's head out in the boonies, while he was dying," Marty said. He studied Kireem closer.

"Did I?" Kireem said, "I don't remember."

"The old man and his dog," Sails said, refreshing his memory.

"Not me," Kireem said. He stared coldy at Sails. "Is your mouth full-grown, or will it keep getting bigger?"

Sails bristled, but kept himself in check.

Marty gave a dark chuckle, liking the idea of a Canadian financier and his tough-talking Kenyon in his office ready to buy heavy dope from him.

"Relax," he said to Kireem, "Nothing we say here will ever leave this room."

Kireem nodded and settled a little. But he gave Sails a final look full of ice picks and poison labels.

"Are we going to sell some blow together, or not?" Augio cut in.

Marty grinned and said, "Mr. Augio, I'm going to sell you all the blow you want, and any other dope you think your people want to distribute up there—" He stopped short and looked at the door as it opened; Maurice stepped inside. Marty AM looked enraged at being interrupted. But Maurice wasn't deterred by the dark look he got from him.

"Excuse me, Mr. AM," he said, "Rudy say he gots to see you in the hall—says it's an emergency." Instead of the pistol he was carrying, the door guard now carried an AK-47 rifle.

Sensing something was wrong the minute the door opened and Maurice and the big rifle came in, Kireem stepped over to an open washroom door and slipped inside, unnoticed by Marty AM and his AK wielding door guard. Augio only glanced around curiously as Kireem closed the door and latched it.

"You wait here, Maurice," Marty said, "Keep everybody comfortable." He gave a quick look around the room, noting Kireem was gone. Seeing the washroom door closed, he nodded at it and said to Maurice, "Watch that one real close."

Uh oh ..., Kireem thought, listening with his ear pressed to the washroom door. He'd been right. Something was about to turn bad and ugly here.

He looked around and stepped over to a narrow door on the other side of the room. He opened the door and stepped inside a dark short hallway with shelves of paper towels and cleaning supplies. He saw another narrow doorway and went to it and cracked it enough to see that it led a few feet back and opened into the main hallway. He listened to angry voices talking in a room near the top of the entrance stairs—Rudy Turbo, Marty AM, others.

Short moments later footsteps resounded along the main hall toward the open office door. He watched until he saw Marty AM pass by, cursing under his breath, carrying a pack of banded cash from the bag in his hand.

Time to arm-up ..., he told himself. As soon as he heard the office door slam shut, he hurried forward and turned into the main hallway. Risking the security cameras seeing him, he raced to the table by the wall, snatched up his big Glock 10mm and racked a round into the chamber. He grabbed Augio's Bersa and French's 9mm and shoved them down in his waist.

(HADTER
TWENTY

Maurice had stood blocking the open hallway door for a tight five minutes, the AK-47 raised and ready. He stepped aside when Marty AM walked in and slammed the door shut behind him. Aaron Augio cut a quick glance to the closed washroom door as if Kireem would come barging out, put an end to whatever was about to happen. But no such luck. The door to the washroom door stayed closed; French and Decampo both looked stunned. Kenny Sails backed away, as if to say he'd seen this dark twist in Marty AM's brow before and wanted none of it.

"Real funny, you moose-fucking *Canuck mother-fucker!*" Marty AM shouted at Augio, hurling the banded bills at him. The pack hit the edge of the desk and flew apart, much of it landing at Augio's feet. Augio looked down at it, then back at Marty AM with a puzzled expression as Maurice stood with the AK half-raised to his shoulder.

"You bring me *funny-money?*" Marty said. "What? Was I supposed to buy *Park Place, The Short-Line fucking Railroad?*"

"The money's counterfeit?" French cut in. He and Decampo inched farther away from Augio. "Mr. AM, we had nothing to do with this. We just wanted to get your product back, like you sent us to do! These two cooked all this up on their own!" He gestured toward the washroom door as he spoke.

"Tough break for you, Sonny!" Marty said. He jerked his head toward the hall and said to Maurice. "Take them to the basement behind the old boiler." He looked at Augio, then at the closed washroom door. "What's with that one?" he asked Maurice.

"I don't know, he never came out," Maurice said. "I'll check on him?"

Augio stood tensed, ready, waiting for any break in the game so he could make his move. *And here it is ...,* he thought, seeing Maurice lower the AK just a little and start to walk across the floor to the washroom.

"No, wait, *stay right there!"* Marty shouted. Maurice stopped mid-step. But it was too late. Seeing the AK lowered, the room broke up in every direction. Sails turned and slung open a big sliding door and ran out onto a narrow balcony; French and Decampo sprang onto Maurice and struggled to get the rifle from his hands. Not giving it up, Maurice's finger made it into the trigger guard and squeezed hard. Augio hurled himself over atop Marty AM's desk and slid off the other side, going for the only gun he knew of in the room.

The AK-47, set on fully automatic, bucked and bounced in Maurice's hands. Decampo and French hung onto him and the gun, keeping the flashing muzzle from pointing at them. A jagged row of bullet holes strung along the walls as the rifle fired nonstop; broken chunks of drywall and paneling splinters filled the air.

On the balcony Sails screamed like a woman, realizing there was no way off the spot he'd put himself on except straight down, nine stories onto traffic and asphalt.

Marty AM had dropped to the floor when the AK started ripping the walls and windows apart. Knowing Augio had gone for the Desert Eagle, Marty yanked a snub-nosed revolver from an ankle holster under his trouser leg and rose into a crouch at the very second the AK fell silent. He fired twice at Augio who had also risen, the big Eagle in hand, when the rifle stopped. Marty's first shot hit Augio high in his left shoulder. His second shot exploded and cut a graze along the side of Augio's head.

But before Marty could fire again, the big .50 caliber Desert Eagle bucked in Augio's hand and let out a roar like cannon fire. The large bullet bored into Marty's left wrist, ripped upward through his forearm and slung blood and fragments of meat and elbow joint onto the wall. Marty flew backwards, but staggered in place instead of falling. His left arm hung in limp meaty shreds. He tried to aim the revolver with his right hand. Augio leveled the big .50 again.

French and Decampo had managed to wrench the AK from Maurice's hands and turn just in time to see Augio's second shot slam Marty backwards. The impact rolled him along the wall, to the open sliding doors and into Sails arms on the narrow balcony. Sails let out another scream and clasped his arms around Marty AM for reasons no one would ever know. The two toppled backwards over the wrought-iron rail and plunged out of sight. Sails left a long scream hanging in the air behind them.

Decampo held Maurice pinned to the floor while French jerked the empty magazine from the AK-47, reversed it and shoved the full magazine taped to it into the rifle chamber. Decampo stepped away from the struggling Maurice and French sent a burst of three bullets into his chest. Maurice melted dead on the floor. French swung the AK toward the door as it swung. But he held his fire as Kireem stopped inside the room, his 10mm out at arm's length.

Looking all around, Kireem got the picture and said to the three, "They coming from downstairs." He looked at French and Decampo. "Lead us down out of here," he said to French. He waved the two toward the hallway. Decampo hurried over and picked up the snub nosed .357 Marty AM had pulled from his ankle holster.

"Why me?" French said. From the far end of the hall running footsteps pounded up the staircase beside the elevator.

"You the man with the *biggest gun,* cracker-boy," Kireem said.

"I don't want to be!" French said, losing his nerve. He turned to Decampo and held the rifle out to him.

"Huh-uh." Decampo shook his head, turning him down. "I'm good." He shook the shiny .357 in his hand.

"This is fucked-up!" French growled, But he hurried to the door and took the lead out into the hallway. Decampo hurried out behind him. Hearing the running footsteps make the turn on the stairs the next level down and keep coming, Kireem stepped over to Augio who stood gripping his bloody shoulder. Blood ran down the side of his head from the bullet graze. Kireem looked all around at the devastated office, broken glass, bullet-riddled walls and furniture. Then at Augio.

"This has not exactly been a win-win transaction, Player. You ready to leave the building?" he said. He pulled the Bersa from his waist and handed it to him. "I got your shiny gun for you."

Augio took the gun and looked at him as the pounding on the stairs grew closer. Outside in the distance the sound of sirens began to swell and wail.

"I thought you ran out on me," he said.

"Huh-uh," Kireem said. "I don't leave 'til I get my money, remember?" He pulled a folded handkerchief from his hip pocket and stuck it against Augio's bleeding shoulder. Augio pressed his free hand on it. "Better not be no funny-money either," Kireem added. He eyed Augio closer and said, "Why did you think that counterfeit shit would work, anyway?"

"It wasn't mine," Augio said in a bitter tone. "The old woman stuck me with it."

"That sweet, pretty woman in Hernando Beach hung you with a bunch of bad paper?" Kireem gave a dark laugh and shook his head. "I love this fucking Gulf Coast," he said.

"I'm going to kill her," Augio said, his eyes glazed with smoldering rage. "I'm going to kill her real slow—piece at a time *slow.*"

At the far end of the hall, French's AK-47 began a deadly hail of gunfire down into the stairwell. Kireem motioned Augio toward the hallway.

"Come on, Player," he said. "You ain't killing

nobody if we don't get out of here, get you fixed up some."

With the AK-47 in French's hands and a pouch of extra loaded clips Decampo grabbed from the gun table, the four fought the uprush of gunmen to a stand-still on the iron and marble stairwell. Behind the roaring chatter of the AK and the countless explosions of handgun fire, the sound of sirens converged on the building from every point of the city. Kireem raised a hand for silence as they listened to the gunmen reloading and whispering on the next level down.

Without a word Kireem hand signaled for French and Decampo to take the stairwell flanking the other side of the open elevator. They got his message and turned and slipped away. Kireem took the Bersa from Augio's bloody hand and aimed it at the stairwell and fired five rapid shots. They heard footsteps hurrying for cover on the next level down as the bullets pinged off of metal and stone.

"I been wondering how your shiny gun shoots," he whispered. He handed the gun back to Augio and gestured toward the other stairwell. As they headed across the front of the waiting elevator, Kireem ran inside the open door, punched the ground floor button and ran back out just as the doors started closing. No sooner than they were headed down the stairwell, the same direction as French and Decampo, four dazed wounded gunmen ascended from the cover of their stairwell and jerked to a halt. They looked up at the descending lit numbers above the elevator door, and at the stairwell leading down on its other side.

"Split up!" said Rudy Turbo to the other three. "Herbert, you come with me," He stared down the stairwell as he spoke, Herbert out in front of him. "You two get to the ground floor before the elevator," he said to the other two. "If they on it, blast them, don't let them off."

The two gunmen nodded, out of breath, and watched as Rudy and Hubert Grist ran down the stairwell out of sight ….

As the patrol cars skidded into a half-circle around the front entrance, another heavy barrage of gunfire, both rifle and handgun, resounded from within the building. The police waited, watched, taking position. A call went in for the tactical deployment unit. But as the call went in, two wounded gunmen staggered out the glass doors onto the street.

Acting quick, the watch lieutenant grabbed the bullhorn and held it close to his lips.

"Tampa Police. Drop your weapons, place your hands above your head," the lieutenant's electronically amplified voice called out. He immediately repeated the same words in Spanish, as if to cover all bases. But in did no good. Neither of the two stunned and wounded gunmen obeyed his order. Instead they raised their guns toward him, seeing him, his bullhorn, and an endless line of officers taking aim across the hoods and trunks of their patrol cars.

"Oh no," said Herbert.

"*Fuuuck you—!*" Rudy Turbo bellowed long and loud, knowing he would finish the day on a stainless steel table no matter how this went. Before his less than eloquent words had left his mouth, a roar of over forty guns resounded as one. The two gunmen flew apart like test dummies in a hand grenade factory. A red mist rained down on them, followed them to the hot asphalt street ....

In an alley behind the building Augio and Kireem had heard the voice call out to the gunmen. They'd heard Rudy Turbo's bellowing reply and the explosion punctuating its ending. They hurried on toward the spot where they'd parked the Explorer, Kireem with Augio's arm looped over his shoulder, helping him stay on his feet.

"Here they come, Player," Kireem said, seeing the big Explorer nose down out of the parking lot and come speeding toward them.

Kireem pulled Augio over out of the way as the Explorer slid to a halt; French threw the side door open, the AK in one hand, and helped drag the wounded man inside. The side of French's shirt was streaked with blood from a graze on his side.

"Aw, man!" he said, seeing Augio's pale drowsy face. "Is he going to bleed out on us?"

"No, I'm not," Augio said. "Am I, K ...?" he asked Kireem.

"No, you're not," Kireem said. "Get us out of here, *Rifleman,*" he said to Decampo. "Drive cool, hang a left over on West Davis Boulevard. I know a guy there who almost went to dental school."

"What does that even mean?" said French, also wounded.

"It means that's where we going," Kireem said. "He lives around the corner from a CVS drugstore ...."

Keeping the Explorer's speed in check, Decampo took a right when they reached West Davis, took a right and drove until Kireem instructed him to take another right. The turn took them out of busy traffic and back a block and a half onto a quiet side street.

"Pull in right here." Kireem directed Decampo to the driveway of a two story stucco house half hidden by hammocks of tropical foliage, bougainvillea, and towering Birds of Paradise. Pulling in along the driveway, Decampo stopped the Explorer at a side door, where a worried looking black face peered out through a partially opened storm door screen and looked both ways.

"It's *you!*" the man's husky voice said as he opened the storm door wider.

"*As-salamu alaykum,* my brother," Kireem said, jumping down from the Explorer, holding a hand back, steadying Augio who stepped down behind him. With Augio came French, AK in hand, stepping down to the driveway.

"*As-salamu,* your ass!" said the man, his eyes widening behind his wire rim glasses. "Every time I see you, there's trouble. What the fuck are you doing here?" He eyed the AK in French's hands. "Aw, man," he added with dread in his voice.

"Hey, can you help a brother out, Dante?" Kireem said in a firm tone. "The kind of brother that gave your ass an alibi, kept you from pulling two to five for—"

"All right, get on in," the man, Dante Byrd said, cutting him off.

Looping Augio's arm over his shoulder, Kireem helped him across the six foot space between the Explorer and the screen door. "We got in some bad business downtown."

"I *know you did,* if you're the ones they talking

about on the news," said Byrd. He nodded toward the sound of a TV inside the house.

"What are they saying?" Kireem asked, hearing a young news reporter speaking in a rapid high-pitched sense of excitement.

"They calling it a drug deal *gone bad,"* said Byrd; he held the door open with one hand and helped steady Augio with the other, helping him up the two short steps into an eat-in kitchen.

"They got that right," Kireem said.

The two sat Augio down in a chair, French standing behind them, looking out the storm door with his AK-47 down his side. Outside, Decampo pulled the Explorer forward a few more feet and shut the engine off. He picked up the remaining dope in the quarter-bag that lay stuffed down beside his seat. Sticking a 9mm down into his waist he got out, closed the driver's door and went inside.

In the kitchen, Byrd stepped away to a cabinet drawer and came back with a clean folded dish towel. He examined the deep graze along Augio's head.

"This one needs clamps and stitches," he said. "But he'll be all right, long as his skull's not fractured." He placed the folded towel over the graze and raised Augio's hand to hold it in place.

"My head's not fractured," Augio said in a weak voice.

"Well, there you have it," Byrd said, stepping back. "The man don't need me. He's his *own caregiver."* He gave Kireem a sarcastic grin.

"Pay him no mind, Dante," Kireem said. "He's a Canadian. Check out his shoulder."

"Sorry, my brother," Augio said to Byrd in a weakened voice.

My brother ...?

Byrd and Kireem gave each other a bemused look. Byrd shook his head; Kireem gave a little chuckle.

"I'll check him out," Byrd said. "They going to be looking for the Explorer?"

"Probably, before long," Kireem said.

"I got a space for it in the garage," Byrd said. "Stick it in there. I'll make a run to the drugstore, get some stuff we need."

"Go, my brother," Kireem said. He looked at Decampo who had just walked in from the Explorer and plopped the bag of blow down on the table. "Ride with him to the drugstore, Rifleman, see that no rustlers get on his tail."

"What, you don't trust me, negro?" said Byrd.

Kireem didn't answer. Instead he said to Decampo, "Get a bottle of scotch on the way back, and pick us up a box of popsicles—all flavors."

"What about some beer?" said Decampo, opening the bag of blow as he spoke.

"Yeah, and some beer," Kireem said.

Dante Byrd shook his head disparagingly, but his eyes went to the bag of blow and he relaxed a little and even managed a twitch of a smile.

"That shit any good?" he asked.

"What do you think?" Kireem said, scooting the bag over closer to him.

On the small TV on the kitchen counter, the Bay News reporter rattled on while the camera scanned up the side of the office building to the balcony where,

"... Martin Ambrose and employee Kenny Sails had plunged to their death when an apparent transaction with unnamed local drug dealers turned violent ...."

(HAPTER TWENTY-ONE

Hernando Beach, Florida:

"... Powerline workers were shocked and horrified today when the decomposing body of a woman fell from the treetops. The yet unidentified female landed on the hood of a maintenance vehicle there doing a routine check and clearing of a firebreak in Pasco County ...."

The young reporter on the small TV screen continued speaking as he gestured a hand toward a background of thick wild foliage and scrub oak. The camera scanned then stopped on a power company truck that sat with its hood crushed and its windshield broken and hanging from its frame. A few feet away emergency workers carried a body bag on a gurney to the open rear door of a waiting ambulance.

      Ray Dylan sat watching, alone, only half hearing the breaking story as he finished his cup of coffee on Sami's lanai. *It felt strange being here without Sami*, he noted to himself—*a feeling akin to being on a beautiful beach, without the sun shining.* In the kitchen behind him sat a cardboard box carrying the mattress bags, the plastic and the roles of tape. With any luck he would still be using the items—hopefully soon.

He'd stood up and turned to carry his empty cup inside when his cell phone hummed and danced in his shirt pocket. He walked on inside, letting the phone ring twice more, then go silent. At the granite counter he rinsed his cup and sat in on the drainer beside the sink. Then he flipped the cell phone open and pressed the message key. The message was short, four words, *Go call your friend.* He closed the phone and dropped it back into his shirt pocket and picked up his windbreaker from across a chair ….

He drove his plain white van to a pay phone out front of a big box supermarket on Cortez Boulevard. Using an anonymous pre-paid charge card he dialed the number he knew from memory.

"It's me," he said when the person on the other end picked up the receiver and waited to hear from him.

"Yeah …?" Phil Rodell said in his unmistakable gravely voice.

"It's me," Dylan said. "You feeling all right?"

"I'm good, thanks," Rodell said. He waited for a second then said with a half-sigh, "Look, you got to come up here."

"The thing we talked about before?" Dylan asked.

"Yeah, that thing," Rodell said. "This guy is getting nuts over the woman thing. Says he don't want her around. He *requests* that you come take care of it." Phil stopped there and waited. Dylan knew it was a bad sign. "He also wants to meet you in person."

"In person …," Dylan commented, letting Phil know he realized the implications of going there and meeting with the man face to face. Dylan knew he might not be coming back. This was how it happened. He'd seen it many times.

"Yeah, in person, is what he wants," Phil said. He paused, then said, "But it ain't like you're thinking. We don't care so much about the woman being there. We want you to meet the guy in person, straighten this out with him, once and for all."

Okay …. He felt relieved, a little. Phil was either telling him that everybody was tired of the guy complaining and wanted Dylan to come and clip him— shut him up. Or, Phil was setting his mind at ease, getting him to come up under the pretense of clipping the guy, then having Dylan himself clipped, which was another way of shutting the guy up. Either way, Dylan figured Phil Rodell had just given him a fifty-fifty chance on coming back alive. That wasn't so bad, he decided with resolve, the kind of work he was in. Anyway, he had to go. What else could he do?

Wear no watch or jewelry …, he cautioned himself.

"When are we talking about?" he asked.

"Next week," Rodell said.

"I get to handle this the way I decide to?" he asked.

Rodell didn't answer. "I'll fill you in when you get here," he said. He paused then changed the subject and asked, "So, how's things going for my friend there, the one with the legs."

"I'm glad you asked," Dylan said. "How good is your phone?"

"Phone's good, go ahead," Rodell said.

Dylan spent the next few minutes telling him about Aaron Augio dying in the Phillipe Pinel Institute. He told him about Augio's psycho lover, Carson Betto, and how Betto had taken on Augio's persona and had put the squeeze on Sami for money in order to finance drug deals. Then he told him Sami had given Betto two hundred thousand dollars from a huge stash of bogus currency the late Sidney Augio had left stored in the guesthouse. He finished by telling Rodell that he'd moved all the money, taken it somewhere and re-hidden it—that he planned to let it lay low awhile then take it somewhere safe and burn it.

"Christ …," was all Rodell said when he'd finished.

"Yeah, I know," Dylan said. "I figure it's some of the old Cuban-Russian spook money from the cold war days," he said. "The sooner it's gone the better." Then he waited for Rodell's response.

"About that money," Rodell said quietly. "Maybe it's not a good idea getting rid of it right away."

Bingo! Dylan told himself. Phil Rodell knew about the money.

"Why not?" he asked, wanting to know more. "It's only going to cause her trouble if she hangs onto it, especially after handing some of it over to this Betto lunatic."

"Listen to me," Rodell said. "I know about the money. It's been there a long time, it belonged to the Augio family since long before Sidney died."

"Oh …?" said Dylan, letting the word hang for further explanation.

"You're right, it is spook money from the cold war," Rodell said. "But it's so perfect you can't catch it with the naked eye. You've got to run it through a counting machine with an ultraviolet detecting system—the kind banks and their drug dealers use?"

"I know about them," Dylan said.

"Even then it's hard to catch," Rodell went on. "These Cubans were good. There's millions in bad paper out there in circulation, has been for years."

Dylan didn't respond; he listened.

"This spook money was coming into Tampa and Miami long before cocaine and smack became a major import. Used to be a lot of it stashed here and there all along the Gulf—thirty or forty million right there in the guesthouse attic. After Sidney's death, I stopped taking *any* in, started moving it out. Now there's maybe ten or twelve million left."

"You're telling me that this has been a drop point all these years?" Dylan said.

"Sort of," Rodell replied.

"How have you been moving it out without Sami knowing it?" Dylan asked.

"Listen to me," Rodell said, "How many pool services you know who use a step van instead of a pickup truck?"

Silky Pool Service ..., Dylan said to himself.

"Damn," he whispered aloud. He hadn't seen that one, and it was right under his nose.

"So, what I'm saying is," Rodell continued, "it's good you moved it, with this unfortunate business going on. But don't get rid of it. Sit on it until all this Aaron Augio thing cools down. I'll tell you when to move it, and where to move it to."

Dylan didn't answer right away. This was why Rodell had him looking after Sami. This was the big interest in her well-being. He should have known—would have known had he not gotten so taken with her.

"You hearing me here?" Rodell said.

"Yes, I hear you," Dylan said. He wasn't going to ask any more questions, not until he decided whether or not Sami was in any danger.

"Good," Rodell said. "You get up here, we'll talk some more about it, okay?"

"Yes," said Dylan, "we'll do that." He listened to the line cut off, then hung the receiver back in its cradle. Sami shouldn't have known about this money. Sidney should never have told her about it. *Wouldn't have,* he thought, *if she hadn't stumbled onto it and demanded an explanation.* Now that she knew, and had even passed some of the money along into circulation, she could be standing on very shaky ground ....

Dylan thought about it on his way back to his van, and on his drive all the way back to Sami's house. Nothing against Phil Rodell, but Dylan didn't believe him, not entirely anyway. Some of it, yes, the part about the spook money, about Silky Pool Service helping him move it out. But there had to be a reason why Rodell didn't tell him about it earlier. The more he thought about it, the more he decided that Rodell had kept the spook money operation going for himself long after the Cubans and Russians had pulled out.

A dangerous thing for Rodell to do, Dylan told himself. The Chicago Outfit was not the kind of men who would take it lightly if they found out they'd been stiffed for hundreds of thousands of dollars. Dylan realized what a bad spot it put him on just knowing about it—him and Sami both, if the whole thing started tumbling down. He thought about it some more as he pulled into Sami's driveway, way back out of sight by the guesthouse. He was going to stick with his notion for now, see how he could better position Sami and himself. One thing for certain, if he went to Chicago right now with all this going on, both there and here, he was never coming back.

Adios, Ray Dylan ..., he told himself. Then he turned the van off, got out and walked into the house through the lanai door. Rodell hadn't asked him where he'd hidden the spook money. That was good. Rodell knew that asking him right now would be a dead giveaway that he planned on having him clipped. Dylan knew if he was right in what he was thinking, Rodell would ask him where the money was before he headed north. He smiled a little to himself. Keeping the spook money out of sight was his ace in the hole, for now anyway.

(HADTER
TWENTY-TWO

Zlata walked from her motel room, across the parking lot to her corner across the street from the Buccaneer Bar in Hudson Beach. She wore clear plastic heels with thin hand-painted serpents coiled upward around them. She had only just arrived and lit a cigarette when she saw a young white man get out of a Toyota Highlander and walk across the street toward her. He wore a dark blue baseball cap turned sideways, Caucasian faux gangster style—*early-warning sign of a genuine pain in the ass,* she concluded at a glance.

He wore an open motorcycle jacket over a white tee shirt and carried himself with the loose jauntiness she ascribed to street punks and vice cops.

"Hey, how's it going?" he said, a thin little grin coming to his three day beard-stubble as he slowed and stopped a few feet back. Zlata saw his hand come around from his hip pocket, saw the badge flash then go out of sight.

"*To mě poser ...,*" she growled under her breath. She drew on the cigarette and blew a thin stream of smoke in his direction, her eyes on him as he walked closer.

The man grinned.

"Hey, I know what you just said." He cocked his head a little.

Zlata only stared at him.

"You said, 'fuck me.'" He shrugged. "That's all right, I get that some."

"How you know Czech language?" she asked.

"Girlfriend of mine in college came from over there," he said, tossing it off.

"Where, *over there?*" Zlata asked.

He didn't answer.

"Do I remind you of her?" Zlata asked, giving him a look.

"Yeah, maybe, a little, the hair, the eyes?" he said. "But she wouldn't be doing what you're doing."

"I am not doing anything," Zlata offered in reflex.

"Come on, everybody's doing something, *Zlata,*" he said.

She looked surprised, him knowing her name.

"That got your attention, didn't it?" he said. Again the little grin. "Anyway, I don't care what you're doing here, Zlata. I'm not a cop," he said. He brought the badge wallet out again and flipped it open; this time he held it closer for her to see. "I'm *Federal Agent* Hughes—one of the big boys. You've heard of us, right?"

Zlata sighed. "Fuck me …," she whispered again, this time in English. They both looked past Agent Hughes' shoulder and saw three bikers across the street at the Buccaneer. The three watched them with interest, slowing to a stop on their way to the front door.

"You work out of here?" he said, gesturing toward the motel behind her.

"No, I am a *guest* here," Zlata said. She noticed that in spite of his seedy wardrobe and beard-stubble, his hair was neatly barbered around his ears, his neck.

"Whatever," Hughes said. He reached up and righted his cap bill. "I thought maybe you'd rather talk inside than out here."

"Talk about what?" she asked with reluctance.

"Come on ..., let's find out *about what,*" he said, cupping her elbow, turning her toward a row of rooms with dingy red doors and water running across the walkway beneath the AC units ....

When they stepped into the room, Agent Jason Hughes walked across the stained carpet to a TV Zlata had left turned on as a ruse to keep any would-be burglar from thinking the room was empty. He picked up the remote, turned the TV off and turned and saw Zlata glaring at him from the open door, a hand on her hip.

"Oh," she said, "so now it has become your room, your television?"

"No, ma'am," Hughes said. He clicked the TV back on but lowered the sound. With that Zlata moved to a table against the wall. She pulled both chairs out and gestured Hughes to one of them.

"Please to be seated," she said. As Hughes sat down she walked to the half size refrigerator and took out a bottle of vodka. She stood the bottle on the table and pulled the sanitized paper covers from atop two glasses and distributed them. "For you a drink?" she said.

"No thanks." Hughes held up a hand, but Zlata poured anyway. Then she sat down and toed her clear heels off her feet and sat with a hand around her glass. She pushed back her pale blonde hair and smiled beneath blue-violet eyes.

"Go," she said in a soft professional voice, "the clock it is ticking."

Hughes looked at the glass of vodka near his hand, a bare foot on the carpet only an inch from his, one leg hiked and crossed beneath her. Her other leg bared itself to the top of her thigh. He cleared his throat.

"All right …." He reached inside his jacket and took out a postcard sized photo of her missing pimp, Johnny Moscow, and laid it in front of her. "You know this man," he said; it wasn't a question.

"Yes, I know him." She stopped there and gave him a look and sipped her vodka.

"Do you know he's dead?" he asked. He studied her reaction with a flat stare.

Zlata only gave the slightest flinch and said, "No, but this does not surprise me. Always he gambles, sometimes without enough money to pay when he loses." She touched a fingertip to her lip, blotted a dot of vodka and licked it. "So, Agent Hughes, do you think I killed him?"

"No, I don't," Hughes said. "Lucky for you I can say where you were when he died." He took out a short stack of grainy enlarged security freeze-photos and laid them in front of her. "You were partying with friends—these *gentlemen* at the Bayside Rental Suites." He slid a photo out of the stack, a photo of Kireem outside the rooms at the Bayside, shoving something into the manager's shirt pocket. "Recognize him, Kireem Murabi? A hard-hitter out of Tampa?"

"He looks familiar," Zlata said, not giving it up easy. "What means this, a *hard-hitter?*"

Hughes gave a slight shrug. His face reddened a little.

"Just a figure of speech," he admitted. "His face shows up a lot. He seems to have his fingers in a lot of pies—" He stopped himself short and said, "Anyway …." He spread the security video freeze-photos out, fished up one of her standing beside Kireem, her arm hooked around his waist. "If they're going to be your alibi for when Johnny Moscow was killed you need to recognize them. If you don't, I'll take my pictures and go home, let you deal with the homicide detectives when they come looking for you."

"Yes, I recognize Kireem," she said, "I do not know his last name."

"Umm-hmm." Hughes nodded, shoved Kireem's photo aside and fished up one of Aaron Augio in the Bayside parking lot, a gun up and pointed out across the street. "What about this one? They call him the Canadian."

"Yes, the Canadian, he was there." Zlata said. "Kireem calls him *Player.*"

"But what's his name?" Hughes asked.

"I don't know." She said. "Player is strange one. I don't think he likes women. I try to make friends, he pulled away from me." She touched her bare toe to Hughes ankle and rubbed it around a little and smiled. Hughes wasn't about to move his foot away, not after what she'd said about not liking women.

"This fellow?" he said. He slid a freeze-photo of Benny Wu, looking bleary-eyed, getting into the back seat of Kireem's Cadillac.

"The Asian," Zlata said, "Kireem called him Benny." She sipped her vodka and slid her toes down away from Hughes' ankle. He looked relieved, even put the photos aside, raised his glass of vodka and studied it. "Is that all?" Zlata said. On the TV, Tampa News played the same simulcast they'd been rerunning all day.

"Almost all," Hughes said. He took a sip of vodka and reached inside his jacket and took out a crisp one hundred dollar bill in a zip lock plastic bag and laid it on the table.

"Oh! For me?" Zlata looked surprised and delighted. She didn't understand the plastic bag, but that was all right. She reached her hand out. Hughes laid his hand down over hers.

"No, Zlata," he said, patting her hand. "This bill belonged to your friend, *Player,* the Canadian? He's left a string of these up along the Nature Coast. We've got him on four different security videos, chicken joints, liquor stores, motels, you name it." He gave a little smile. "Somebody should have told him everybody's a video star these days."

"Player is a—*how-you-say-it*—a *counterfeiter?"* she asked, with a puzzled look.

Hughes nodded. "Yes, that's exactly how we say it. You need to tell me where we can find this guy, and his pals." He raised the vodka and finished it, and sat the empty glass down with his hand still around it. He made no effort to stop her from refilling it.

"Tell me about your girlfriend, Agent Hughes," she said. Her toes found his ankle again—getting playful. This time he moved his foot.

"No, we're still talking about this," he said. He tapped his finger on the bill in the plastic bag. In the bottom corner of the bag an ID tag read: Popeye's Fried Chicken, Commercial Way, US Highway 19. "This is the last place we know of, the Canadian passed a bill. What happened, everybody get tired and break up?"

"I don't know," Zlata said, "I do not pass the counterfeit money."

"What about your friends here?" he said, pushing a single photo across the table to her.

"My friends?" Zlata said? She studied the photo, seeing Tisha and Sarita walking across the Bayside Rental Suites parking lot, a halo of security light falling around them. She shrugged. "I do not know these women."

"Too bad," Hughes said. "We'll have to charge them with being a part of all this unless you can tell us otherwise."

"All right," Zlata gave in. "They are Tisha and Sarita." She tapped a fingertip on each girl in turn. "They know nothing about counterfeiting."

"Where can we find them?" Hughes asked, making mental note of their names for the time being.

"Tisha said she was going to her sister's in Tampa to let her nerves rest." Zlata fished a cigarette from a pack on the table and lit it and blew out a stream.

"And Sarita?" Hughes said.

"Sarita is there," Zlata said matter-of-factly, gesturing her cigarette past Hughes to the TV screen. The young agent jerked around in his chair as if expecting someone behind him. His hand dropped near the gun on his side beneath his jacket.

"What are you *talking about?*" he said, seeing

no one, only the TV playing against the wall—the same simulcast segment that had been repeating itself all day.

"*There,*" Zlata repeated, nodding at the somber scene, the yellow tape, the workers sliding the gurney into the ambulance. "That is Sarita—the one in the bag," she added for clarification.

Hughes stared at her for a moment, letting it sink in.

"You're saying this is Sarita, one of the women we're talking about?"

Zlata blew out another stream of smoke.

"Yes, three times I tell you this," she said.

Hughes glanced again at the TV and took his cell phone from his jacket pocket.

"And you're sure that's her ... this Sarita we're talking about?" he asked, even as his thumb touched a speed dial button.

"Yes, I'm sure," she said. Then, as if to get everything off her chest, she said, "There are also bodies of a man and his dog not far from there." She poured vodka into both their glasses, drew on the cigarette and stared him squarely in the eyes. "That got *your* attention, didn't it?" she mimicked.

Hughes took a deep breath. He fished a notebook and pen from inside his jacket and laid them on the table. "Tampa Homicide is going to want to talk to you," he said, nodding at his cell phone. He pushed the glass of vodka away. "So we're going to sit tight, get them over here."

"I thought if I talked to you I would not have to talk to the police," she reminded him.

"I know," Hughes said. "But if this dead woman

was with you, partying with these guys, we've got to bring in Tampa PD. This thing is getting bigger than I expected." He looked at the glass of vodka he'd pushed away, changed his mind, picked it up and drank it down. "One thing they're going to ask you is how the dead woman got up into the tree."

Zlata gave a little shrug and said, "She flew out of a—how-you-say—*Ferris Wheel?*"

Hughes stared at her, his hand covered the cell phone as a police dispatcher's voice came on the other end.

"That's real cute," he said to Zlata, lowering his voice. "Tell that to Tampa when they get here, you'll get free bed and board for a couple of nights—"

"But it is truth," Zlata said. "How could I make up such a thing?"

Hughes thought about it.

"You got me there," he said. He raised the phone to his cheek and asked for *Homicide.*

(HAPTER TWENTY-THREE

At midmorning Kireem and Hal Decampo left the Explorer out of sight in Dante Byrd's garage and drove Dante's 90s Oldsmobile Regency into downtown Tampa, to the place where Kireem had stashed his maroon Cadillac before the shootout. Following Kireem's instruction, Decampo circled the block twice, then parked a half block away across the street. They sat watching the big Cadillac and the surrounding neighborhood for a few minutes until Decampo grew restless.

"I say everything's cool here," he said. He sat with his palms on the bottom of the Explorer's steering wheel, tapping his fingers to *Sweet Home Alabama* on the radio.

Kireem sat with his 10mm Glock on his lap, loosely pointed sidelong at Decampo.

"Really?" he said. He reached out and turned the blaring music down by half. "You saying everything's cool doesn't do much for me, *Rifleman.*"

Decampo looked at the Glock, Kireem's big hand resting on it.

"Hey, man," he said, "don't go blaming me for things going wrong yesterday. I did what I was told to do. Your boy, *Player,* screwed us all with his play-money. French and I lost big-time on this deal. Now, whoever takes over Marty AMs business will be out to kill us both."

"You trying to say you and French are out, without paying me like you agreed to do?"

"Damn it!" said Decampo, "pay you how? We've got no money."

"You still owe me," Kireem said.

"But we can't pay you until we come up with a way to raise the money," Decampo said.

"I don't care how you raise it," said Kireem. "Maybe you can take down a dealer, like Jamal and Baker and Benny Wu did."

"Jamal put all that together," Decampo said. "He was a crazy motherfucker."

"You and French better start being crazy yourselves." Kireem warned. "You said you had connections—said you would hook me up with them once you straightened things out with Marty AM."

"We didn't exactly straighten things out, did we?" Decampo said with sarcasm.

"Too bad," said Kireem. "Don't start talking like you're backing out. We've still got a deal." He picked up the Glock 10mm and hefted it in his hand. "When you act like we don't, it sort makes me want to shoot you in the head."

"Whoa, easy man," Decampo said, "we're just talking here." He held a hand up as if it would ward off a bullet. "We said we'll hook you up with dealers, and we will. Don't go bat-shit on me. The more I think about it, the more I can see Marty AM's connections looking for somebody to move in on his turf. We take you to them, you and Augio set yourself up."

Kireem noted a complete shift in attitude come over Decampo with the Glock staring at his chest.

"That's more like it," he said, wagging the gun, encouraging Decampo to continue. But when Decampo started to say more Kireem cut him off "—hold on, what'd he say?" He turned the Regency's radio back up and listened to a breaking news report.

"... in a bizarre twist involving the story coming out of Pasco County, while investigating the case of a female body believed to have fallen from the treetops in a remote woodlands. Authorities discovered the body of long sought after serial killer, Former Army Sergeant James Edmunds, known to state and local law enforcement as Mundo the Swamp Cannibal ...."

"What the fuck?" Decampo blurted out; Kireem raised a hand hushing him as the news continued.

"... authorities found Edmunds body and that of his slain dog Rebel while acting on a tip from a local woman being held as a person on interest involving a string of counterfeit money violations across Pasco and Hernando Counties. In related news, counterfeit money of the same quality and binding has been found at the location of that shooting in Tampa that rocked the downtown area and backed-up traffic for hours following the incident ...."

"I don't believe this shit," said Decampo. The news went on.

"... searchers continue to scour the area surrounding a deserted cookie factory and a lot full of abandoned carnival rides that may have contributed to the death of the woman now being called the Treetops Lady ...."

Kireem and Decampo sat quietly as the newscast cut away to a new truck commercial.

Kireem turned the sound down on the radio.

"Did he say, Mundo the Swamp Cannibal?" he asked Decampo.

"That's what it sounded like," Decampo said. "Just think, you killed him." He gave a lopsided smile. "You killed Mundo the Swamp Cannibal."

"Hey, don't be saying that," Kireem responded quickly. "I didn't kill him. He was already dead."

"I saw you shoot him in the head," Decampo said. "What's the problem? They had a reward out for him. Maybe you'll get something out of it."

Kireem considered it.

"Yeah, like a lethal injection," he said. He eyed the Cadillac closer and said, "We got to get out of here, Rifleman. Swing around, let me out. Follow me to an alley so's I can change the plates."

"You got it," Decampo said. He put the Regency into drive and swung a wide turn on the inactive side street ....

Having stopped long enough to change the license plates on his Cadillac, Kireem followed the

Olds Regency. When both vehicles pulled into Dante's driveway the two drivers saw the open garage door with no sign of the Explorer parked inside.

"What now?" Decampo asked Kireem, the two of them getting out of their vehicles and walking to the side door, guns in hand. Kireem didn't answer. He leaned and looked into the kitchen through the screen door.

"Aw, man …," Kireem said, seeing Dante lying on the kitchen floor in a surrounding circle of blood. Dante's eyes were stretched open wide in terror, staring at the ceiling. His throat had been cut deep; a large butcher knife stood on his chest buried to its hilt. Tightening his hold on the 10mm Kireem shoved the door open and stepped inside, Decampo right behind him. On the kitchen counter a daytime soap opera played on the TV. A broken coffee carafe lay strewn in shards and pieces on the floor.

Walking wide around the blood on the floor, Kireem led Decampo into the bedroom where Augio had slept overnight. A blanket-covered cot lay along the wall where French had slept. Another small TV sat playing on a dresser facing the bed. The soap opera theme music faded and switched to a news update on the Treetops Lady and Mundo the Swamp Cannibal. Kireem and Decampo stood in silence for a moment, their guns half-raised, looking all around the empty room.

"They're gone," Decampo said. He gestured toward the news reporter coming on the TV, his story the same as the story they'd heard on the car radio. "They must've heard all this and *freaked,*" he said.

"*Freaked …?*" Kireem said, giving him a dark critical look.

"Not *freaked,* but maybe … well, you know, whatever," Decampo said. He shrugged. "Anyway, they're gone."

"Yeah, they are gone," Kireem said. He thought about it.

The two saw the blue-lined bag of dope lying open on a nightstand beside the bed, most of its contents gone. Beside it spilled residue left a powdery sheen where Augio had dipped the powder from the bag into a pill bottle. "At least they left us some blow," Decampo put in. He stepped over and raised the bag to take out a snort for himself.

Kireem watched him raise a mound of blow on the inside on his long pinkie nail and suck it up his nose.

"I know where they'll be going tonight as soon as it's dark out," he said to Decampo.

"Yeah, where?" Decampo asked in a strained voice, his face red, his eyes watering.

"Hernando Beach," Kireem said. "Player's wanting to kill the woman who stuck him with the bad cash."

"I can't say I blame him for that," said Decampo. "She put the screws to all of us, big-time." He wiped his palm back and forth under his nostrils, clearing the white powder.

"Yeah, *big-time,"* Kireem said in a sarcastic tone. He wagged his fingers at Decampo, motioning for him to hand over the bag of dope.

"Are we going to wait right here for them, sort of chill for awhile?" he asked with a clipped little cocaine smile.

"You do that, Rifleman," said Kireem, "wait right here. When the police get here, tell them all about Dante laying there dead while you're *chilling.*"

"How will the police know to come here?" he asked.

"*How will they know?*" Kireem said in disbelief. "I don't know how *they'll know!* But they'll come here and find his dead ass laying there!" He gestured toward the kitchen, then at the TV. "You see how they've already started tracking all this stuff, tying it all together … swamp cannibal … counterfeit money, Treetop Lady falling out of a tree, *dead!*" He glared at Decampo. "We got to pull our boys together and get out of here."

Decampo winced.

"All right, I get it," he said. "I'm with you, man. Where we going?"

Kireem didn't answer; he looked at him, then he looked away and shook his head.

"You cowpokes are killing me," he said under his breath. He closed the dope bag, shoved it down into his pocket. "Come on." He wagged his 10mm toward the storm door.

Hernando Beach:

Ray Dylan had spent the night at Sami's house alone, awake, armed and ready, still running things over and over in his mind. He'd watched the wavering image of the moon move across the dark Gulf waters, thinking, staring out at the canal from the rope hammock on the lanai. A warm fleece blanket pulled around his shoulders, he'd replayed his conversation with Phil Rodell until he knew both their words by heart. He'd been in tight spots before but never anything like this. He recognized this was the place where the bad stuff came down. There'd been no anger, no threats made, no raised voices or warnings. There was only this slight problem, the woman, Jill Markley. It was something —*you need to come up here and deal with, make everybody happy* …, he could hear Phil Rodell say. He must've heard it a dozen times over as the night drew closer around him ….

He didn't fall asleep until well after daylight. He awakened in the afternoon. Still he lay in the hammock a while longer, watching a fishing boat idle along the canal and turn out toward open water. All right, he got it, he told himself, picking up the same conversation he'd fallen to sleep with. Finally he pushed himself up and sat on the side of the hammock, feeling the heat of the afternoon sun. He pushed his hair back from his face with his fingers.

See how easy that was …? He heard Phil Rodell say again. He pictured him smiling, friendly, almost fatherly. Only now he pictured Phil talking to somebody else, about him.

So, this is how it ends for me …? Dylan asked himself. *One little slip up and the walls come tumbling down …?* It wasn't even his mistake, he reminded himself. The old man was supposed to be alone. Now he even wondered if that might have been a setup.

No, he told himself, wiping his face with both hands. *That part had been legitimate,* he was certain. The thing with the woman, Jill Markley had come up—a wild card in an otherwise perfectly stacked deck. Phil Rodell could have moved the matter along any way he wanted it to go. Rodell had the power, he could have told the son to go fuck himself, that it had been his responsibility to make sure his father was alone that day. But now, with the spook money starting to surface and Dylan knowing about it, knowing Phil had gotten greedy and kept the spook fund in operation for himself, Phil was giving him up. And that was that. *Good ole Phil Rodell ....*

Dylan felt a little foolish now, thinking about it. He'd actually thought Rodell had been looking out for Sami Bloom just for old time's sake, just because he and Sidney Augio had been friends, and you know, *What're friends for ...?* He'd even thought it meant something, Phil asking him to look after her. Kind of a personal favor, he'd thought, doing it as a friend of a friend, part of being on the inside of something—one of the guys. He gave himself a tired little smile, got up from the hammock and walked inside and filled the coffee carafe with fresh water.

Had it not been for Sami, he might ease away and drop out of sight. He'd thought about it from time to time, sort of a getaway plan for just such an incident as this. But Phil had figured him and Sami were close now, too close for him to walk away and leave her hanging. He thought back to the day he'd told Phil they were seeing each other and Phil considered it and giving his blessing.

That had been a bad move, Dylan told himself. He should never have let Rodell know anything about him and Sami. *Damn it ....* Now he had to dance when his strings were pulled. Not offering himself up in Chicago was the same as offering Sami up to them right here ....

When the coffee was ready, he poured a cup for himself and sat down and cleared his head. Halfway through the cup, he took a deep breath and picked up Sami's house phone from its charge station. He touched

Millie's number in Clearwater on the contacts list.

Sami answered.

"Hello, Sami?" Dylan said. He must've sounded a little surprised that she answered.

"Hi, Ray," Sami said. "I saw the call was from my home number."

Ray nodded to himself.

"You two having a nice visit?" he asked. He noticed the tired sound of his voice.

"Yes, we are," Sami said. She paused then said, "Is everything all right, Ray? You sound worn out."

"Yes everything's fine," he said. "I spent the night here. No sign of anybody. So far so good."

"Yes, that's good," she said, sounding relieved.

"Is this a good time to talk?" Dylan asked.

"Yes," Sami said. "I've got the house to myself. Millie's taking her poodle in for therapy."

"*Therapy?* You mean …," Dylan paused, tried not to make it sound frivolous. " … the dog has had a *troubled past?*"

Silence. Then Sami said, just a little put out, "No, Ray, the poor thing has a terrible skin condition."

"Oh, right," Dylan said, "skin therapy."

"Ray, something's bothering you," Sami said. "Don't tell me it's not. I know you well enough to tell. Is everything all right there, *really?*"

"Everything's good here, Sami," Dylan said. "But you're right, you do know me pretty well." He smiled a little to himself. "I got some bad news from Sarasota." He made it up as he went. "It looks like I will have to go down there for the closing after all."

"Oh, that's too bad," Sami said. "When do you

have to be there?"

"Next week some time," he said. "I'm waiting to hear when."

"Would you like me to go along?" Sami said. "You could come by here and pick me up. I can leave my car in Millie's drive. We can make a Christmas vacation of it—"

"Let's see how it goes, Sami. It can be hard getting good reservations this deep into the holidays."

"I can check online?" she offered. "I mean, if you'd like me to come with you. I don't want to be in your way."

Dylan stopped short and caught himself before nixing the whole idea.

"Yes, I'd like for you to be with me, Sami," he said. "Check around some, see what you can come up with. But don't reserve anything until I know more about this closing. If something happens at the last minute, we don't want to pay cancellation charges." Okay, now he had time to figure a way not to take her with him. He didn't like it but what else could he do?

"Don't worry, I'll just get some rates for us," she said. "You tell me when to set it up, and I'll …." She stopped herself and waited for a moment. Something was bothering her; she didn't know what. Ray caught it in her voice. He didn't know either.

"You'll what, Sami?" he asked.

"Oh … nothing," she said, ponderously. She stopped again.

"Are you okay?" now it was Dylan's turn to ask.

"Yes, I'm good," Sami said. "I think with all the craziness that's been going on, it would do us both some good to get away a few days. Don't you?"

"Yes, I do think so, Sami," he said. "I've got some things to take care of today. I'll call you tomorrow, see what you've found out on rates. Okay?"

"Okay, Ray." She waited for a second, then said, "Bye?" She could tell there was something more he wanted to say. *What was it? Why wouldn't he say it?*

"Bye, Sami ... tomorrow then," he replied, quietly, leaving whatever it was unsaid; and before she could inquire further, the line went silent in her hand.

(HADTER TWENTY-FOUR

Sami hung up the phone and heard Millie's car door shut in the driveway. Through the window she saw Millie leading her poodle, Trixie, from the car, across the drive to the front door. In the seconds it took for her to walk to the door and open it for Millie and Trixie, Sami thought about the conversation she'd just had with Dylan. Something about it left her ill at ease. She couldn't put her finger on it, but something was troubling Dylan, she was certain of it. Had she put too much on him, this sordid business with Aaron Augio and his big thug of a bodyguard *slash* accountant? She could picture the smug nasty smile on Aaron Augio's face as he'd said it.

She knew Ray Dylan was a good man. She knew he was no coward, yet, she was starting to realize, he was no match for those two. Sure, he owned a gun; he'd even carried one for a time. But by his own admission he had no idea what he would do if it came right down to shooting someone. A flash of panic ran through her as she realized she should have never left him there alone to deal with this.

What were you thinking ...?

Mille stopped short, key in hand, a small container of mace hanging from her key ring. She looked a little surprised as Sami opened the door and stepped to the side.

"On my, Sami," she said with a nervous laugh. "I'm so use to coming home to an empty house ...." Noting the worried look on her friend's face, she let her words trail and said, "Are you all right, dear?"

Sami relaxed, managed to smile.

"I'm all right. Something has come up with Ray and his real estate." She stooped a little and scratched the poodle's curly snow white head, trying to play down her uneasiness. "How's this little girl doing?"

"Much better, thank goodness." Millie unsnapped Trixie's leash; Trixie cut a quick nail-tapping circle on the tile floor and sprang up onto the sofa.

"Her skin is clearing up," Millie said. "The doctor wants to see her next week."

Sami cut in almost before Millie stopped talking.

"I've got to get home, Millie," she said.

"Oh ...?" Millie studied her eyes. Seeing the worry still there, she said, "Before you go anywhere, sit down and relax. I should tell you the traffic is backed up something awful. You could be two hours or more getting to Hernando Beach. It'll be after dark—"

"I'm used to this snowbird traffic," Sami cut in. "I'll be all right."

"Is Ray expecting you?" Millie asked.

"No," Sami said. "I'll call him when I stop for gas in Tarpon Springs. I don't use the phone while I'm driving."

Millie said, "Stop for gas at the new place there on the corner, they have a Starbucks. I don't know the name, but it's next door to a gun store, where I bought this. I chose Glittery Pearl, but they have it in other colors." She jiggled the spray container of mace. Then she stopped and took Sami's hand. "Look at you. You seem awfully tense to be driving."

"No, I'm fine, Millie, stop it," Sami said. She smiled and squeezed her hand a little then turned it loose. "Driving helps me think."

"Okay …." Millie sighed, opened her shoulder purse and dropped her key ring, deco mace container and all, inside. She closed the purse. "Give Ray my love … and I want you back here *real soon.*"

Sami touched a light kiss to her cheek.

"Thanks for understanding, Millie," she said. "I *will* be back real soon. I'm not even taking my things with me—just my purse and sunglasses." She stepped over to the sofa, slipped into her scandals, picked up her purse with her sunglasses in it and walked to the door.

"Sami, should I be going with you?" Millie asked in afterthought, looking concerned. "I get the feeling this is bigger than you're saying."

Sami thought about the pistol in her purse, the way she had deliberately stopped herself from putting a bullet in Aaron Augio's head when she had a chance.

"Thanks for offering, Millie," she said. "But I've got this."

After talking to Sami on the phone, Dylan had gone out and driven the van into the backyard and parked it on the grass between the pool and the canal. A tall row of mature Azalea hedge hid the van from sight. With gray evening creeping in around a red setting sun, he walked back inside and shoved a Chicken Brie dinner in the microwave. He walked through the shadowy house making sure every door and window was locked, and turned off all the lights except for the nightlight in the master bath and the light of the TV playing in Sami's bedroom.

When the microwave stopped, he took his food out and carried it on a tray into the living room, along with a freshly brewed cup of coffee. On the kitchen counter a carafe of hot coffee sat as if on duty with him.

Bon appetite, he told himself.

He ate his meal in grainy darkness while the night light glowed down the hallway and the TV resounded from the empty bedroom. Finishing the meal, he laid the tray down and set the coffee cup on the table beside his chair. He sat in stone silence, wide awake and listening. Ready for more night work. On his thigh lay his silenced small caliber pistol. A strong 48 inch black nylon cable tie hung at his waist, garrote style, looped and ready to tighten. A couple more shorter cable ties—the ratcheting kind some police used as wrist restraints—hung beside it.

A pair of Klein diagonal wire cutters stood in a leather sheath down in his trouser pocket. On his left side he carried his .45 in a cross draw behind-the-belt holster. Should all else fail and the going get rough and noisy, the .45 would be, as always, his backup plan.

He wore a utility style wristwatch, one with a quiet pulsing alarm. A perfect watch for this kind of tedious work, he'd set the watch's alarm to go off on the half hour and require a manual reset to make sure he would deal with it each time it went off. It was just enough detail to keep a man from falling into a lull at the wrong time and ending his life with his head tilted back, seated above a deep puddle of blood.

This was dark, gruesome work, he reminded himself. It required all the discipline and proficiency that he'd spent a lifetime cultivating. He knew without reservation that if the two men he expected moved in out of the darkness tonight, ready to harm Sami Bloom, he would kill them with quick proficiency—no further thought on the matter ….

An hour later when he had set the wristwatch alarm for the second time, he pushed up from the chair, the silenced gun in hand, and walked to the kitchen in the dark. He poured himself a cup of coffee, brought it back to the living room and started to sit down. But he stopped and listened to a vehicle moving along the dark quiet street toward the house. He sat the cup down and stepped over beside the front window; he waited until the beam of head lights shone through the curtains and circled around the inside walls as the vehicle pulled into the driveway. When he saw the lights click off, he peeped out at the familiar white step van and saw the driver's door slide open.

Silky Pool Service. What the hell …?

Watching the stocky mustached driver step out and walk along the driveway, Dylan moved to a side window and kept him in sight. Though he had only seen Henry Silky a couple of times coming and going from servicing the pool, Dylan thought he recognized the older man's thick gray mustache, his stocky build, the turned up short sleeves of his green uniform shirt. Yet, upon closer look, *Hunh-uh,* Dylan corrected himself. He was sure this wasn't Henry Silky.

Who then ...? He continued to watch as the man reached the guesthouse where he looked all around, unlocked the door and slipped inside. Even if it were Henry Silky, he asked himself, what was he doing coming here at this time of night? After Rodell telling him he'd had Silky watching this place for him, he had no reason to trust Henry Silky or anybody connected to Rodell's secret cash smuggling enterprise.

He saw a flashlight move inside the guesthouse near the fold-down stairs. He saw the glow of the light as the man ascended the stairs. A moment passed, then he watched the flashlight glow move back down the stairs and shut off. He watched the darkness until the door opened and he saw the man come out and walk toward the lanai. The flashlight was gone from the man's hand, replaced by a gun with a silencer on its barrel, much like the gun Dylan held down his thigh.

Here we go ....

Dylan stepped out of his shoes; he moved quick and silent in sock feet, down the dark hall and into the bathroom where he partially closed the door and turned on the light. He stood beside the commode with his hand on the chrome handle until he heard the slightest jimmying sound at the lanai door opening into the house. When he heard the rear door open, he pushed down on the handle, and slipped out of the bathroom as the commode flushed behind him ....

At the open door to the lanai, the man stopped at

the sound of the toilet flushing. Dylan had slipped into the spare bedroom which lay halfway down the hall to the lanai. He stood waiting, the black looped restraint in his left hand, the silenced pistol shoved down in his waist.

"Misses Bloom?" he heard a voice say down the hallway toward the bathroom. "It's Silky Pool Service."

Sloppy work, this guy. An amateur, maybe ...? Dylan wondered. But he wouldn't allow himself to underestimate this man. He would stick to his plan, amateur or not.

"I know it's late, Misses Bloom. But I had to tell you I found a problem with your pool today," the man said. Dylan heard footsteps venture forward in the hall, drawn as he had hoped and planned for toward the bathroom light, the sound of the commode tank filling.

"Hope I haven't frightened you. Are you there, Misses Bloom?" The man asked just as Dylan stood watching him ease past the dark open doorway, his gun out, pointed toward the sound of the toilet tank filling. "We always like to let our customers *argh—*"

His words stopped with a violent choking sound as Dylan stepped in behind him, slapped the looped cable tie down over his head and gave a hard solid yank on it, jerking his head back by his hair with his free hand. The nylon tie bit deep, ratcheting tight just below the man's Adam's apple. With the tail of the tie wrapped around his left hand, Dylan held on, pulling even tighter, dragging the man backwards and down. He turned loose of the man's hair, reached forward and grabbing the man's gun hand, keeping the flailing gun pointed away from him.

The man's strength waned quickly. He made sounds that no man could make for long; he began melting on the hall floor. Dylan had brought the cable ties for Augio and his pal, but this worked out well. He took the gun easily from the man's trembling hand, turned loose of the tightly drawn cable tie and let the man flop and struggle on the floor. In the slanted light from the bathroom doorway, he looked down at the swelling red-blue face staring up at him, eyes bulged and watering.

Back in the day, he reminded himself, he would have had to use a wire garrote, the two-hand kind. He would have had to hold on no matter what, even if the wire cut into his palms, even while the man kicked and thrashed and more than once emptied his bladder on him, or worse. This way the man might still spill his waste, but at least Dylan didn't have to be down there in it with him.

High tech had its plus side, he had to admit, watching the man gasp and claw an ineffective hand at the deeply tightened nylon. The cable tie had a tensile strength of 175 pounds. It wasn't coming off. Dylan studied his face, watching life starting to dim away in his eyes.

"Arturo Lamato …," he said, recognizing the distorted face upon closer study. He gave a grim smile, stooped down, drew the cutters from the sheath in his trouser pocket. He worked the smooth metal nose under the tight nylon tie and squeezed hard. The cutters sliced through the tie and sent it flying away from the man's red swollen neck. But seeing the hapless man's breath was almost too far gone to revive, Dylan slid the cutters into their sheath, doubled his fists together and swung them down solidly on the stalled chest. "Come on, Art, start breathing, or I'll let you go." He hit the chest again, then stood up and stepped back.

The downed man sucked in a horrible sounding breath, held it for a second and managed to exhale with the same force.

"Okay," Dylan said. He walked away, to the kitchen down the dark hall, filled a glass with tap water and walked back. Lamato had tried to collect himself and get on his feet. He'd made it onto one knee. Dylan, water glass in one hand, Lamato's gun in his other, planted a foot on his shoulder and shoved him backwards. Lamato landed on his back, half-leaning against the wall. His thick fake mustache had pulled loose from one side of his lip and hung down to his chin. Still gasping a little, the man peeled it the rest of the way off and let it fall.

"Here, drink this," Dylan said. He handed the glass down to him and stepped back while the man tried to drink. "Watch the water," he said, seeing a surge spew out of Lamato's gaping mouth and spill down his shirt, onto the clean tile floor.

Lamato coughed and wheezed, sending more water flying from his lips.

"That's enough." Dylan reached down and took the glass back from him. "Why are you here trying to kill my friend, Sami Bloom?"

"I—I wasn't," the man stammered, still struggling to get his breath, his voice raspy and shallow.

Dylan gave him a look, aiming the man's own gun down at his face. Lamato raised a hand as if to protect himself from a bullet.

"Okay, wait, please ...," he said in a halting

voice. "Yeah, I was going ... to whack the woman. I was paid to ... what do you want from me?"

"Paid by Phil Rodell ...," Dylan said. "You went back there first and saw the money's gone." He nodded toward the guesthouse. "Were you supposed to take it, too?"

"I was supposed to check ... if it was still here ... I was told to take it," Lamato said. He rubbed his aching throat as he spoke. "How you ... know so much?"

Dylan didn't answer.

"Did your *friend,* Phil contact you himself to do all this?" he asked.

"Maybe ...," Lamato said, hesitant, suspicious. "You going to cut me loose ... I tell you everything?"

Still no answer.

"Did he ask you *himself?"* he insisted in a stronger tone, pointing the gun closer to his forehead.

"Yes ... yes he did," said Lamato. "He told me keep it all on the hush-hush. He sounded scared ... real scared—didn't want nobody knowing nothing. Even told me to pick up my envelope from him in person ... in Chicago."

"He was going to whack you, Art," said Dylan. "Didn't you see that coming?"

The gunman rubbed his throat some more, thinking about it.

"Yeah, I guess I did," he said, his voice less gravely. But then he said as if in revelation, "So, you jumping me might've saved my life?" He coughed and shook his big head. "That's fucked up," he said.

Dylan let out a breath and pulled one of the shorter, black nylon cable ties from his belt.

"Yes, it is," he agreed. He reached down, helped the man onto his feet and turned him facing the wall. "Put your hands back," he said.

Lamato did as he was told. Dylan drew his wrists together, slipped the loop around them and yanked it snug. Lamato gave a little grunt.

"Can you … give me a pass on this, Ray?" he asked humbly. "For old time's sake … you know, like the guy in the movie asked for?"

"I can't see it happening," Dylan said quietly. He gave the man a little shove toward the rear door. "You know how this business works."

"Yeah, I do," Lamato said with regret. Walking to the door, he coughed again and shook his head, his hands secured behind him.

"I thought I heard somewhere … that you'd gotten out of this game," he said.

"I have, more or less," Dylan said. "But something like this pops up now and then, what're you going to do?"

"Yeah, really," Lamato said over his shoulder. He shook his head as if in contemplation and said as if in regret, "Things are bad. I can tell you that."

Dylan didn't answer. He watched for any trick the man might still have in mind as they walked on.

"You hear about the old man going down?" he asked.

"I heard something about it," Dylan said, keeping his interest from sounding piqued. "Bad health, I heard."

"Bad health, *ha,*" said Lamato, "we all know his son had him put to sleep. He couldn't wait to be next in line—sit in the big chair."

Dylan didn't answer.

"Even the kid must've known it," Lamato said. "Word is that's why he shot his father—"

"*Whoa,*" Dylan said cutting him off. "What do you mean *the kid shot his father?* What kid?"

"You know, the old man's grandson, the *ball player,*" Lamato said. "The kid was still in high school, already had the Cubs interested in him. But he couldn't keep his nose clean. He got hooked on the shit and blew his chances. Now he's all fucked up."

Jesus ...! Dylan said to himself. "You mean *that* kid shot his father?" He shook his head. "When was this?"

Lamato gave a little shrug, Dylan keeping watch on his banded wrists as they stopped at the rear door of the step van.

"A couple of days ago," Lamato said. "The kid took his grandfather's death real hard, stayed knocked out on dope ever since the funeral. He accused his father of killing the old man—not publicly you understand—but in our circle of friends. Luckily, our people got ahead of it and smoothed things out. They came up with a witness who said it was accidental. But everybody knows the kid did the deed. He had a hard-on at his father for killing the old man. He fueled up on eight balls, nailed his father in the eye with a .357 magnum. *Bang!* End of story." He gave a dark little chuckle. "Killing their fathers must *run* in that family."

"Jesus ...," Dylan said again, this time out loud. He reached past Lamato and opened the van's rear door. He saw two feet in scuffed work shoes through layers of rolled up plastic drop covers.

"Henry Silky?" he asked Lamato.

"Part of the job," Lamato replied. "Phil wanted him gone." He looked Dylan up and down, at the gun in his hand, and said, "Look, I don't know about you, but I've been hedging up for this day for a long time. I've laid back a hundred thousand just in case I needed it." He studied Dylan eyes. "What do you say, Ray? A hundred bucks and I walk? Who's ever going to know?"

Dylan shrugged. "What can I tell you, Art? You came here to hit a very close friend of mine, me too for all I know."

"But I didn't hit your friend," Lamato pointed out. "No harm no foul, right? As for you, Ray, you were never a part of the package." He shook his head, adamant about it. "No, I wouldn't have taken the deal had you been part of it. You've always been straight-up in my book."

"That's good to hear, Art," Dylan said in a quiet tone. "Man, if only I thought I can trust you." He turned Lamato around, facing into the dark van.

"Hey, you can!" said Lamato. "I swear to God you can! Jesus, Ray. Don't do this!"

"Take it easy," said Dylan. He tugged at the band on Lamato's wrists.

Huh ...? Lamato caught himself on the verge of sobbing. But he stopped suddenly, feeling the nylon restraint fly away from his wrists as Dylan's wire cutters bit through it.

"When do I get the hundred bucks?" Dylan asked. He shoved the cutters into his pocket as Lamato turned facing him, rubbing his wrists in disbelief.

"Hey, buddy, any time you want it, you got it. I'm never going to forget this, Ray! The hundred thousand is yours!"

"All right, you owe me," Dylan said. "Now get out of here. I've got things going on."

"You got it, Ray," Lamato said. He started to turn away, but stopped himself and said in afterthought, "Oh— one thing, can I have that gun back? It's been with me a long time."

Dylan smiled, flipped the gun around in his hand and handed it to him, butt first.

"There, now get out of here," he said.

A slow strange grin came across Lamato's face. He shook his head real slow, raised the silenced gun arm's length an inch from Dylan's forehead.

"You sorry prick," he said with a dark chuckle. "Phil warned me to watch out for a trick when I go to nail you. But it looks like you're all out of tricks, hunh?"

Dylan just stared, raising his hands chest high away from his own silenced gun stuck down in his waist.

"You're really going to do this," he said, "after me cutting you a break?"

"There's no breaks in this game, you should know that, Ray," he said. "You got old and you've gotten easy. No way I could have put this over on you ten years ago." He widened his grin, revealing a gold-capped tooth. "Time's up. *Adios*, Ray Dylan. FYI, I never really cared much for you."

Dylan watched him pull the trigger, saw his grin melt as his gun snapped without firing. Lamato shook the gun as if that would fix it. Then he tried again—still nothing. Twice more he tried. No dice.

"Oh, *shit!*" he shouted. While he struggled with the gun, Dylan took his time, raised his own silenced gun from his waist and stuck it against Lamato's forehead.

"Wait!" said Lamato. "Listen to me!"

"Why?" Dylan said flatly, "you've told me everything I wanted to know." He pulled the trigger twice, a double tap, and sent both small caliber bullets boring halfway into Lamato's brain. Then he stepped forward, clutched the man's limp shoulder and guided the body down to a sitting position on the van's step bumper. Lamato's eyes appeared to have snapped loose from whatever elastic membrane held them in sync and gazed off in different directions.

The dead gunman weaved in place until Dylan gave him a little backwards nudge. Lamato tipped over, his unloaded gun still in his hand and flopped down beside the plastic-wrapped body of Henry Silky. Dylan tipped the lifeless feet up and rolled his legs inside. He took Lamato's bullets from his trouser pocket and tossed them in on the van floor. Closing the rear door, he looked all around carefully, making sure no one had seen what happened.

So far so good ..., he told himself, turning, walking to the guesthouse. He checked his watch; he was still certain he had a long night ahead.

(HAPTER TWENTY-FIVE

Augio and Sonny French had both been snorting spoonful hits of blow from the pill bottle they'd filled before leaving Dante's house. They'd circled the Hernando Beach neighborhood twice before French backed the Explorer in and parked it at the lower right edge of Sami's driveway in case they needed a quick getaway. The two sat for a moment, French taking down a deep lungful of smoke and passing the joint over to Augio. He studied Sami Bloom's house in his rearview mirror.

"I got to tell you, Auggie," he said, squeezing his words out while he held his breath. "This don't strike me as some big-time counterfeiter's crib."

"I never said this woman is a big-time counter-feiter," Augio said, sounding agitated. Lit high on the coke, and on the reefer they'd smoked on their way, he gave French a look as he took the joint from him. "Don't ever call me Auggie again," he added in a deep, tightly wound voice. "I don't like it."

"Cool," said French. He noted Augio's voice had deepened, taken on a menacing tone. But he shrugged it off, having noticed it before the past few days. He waited and took the joint back when Augio had taken a deep draw.

"So …. You want me to call you Player, then," he asked, "Like K does?"

Augio didn't answer right away, not until he'd held his breath long enough that he needed to let it go.

"Yeah, *cracker-boy,"* he answered in the same deeper tone. "Call me Player, like K does." He sat looking in the rearview with French, checking the darkened house, tapping Marty AM's big .50 caliber Desert Eagle on the side of his thigh. His Bersa 9mm stood tucked behind his belt. "When you're talking to me, *you are talking to K."*

"Okay …, that's weird," said French, taking the joint back, his gun lying on his lap. The silenced .22 caliber pistol lay on the seat between them, smiling-face yellow duct tape still wrapped around the barrel.

"What's weird?" Augio asked.

"You doing an impression of Kireem," French said.

"Who said it's an impression?" Augio asked. "Who says I'm not Kireem right now, *right this minute.* Only difference is you can't see it."

"See? That's even weirder," French said. He gave a little scoff; took a draw on the joint. "Sounds like you've going whigger on us," he said, holding his breath.

"Whigger?" Augio queried.

"You know …," said French letting out the smoke, "a white dude trying to be—"

"I know what a whigger is," said Augio, cutting him off. He picked up the silenced .22 and aimed it at

French's heart, an inch away. "That's some racist shit, cracker-boy," he said in Kireem's voice.

"Whoa! Hold it, man!" French shouted, jerking away from the gun. In reflex he started to raise his own gun, but Augio caught his hand and gave a dark chuckle. Then he flipped the .22 around in his hand and held it out to French, butt first.

"I'm just fucking with you, French," he said. He turned French's hand loose and stuck the butt of the silenced .22 in it. "Grab this head popper. Let's go on get this thing done."

The two got out of the Explorer and walked up the driveway to the house.

"Stop it with that voice," French said. "You're starting to freak me out." He shoved his 9mm into his belt and held the .22 at his side.

"Tell me something," Augio said looking around at him, his dilated eyes shiny and wild in the light of a three quarter moon, "do you believe a man can be more than one person at a time?"

French tried to make sense of the question for a second, but couldn't do it. He gave a little chuff.

"I believe a man can get so *high* he don't know his ass from his elbows ... is what *I* believe," he said, stepping up onto the porch behind Augio. Looking around, Augio tried the door and found it unlocked. He gave the door a little push and watched it open ....

Inside the house they went from room to empty room, turning on the light, checking, then turning the light out. When they finished searching, they stood in the kitchen, staring down at the little red light glowing on the half full coffeemaker. French still held the short joint—

smoked down to a roach—pinched in his fingertips. He sucked air around it and held the smoke.

"Looks like she forgot to turn it off," he said, seeming unable to look away from the tiny glowing light.

"Hunh-uh," said Augio, in an entirely different voice, one that wasn't his and wasn't Kireem's. One that French had not heard until now. "I know her. She always turns this off."

"You know her?" French asked. He laid the roach on the glass top of the white wicker table.

Augio came back from some far off place.

"I know people *like her,*" he corrected himself. "She left it on because she's coming back, real soon."

"Meaning?" said French. In the slanted moonlight through the window, he took the pill bottle of coke from his shirt pocket and unscrewed the top. He shook out a mound of the blow into a green-tinted mermaid dish sitting on the tabletop. Snorting it down, he shook out another mound and handed the little dish to Augio.

Augio snorted his portion and smiled to himself, staring at the little raised mermaid figure embedded in the bottom of the dish.

"Meaning, we're waiting right here for her," Augio finally replied. "Go move the Explorer down the street. I'll pour us some coffee." He licked his tongue across the little mermaid, picking up any residue. Then he wiped the residue along his gums.

The seasonal traffic between Clearwater and Hernando Beach had been a nightmare the whole way, Sami recounted to herself. At Tarpon Springs she'd stopped and filled her gas tank and bought herself a cold bottle of water. Finishing at the pump, she parked over to the side of the asphalt lot, got out and walked next door to the gun store where Millie had purchased her key ring container of mace. Ten minutes later Sami walked out with the same deco spray container, *Glittery Pearl* hanging from her key ring.

Yes, Glittery Pearl ..., she reminded herself.

She shook her head as she got back in the car and stuck the key in the ignition. She looked at the mace and dropped it into her purse. It was a chic sparkling little item, she thought. Solely designed to be sprayed in a person's eyes. Jesus. Something about carrying it made her feel a little ... *what*, she asked herself, *vulnerable, foolish?* Maybe just sad, sad for herself and for Millie. She saw them both as two aging mystical mermaids coming to grips with the real world.

She reminded herself that not only was she carrying a can of mace in her purse, right there beside it she was carrying a loaded gun—a gun she had bought and learned to shoot for the sole purpose of killing a man.

And there you are, Mystical Mermaid, she told herself with a sigh. She turned the key, brought the car to life, and drove on ....

An hour and a half later, she'd turned off the crowded highway and wound around through the Hernando Beach community until she turned onto the empty quiet street leading back to her house. Drawing closer, she noted that Ray Dylan's van was not in the driveway, but as she turned in she caught a glimpse of it through the hedge in the backyard. She also took note that the house was dark. It was too early for Ray Dylan to have gone to bed, but under the circumstances, she could see him leaving the lights off, watching TV, maybe listening to the radio—cool jazz out of Tampa.

Ray Dylan ..., she said to herself, glad he was around, glad he'd shown up in her life when he did. She liked his ways, cool, calm, confident without being cocky. She liked the way he had been through all of this—right there by her side. Okay, she was more than just glad he was around, she told herself, turning the engine off. She smiled to herself getting out the car, purse in hand and walking onto the front porch. She was *very* glad ....

She stopped suddenly as she reached to push the doorbell and saw that the door was standing open a few inches inside the glass storm door. She tried the storm door; it was unlocked.

"Ray ...?" she said, opening the door a little and speaking into the dark living room. "Ray, are you in there?"

Hearing no reply, she started to take a step into the dark and switch on the light. But she stopped herself. *Hunh-uh,* something wasn't right in there; and she wasn't going in. She started to turn away.

Wait! She stopped again, seeing a black silhouette move across the floor toward her.

"Ray?" she repeated. But as soon as she said it, she realized the person coming toward her wasn't Ray Dylan; and she turned and ran back toward her car, hearing the storm door fly open behind her. She wasn't about to look back, or stop. She rushed to the car and jerked the door open; but she didn't make it inside. Her key ring and purse flew out of her grasp, a strong pair of hands grabbed her from behind, lifting her backwards away from the sanctuary of her car.

She tried to scream, but one of the hands clamped across her mouth, stopping her. Her feet were off the ground. Her purse and key ring lay spilled on the grass. She saw them lying there in the moonlight, her purse flung open, items strewn on the grass, the key ring among them, the *Glittery Pearl* can of mace. A lot of good it had done her—the gun either for that matter. She didn't see the gun lying among the spillage.

She struggled hard, but it did no good. Neither her flailing fists nor her clawing nails did any damage. Her abductor seemed impervious to pain. He carried her back to the open front door and shoved her inside the dark living room. Another pair of hands caught her and slung her across the room. She landed on the sofa.

"Make a sound and I'll kill you, *Sa-mantha,*" Augio said, standing over her. His mocking voice sounded different, deeper, yet unmistakable to her.

She dared not speak. Trembling, she looked past him and saw the other silhouette standing, watching, a gun hanging down his side. But this wasn't the black accountant *slash* bodyguard; this was someone different, someone not as big.

"Go get her purse, cracker-boy," she heard Augio say over his shoulder. As the other man went out the door, Augio grabbed her wrist, yanked her to her feet and pulled her along toward the darkened bedroom. "You, come with me," he demanded. "I've got a lesson to teach you."

She found her voice, yet she dared not scream; she believed he would make good his threat and kill her.

"Aaron, listen to me, please, don't do this," she pleaded, thinking about the knife holder, its sharp contents standing on the counter beside the stove, right in there. She saw the kitchen doorway move past her as he dragged her along. *Too late! My God!* It seemed there was no way she could save herself. "Didn't I do everything you asked me to?" she said.

"What you did is, you stuck *Player* with a bag full of bogus money!" the darker, deeper voice shouted at her. He dragged her around the dark bedroom doorway and threw her over onto the bed.

She heard the other man's footsteps on the tile, hurrying down the hallway. In his own voice, Augio shouted, "My backers sent me here with *real cash* to set up a drug supplier. I sent them back a bag full of *counterfeit money!* Before they kill me, you're going to die!"

"I—I didn't know it was counterfeit!" Sami said, trying to spring right up, not wanting to be trapped there in her own bed at the mercy of two monsters. "I can get more money! You can take me to the bank yourself!"

As she tried to rise, a hard backhand slap came out of the dark, streaked across her face and sent her backwards on the mattress, stunned.

"I got her stuff out of the yard," the other voice said, tossing Sami's purse aside onto the floor. Contents spilled out again onto the carpet.

"All of it?" Augio asked.

"Yeah, I guess," French said.

"You *guess?*" said Augio, drawing a folded knife from his trouser pocket.

"You want me dicking around out there with a flashlight?" French asked in a sharp tone.

"No, cracker-boy," said Augio, "I just want to know that you're up on your game."

"Don't worry about it," said French. "Hurry up

and do her, let's get out of here."

Sami heard the metal click as Augio flipped the knife blade open.

"Don't tell me what to do," Augio warned French, his voice back to normal. "All the trouble she's caused me, I'm in no hurry. I've got to cut on her some."

"Fuck all this, I'll do her then," said French, agitated. He stepped forward in the darkness, holding the silenced gun out at arm's length.

"Get away, cracker-boy, she's all mine," said Augio. He shoved French hard. Sami started to rise up again; Augio shoved her back down, his hand catching the front of her blouse, ripping it open. French had stumbled backwards and caught himself against the door frame.

"Hey, don't push me, *Auggie!*" French said. "I'm not your damn flunky!"

Augio fell silent for a second, then he said to French in the deeper tone, "Turn on the light, cracker-boy. I can't see shit in here."

"Don't call me that again," French warned, the coke boiling in his brain, the weed not keeping him grounded. He ran his hand along the wall by the door frame, found the switch and flipped it on. Seeing the woman in the sudden burst of light, her breasts exposed, her arms trying to cover her, French's senses jolted in place.

"Whoa, *mama!*" he said. He looked Sami up and down, his eyes wide and shiny. A wet grin spread across his lips. "Hey man, you're right. We don't have to be in no hurry here." He stepped forward, the silenced gun with its happy face tape hanging in his hand.

261

(HAPTER TWENTY-(IX

Ray Dylan held the gas feed wide open on the little Cushman the minute he rode away from the van with the two bodies in it. He'd driven the van eleven miles from Sami's house, to a swampy back road reaching out into deep tropical overgrowth. Taking the back road to where it ran out in a small clearing, he'd parked and rolled the little Cushman motor scooter out the rear door and took out the can of gasoline he brought with him. He'd poured the gasoline all over the van's contents, bodies and all, and took a cigarette from a pack in Art Lamato's shirt pocket.

Stepping out the back door, he'd lit the cigarette with a match from a matchbook and took a few functionary puffs. Then he'd folded the matchbook around the burning cigarette, closed it, laid it inside the van and shut the door ....

Moments later, reaching Sami's neighborhood, Dylan looked back to his right and saw a glow of smoky fire roiling atop the tree line. There was nothing to connect the van or its contents to him other than the fact that one of the dead men inside happened to be Sami Bloom's pool man. *Not a big thing,* he assured himself. Knowing Phil Rodell, he wondered if there would even be a record of Sami being on Silky Pool Service's client list.

Good point ..., he told himself. Rodell kept much of what he was involved in to himself. The more Dylan thought about it, the more he wondered just how much Chicago knew about any of this. Suddenly it struck him. What about the hit Rodell had him make on the old man? Was Chicago behind it, or was that some private setup between Rodell and the old man's son? That would explain things not going as they should have—the woman being in the room. Chicago didn't make mistakes like that. *Another good point ...,* he told himself. He'd have to give that some more thought, first chance he got ....

When he cruised past the Explorer, he eyed it closely, for no other reason than it hadn't been there when he'd driven the van out. Ordinarily he would have thought nothing of it—*but this is not ordinarily,* he told himself. He didn't even slow down as he guided the little scooter past Sami's house. But his heart almost dropped inside his chest when he saw her car parked in the driveway.

For God sakes, Sami. What are you doing here ...?

Two houses past Sami's front yard, he drew the Cushman in a wide circle on the empty street and rode back, idling at first. Then clicking the headlight off and killing the engine he coasted in silence the last few yards, kicking himself along with his feet. Beside a palm standing between her house and her neighbor's, he laid, the Cushman over on its side and moved along in a crouch, staring up at the dark house.

Okay, Sami. You come home, into a dark house, don't even turn on a light?

He dropped down lower and started to move up along the edge of the driveway—but he stopped short. Right there in the grass at his feet he saw Sami's tiny jar of lip gloss; a purse-sized pack of tissues lay among strewn coins, a quarter, a dime, some pennies. Sami's petite silver ink pen lay atop the plush carpet of grass. As he stared at the items in the shadowy moonlight, he heard the distant sound of sirens from every direction—volunteer firefighters converging, headed down Cortez Boulevard in the direction of the burning van. Looking back the way he'd ridden in, Dylan saw a pair of headlights swing into sight. As quiet as a ghost he slipped farther up the driveway, toward the back of the dark house ....

Without seeing Dylan slip out of sight, Kireem slowed his Cadillac to a stop, killed the engine and headlights and sat studying the quiet neighborhood hawk-like, having spotted the Explorer on their left a few yards back. Beside him Hal Decampo sat with a joint in his hand, a tall can of beer between his legs. He took a draw and held the joint over to Kireem. But Kireem turned it down, not taking his eyes off the street. Thirty yards ahead, a steel-gray Taurus that had driven past them real slow, pulled off onto the grass facing in the same direction.

"What, you quit smoking?" Decampo said in a tightly squeezed voice.

"Naw," Kireem said quietly without facing him. "I think we got some serious shit about to go down here."

"Hunh-uh, I don't think so," Decampo said, "you're just getting paranoid."

"I've never *been* paranoid myself," said Kireem. "I make *others* paranoid."

"First time for everything," said Decampo. He let his breath out in a rush and nodded at the parked Taurus. "I figure it's probably just some dude and his dudess making friends in the dark," he added. He chuffed at his little joke.

Kireem looked him up and down with disdain and shook his head.

"*Rifleman,* you can't know how glad I'm going to be getting rid of your ass for awhile."

Decampo gave him a puzzled look.

"What about you saying me and Sonny owe you?" he said. "I thought we were going to be doing business."

"Oh, we are, for certain," said Kireem. He grinned. "First, I wants us to take a little time out—get away from you cracker-boys. Anyway, I gots to get some clothes washed."

"I hear you," Decampo said.

Kireem reached over, picked up the AK-47, dropped the ammo clip and jacked the round from its chamber.

"The fuck are you doing?" Decampo asked, grabbing the rifle.

"I want you to wait right here, Rifleman," said Kireem. "I gotta check on Player and your boy, French."

"I'm going too," Decampo said. He started to reach around for the door handle; Kireem reached in with his 10mm and gigged him in the ribs.

"Sit your ass down and shut the fuck up!" he said. "Wait right here or I'll burn you down."

"What are you going to do?" Decampo called out, trying to keep his voice down. When he got no reply, he sat watching, stoned and bewildered, as Kireem eased away and walked up the driveway toward the front porch ....

Inside the parked Taurus, the man behind the wheel spoke into his cell phone, watching Kireem moving toward the house.

"Heads up, everybody," he said, "Kireem Murabi is entering the building."

"Copy that," a voice replied.

The wheelman turned a little in his seat and picked up his .40 caliber lying beside him. Beside him, another man in a wrinkled suit sat watching Kireem.

"He's been on a run. It's time we caught up to him," he said under his breath.

The wheel man said into the cell, "Agent Kim, Agent Blanco, you two get in behind him, keep close, keep out of sight as long as you can."

"Copy that," said another voice.

"Peterson, Danner," the wheelman said, "get the back of the house covered. Nobody gets away tonight." He clicked the cell shut, nodded over his shoulder and said to the man beside him, "Let's get this one behind us."

Inside the house, standing at the light switch he'd clicked on only a moment ago, Sonny French turned his grinning face to Augio, just in time to hear the roar of the big Desert Eagle, and see it buck in Augio's hand behind a belch of blue-orange fire.

Sami screamed at the sound of the gunshot, at seeing the hole appear on the right side of French's chest, at seeing the blood splash on the wall behind him as he spun around and slapped the wall face first. She screamed again as he slid down the wall and flopped back around facing her and Augio, the big smoking .50 caliber pistol still leveled at him.

There was not a doubt in her mind she was witnessing him murder a man. This manic would kill her before he left her alive to identify him. In panic and fear, realizing she had nothing to lose, she hurled herself from the bed and tried to run through the open bedroom door. In doing so she stumbled sideways on the carpet and plowed headlong into Augio, knocking him sideways, unbalanced. Just as he fired what he intended to be his killing shot into French's head, he had to grab Sami and throw her across the room toward French to keep her from escaping. His second big .50 caliber bullet missed French and ripped through the bedroom wall. Pictures flew off their hooks and crashed to the carpet.

"You're not going anywhere, you crazy old bitch!" Augio shouted at her. He swung the big Desert Eagle away from French toward Sami, his knife still open in his other hand. But Sami had gone too far to stop now. She lunged onto the floor where the contents of her purse lay scattered. She didn't see her gun, but she saw the little *designer* mace can and snatched it up. Augio stepped forward looming over her, the gun pointed, the knife raised in his other hand, ready to swing the blade down on her.

Sami, rising onto her knee, reached up with both hands and shot a hard spray of mace into his unguarded eyes. He didn't even have time to squint before the fiery liquid hit the soft tissue of his cornea like a flamethrower.

"Kill … him!" French managed to say in a broken voice, blood spewing from his chest. Augio stumbled backward a step; the knife flew from his hand. He screamed into his palm. The .50 caliber started firing wildly, blindly, searching for Sami. But Sami wasn't finished, she glanced all around for her gun. Didn't see it. It had either been spilled with the other items in the yard, or fallen deeper down in her purse. Either way, it was gone. Frantic, she saw the silenced .22 with its happy-face duct tape grinning at her; she grabbed it, sprang to her feet and held it out arm's length.

Now what? She looked at the gun, with no idea how it worked.

Augio collected himself ten feet away, standing between her and the doorway. He batted his red eyes, managing to see her watery image. He aimed the big wobbly .50 caliber pistol and fired. The bullet went wild; her bed lamp exploded.

"You're dead!" he shouted.

Sami glanced again the gun, tried to remember what Ray Dylan had taught her about shooting—*get a good balanced stance, take a breath, hold it*— Fuck all that! Out front she heard a hard pounding on her front door. *Someone crashing in? The police? God,* she hoped so!

She pulled the trigger knowing she had no time to wait for help. The little gun made a snapping sound. She saw Augio flinch as the bullet struck him dead center. A little teardrop size spot of blood appeared on his chest; but why didn't he fall, stumble, something?

God, it's a nightmare! She fired again; again the quiet little snap, no recoil, no power. How was she supposed to kill this man! She looked wild-eyed at the little gun, the happy faces staring with their same stupid grin! From the other room she heard glass break in the louvered door opening to the lanai.

"That's it, you washed out old bag?" Augio said, his eyes better now, focusing on her. He gave a dark little chuckle in spite of the two little blood spots on his shirt. "That's all you got?" He stepped forward; the big gun steady in his outstretched hand. "Really?" He grinned. "So long, bitch."

Sami saw him brace himself, ready to pull the trigger. All she could do was try to back away. She pulled the little gun's trigger again. There was still no recoil, no power, yet this time even with its silencer, she heard two load blasts back to back, like that of a double-barreled field cannon.

A double tap? Oh my God ...!

Sami stood frozen, stunned, seeing the madman's forehead explode outwards, streaking across the ceiling above her in a black-red cloud filled with brain and bone matter. She felt warm blood shower down the front of her—down her exposed breasts, her shredded blouse. She watched him fall forward to the floor, and saw Ray Dylan standing behind him in the doorway, his trusty .45 out at arm's length, a curl of smoke doing a slow waltz on the tip of its barrel.

"Hey, are you all right?" He asked almost in a whisper. He saw her give him a stiff slight nod, knowing it was taking all of her effort. He saw the little gun still in her hand, pointed squarely at him. "Easy, Sami, lower the gun," he said stepping in, looking all around, his gun muzzle probing the room.

"Why? It won't kill anybody, Ray," she said in a shaky voice. He realized she was half in shock.

"But *still,* Sami …." He gave her a look, stepping around the dead man on the bloody carpet, seeing the badly wounded man lying nearby, leaning against the wall.

Sami let the gun down to her side, but she held onto it. They both heard movement on the hallway tile. Dylan turned facing the doorway with his .45 raised and ready. He stepped over beside Sami and slipped his arm around her, gun hand and all.

"Drug Enforcement Agency! DEA!" A deep booming voice called out from the hallway, "Stand down in there!"

"DEA?" Dylan whispered sidelong to Sami.

"Stand down?" she whispered back. "I recognize that voice, it's a trick, Ray!" she said just a little louder.

"She's right … it's a … trick," French managed to say in a waning voice, clasping a hand to his chest against the flow of blood.

"Show some proof," Dylan called out. As he spoke he guided Sami around the bed; the two lowered down to bed level, Dylan with the .45 out and ready across the mattress.

"There, see that?" the voice said. Dylan and Sami saw a black hand hold out an ID wallet and flipped it open, showing a badge and a photo ID inside it. "Agent Cornell Mayes. Stop the shooting. We're coming in."

We're coming in? Dylan asked himself. *How many men were out there?* He kept the .45 aimed at the doorway.

"He's lying, that's Kireem!" Sami shouted, seeing

the familiar black man step into sight holding the ID wallet to the side. She pointed the little gun and started to pull the trigger. Dylan shoved her hand just as the little gun made its silent snap.

The black man flinched and jerked sideways, holding his upper shoulder.

"She got me—" he said. As soon as he said it, he held out his hand toward unseen faces in the hall. "—That's all right, no harm done." He looked over at the bed, saw Dylan taking the small gun from the woman's hand.

"She's okay!" Dylan called out, seeing two more men step inside the room behind the black man. They had badges and IDs on chains hanging around their necks. Dylan held the little gun out and dropped it on the mattress. "She's upset—in shock maybe!"

The black man looked at the body on the floor, French lying bloody against the wall, the bloody shot-up room.

"*Copy that,*" he said quietly. A drop of blood appeared on the shoulder of his polo shirt.

Dylan eyed the big Glock standing in the black man's waist. He held his cocked .45 up and let the three DEA agents see him ease the hammer down. He was already planning how he was going to act, what he would say—his version of what had gone on here—what he would or would not mention. Then he let them see him lay the .45 on the mattress. He rose to his feet, holding Sami against his side. She held her blouse gathered across her breasts.

"I— I shot you, Kireem," Sami said in a weak trembling voice.

"Yes, ma'am, you certainly did," the big man said, crooking his neck and looking at the tiny blood spot. He looked back at her and smiled. "But I'm not Kireem anymore. I'm agent Mayes—Cornell Mayes. I know I scared you before. I want to apologize. I was just doing my job."

"You son ... of a ... bitch," French said, looking up at Kireem Murabi—now Agent Cornell Mayes. "You're a ... fucking narc."

"Hey, watch your language, French," the black agent said, stepping over, stooping down beside him. He brushed French's hair back from his eyes and said in a milder voice, "Hang on, we've got an ambulance coming for you." He called back over his shoulder to the other two agents, "One of you got a handkerchief or something?"

"Here, I've got one," said Agent Andrew Kim, a young Asian with a small bandage on his forehead, a few scratches down his cheek. He held the folded white handkerchief down to Kireem—Agent Cornell Mayes. French looked up at the Asian in surprise and disgust.

"Benny Wu, you rotten ... little narc prick," he said. "All the dope ... we smoked—"

"Hey, French," Mayes cut in, "want us to cancel that ambulance?"

French settled down; Mayes placed the handkerchief over the wound and pressed French's hand on it.

"Where's Hal ...? Did you ... kill him?" French asked.

"No, Decampo's out there right now, *disarmed.*" Mayes held up his shirt and showed the AK's magazine shoved down behind his belt. He looked around at Ray

272

Dylan and Sami. "I was joking about canceling the ambulance," he said. "French knows that, right, French?"

"Prick …," French said under his breath. From the front door came the sound of more footsteps. In the distance an Emergency Medical siren wailed.

"Are you all right, Sami?" Dylan asked.

"I want to sit down," Sami replied.

"Are you going to be sick?" Dylan asked quietly.

"No, Ray," she said, giving him a look, "I just want to sit down. This is all too much for me … shooting people." She shook her head as Dylan helped her sit down on the edge of the bed.

"I know what you mean," he replied to her, giving the agents a glance. "Neither of us are used to this sort of thing." He sighed and shook his head and sat down beside her.

EPILOGUE

"... When we return, we'll have more on that attempted home invasion in Hernando Beach that cost the perpetrator, Carson Betto, his life. Spokespersons say Betto had a troubled history of mental illness and was believed to be trafficking illegal drugs between Canada and the US .... Plus, coming up, more on that raging vehicle fire that claimed the life of two campers in a secluded wetlands along the Hernando County coast near Pine Island—"

A hand reached out, pointed a remote at the TV sitting on a shelf across the office, and clicked it off. The hand, remote and all, gestured for Agent Cornell Mayes to have a seat across the wide polished desk.

"I commend you for the job you and your support team have done in toppling Martin Ambrose. Sources say the Tampa Bay area is already feeling a cocaine shortage."

"Thank you, sir," said Mayes, out of his street clothes now, wearing a dark suit, a black tie, a light blue dress shirt. "It would have been nice taking him in. We could have used him to get us farther along in the pipeline."

"Yes, it would have been nice," the man behind the desk said. "But I'll settle for *dead.*" He gave a thin smile. "Think of all the resources it saves us." He lowered his eyes for a second, consulted the report on his desk and shook his head. "And this all stemmed from your informant, Willie Hopps, AKA *Psycho Willie?*"

"Yes, sir," said Mayes, "Hopps is looking at seven to ten for possession with intent to sell. He set me up with the Canadian. The two had served time together in Detroit, in a mental facility."

"Remarkable story," the man said, consulting the paperwork lying before him. "Carnival rides, this Canadian maniac, a cannibal, counterfeit money." He gave a little chuckle. "Imagine the faces on those Canadian hoods when they find out their own man stiffed them with a load of funny money." He raised his eyes and said, "By the way, I've spoken with Washington; the department is backing off this thing for the time being. The only counterfeit money they've located is what they confiscated from Ambrose's office. They can't connect it to anyone, at least to no one alive. According to your report, Carson Betto informed you that it came from the woman, Samantha Bloom?"

"Yes, he informed me of that, sir," said Mayes. "Agent Hughes and his men searched the residence and found nothing. The woman and her boyfriend claim to know nothing about it."

"I see." The man considered it. "Then this entire issue would only amount to hearsay in a court of law," he said. "At any rate, that's for Washington to deal with. I'm going to call this a wrap, for us—" He removed his glasses. "—Unless you have something to add, *officially* that is."

"No, sir," Mayes said, "my report is complete."

"How about, *unofficially* then," the man asked, scrutinizing him closely. "Need any time off … say, to clear your head?"

"My head is clear, sir," Mayes said. "I do have two weeks vacation I'd like to take, effective immediately." He offered a slight smile "—A couple of young ladies I'd like to spend some time with."

"Certainly," the man said, "go your way." As he pushed up from his leather chair, he said, "One more thing. The local coroner found no bullet wounds in the *Swamp Cannibal's* head. So, this Hal Decampo's statement that you shot the man is completely false."

"Yes, sir," Mayes said, rising. "I did fire two shots in the ground near the man's head once I saw he was already dead. I knew I'd never get in to see Martin Ambrose unless he saw I was as bad as the rest of them."

"I understand," the man said. He walked around his desk and ushered Mayes to the door and shook his hand. "Give my best to those two young ladies."

"Yes, sir," Mayes said. He walked out into the long marble hallway and down the corridor toward an ornate wooden bench. As he approached the elevators, a woman stood up; a little girl stood up beside her.

"Daddy, Daddy," the child sang out, running to Mayes, her small shoes resounding in the long hallway.

"Watch Daddy's shoulder, Jessi," the woman called out, staying close behind the running child.

Agent Mayes stooped and caught the little girl in his arms.

"She's not hurting me," Mayes said, turning full circle with the child against his chest. "Daddy's doing fine," he said against her cheek, "just fine."

The woman stood beside the two of them, her arms around them both.

"Well …?" she asked. "Are we good to go?"

"Two weeks, Terese," Agent Mayes said to his wife, "Anywhere you womenfolk want to go, we are on our way."

They turned and walked to the elevator. Mayes held the child out and let her push her tiny finger against the ground floor button.

Terese Mayes looked all around. Seeing the hall lay empty, she said, "Someday, Cornell, we're going to sit down and you're going to tell me all about these *cases* you go on."

Mayes kissed little Jessi's cheek and looked at Terese.

"It's mostly just day-to-day routine stuff. I know you'd find it uninteresting."

"Even when you stabbed yourself walking into a coat rack?" She smiled and placed a hand carefully on his shoulder. "That's unbelievable." She gave a little laugh.

"See? I'm never going to hear the end of that," Mayes said, "I never should have told you." He smiled. "Trouble is, like most folks you see Hollywood's version of all this drug war stuff—breaking down doors, millions changing hands—shootouts and whatnot. It's almost never like that. If it was I wouldn't be doing it. I'm no hero. I'd go somewhere and hang out my shingle."

"Well, you're our hero," Terese said. "That's all that matters to us, right Jessi?"

The child nodded her head and snuggled against her father's chest. Agent Mayes smiled at her and drew her closer.

"That's all I care about too," he said. He closed his eyes for a moment and felt his daughter's little heart beat against his while the elevator rose and halted before them. *Yeah, that's all that matters ....*

Ray Dylan and Sami Bloom sat in lawn chairs looking out across the water at two teenagers wrestling with a little sailboat where the mouth of the canal opened onto the Gulf. Dylan was a little surprised when his cell phone rang and he looked at it and saw the Chicago area code. But *okay* .... He was ready. He wasn't going to Chicago, not on Phil Rodell's summons. Rodell's attempt at having Art Lamato kill him had failed. Dylan wasn't putting himself out front again. By now Rodell had to be anxious, wondering what happened down here—send out a hit man and he never comes back. Rodell had been doing a lot of things without Chicago's blessings. Knowing that would be Dylan's ace in the hole.

"Excuse me, Sami, I've got to take this," he said, pushing his sun glasses up above his forehead. He stood up with the phone in hand, walked down from the lanai to the edge of the canal and answered it.

"You know who this is?" the voice said. It wasn't Phil Rodell. Dylan was surprised again.

"Yes, I do," Dylan replied, then he waited.

"Is your line good?" the voice asked.

"Always," Dylan said.

"Okay," the voice said. "I'm going to talk to you. You good with this?"

"Go ahead," Dylan said, already sensing something different was afoot.

"First thing," the voice said, "Your friend who calls you, won't be calling you like before." A silence followed.

"For how long?" Dylan asked, trying to put it together as it went along.

"From *now on,*" the voice said, flatly, leaving Dylan little doubt that Phil Rodell was dead. He breathed in relief.

"Okay …," he said. He waited, the way he knew he was supposed to.

"From now on anybody calls you, it'll be me," the voice said. "I understand it's been awhile since you been up here—since anybody called you for anything."

Hunh …? Dylan didn't answer; he listened, learning something here. *Bingo*, just like he'd suspected. Rodell and the old man's son had set up the hit on the old man without Chicago even knowing about it. Now Chicago was fishing around trying to find out who knew what, probably who did it, too. Here was his chance to back away from the matter, take his name out of play on it for once and for all. "It's been awhile," he said. "But I always come when I'm invited."

"Everybody knows that," the voice said. "You've got friends here." He waited then said, "You heard about the old man, about his son?"

"Sure," said Dylan, "I heard about it. But I heard it too late to make the funeral." He paused then said,

"Natural causes is what I heard—but then I heard the grandson had doubts."

"Crazy stuff," the voice said without offering opinion. "But that's old news. Anyway, your friend is gone, and I'm your new friend. Nobody here wanted you to worry about any of this. All right?"

"Yes," Dylan said, even more relieved.

"So, I need you, I'll call you," the voice said. "Anything we can do for yas down there?"

"Thanks," Dylan said, "I'm good here." He looked all around, up at the sky and out across the water. A gull careened in and dipped and circled a few feet away.

"Be well, my friend," the voice said.

"And you," Dylan replied.

And that's that ....

Dylan let out a breath. He knew that was as much as he would ever hear on the subject of the money, or of Phil Rodell. He wouldn't bring the matter up ... *not ever.* He was known for keeping his mouth shut. It was that kind of reputation that had followed him throughout the years. For him to have friends, he had to be the kind of friend they wanted to have. He got that, he always did.

Good enough ....

He closed the phone and walked back to the lanai. Sami handed him one of the vodka tonics she'd poured. Dylan took the drink and sat down. He stretched his legs out and crossed his ankles as Sami sat back down in her lawn chair beside him.

"That was Sarasota," he said. "Good news, I don't have to go there after all. Everything got worked out without me." He breathed deep and took a sip of his drink. "I'll be home for Christmas." He smiled.

"Oh ...." Sami thought about it. "I was sort of looking forward to going with you." She paused then said, "I guess it's for the best though." She smiled.

"How so?" Dylan turned his head a little and looked at her.

Sami shrugged.

"I never made us reservations," she said.

Dylan only nodded and turned his face back to the sun.

"Anyway, after all we've been through," she said. "We should take it easy a while longer, rest up, don't you think?"

Dylan shrugged. "Yeah, I'm still pretty shaken by the whole thing," he said. "I never want to go through something like that again." He reached over and took her hand and squeezed it a little, just enough to let her know he was there.

"Me neither, Ray," Sami said. "But if I ever did, you're the person I'd want by my side."

"Same here, Sami," Dylan said. "Nice of you to say so."

All right, he felt bad keeping things like this from her, he told himself ... *but what're you going to do?*

They sat in silence gazing at the young people and the unruly sailboat.

"Look at those two," Sami said after a moment. "Where on earth do they get the energy?"

"Beats me," Dylan said with a half-smile, breathing deep, taking in the salt air, letting it out slowly. He lowered his sunglasses back over his eyes and watched a wide distant sun melt down over Mexico.

SEASON OF THE WIND

Here are some unedited pages from Book 2 in Ralph Cotton's Gun Culture Series: **Season Of The Wind,** *currently in production.*

Punta Rassa, Florida –August 1981

Ray Dylan drove an army surplus Jeep along a secluded two lane road. There were no doors on the battered vehicle. It had a rattling after market air conditioner that blew a weak steady stream of tepid air at Dylan's knees. It wasn't his Jeep. It belonged to Randall Parks, the man seated beside him. Parks, a tall swarthy man with a pockmarked face sat leaning forward, watching the road through thick black-framed glasses. It was late afternoon and the day's storm had come and gone, leaving the land swollen and plush, beneath a steamy veil. More than once Parks had taken off his glasses and wiped a sheen of fog from the lenses with a yellowed handkerchief.

Merciless weather ....

But he'd seen worse, Dylan reminded himself.

Sweat crawled along the middle of his back beneath his cotton shirt, under his arms, at his collar, his hair line. He'd be glad to get this thing over with. He checked his wrist watch, 6:00 pm, getting dark soon. He looked down at the big-framed .45 Colt stuck behind his belt, cocked and locked. He looked over at Parks who held a *Grease Gun* style FMK Argentine submachine on the seat against his thigh. His left hand rested on the gun's retracted wire stock, near the trigger, under a selection switch. The switch had three settings, S for safety, R for repeat fire, and A for full Automatic. Dylan had noticed first thing that the switch was set on A –*full automatic. No big deal*, he thought. But he'd found it noteworthy.

If push came to shove, he hoped Parks—if that was his real name—was the right man to be carrying automatic firepower. Situations like this, submachine guns were often as much for show as for actual protection. *The message being, don't fuck with us, we've got a machine gun,* he told himself. He studied Parks for a second, his glasses, their thick lenses. The man appeared to struggle with seeing the road ahead. No wonder he'd asked him to drive, Dylan speculated. He turned his attention back to the worn and crumbled asphalt.

He'd never laid eyes on this man until three days ago. Odds were good he'd never see him again after today. The man could be CIA, for all Dylan knew. Not that it mattered. He'd worked with CIA before. The agency had such a high turnover in personnel, it was hard to see a familiar face twice. But if Parks was CIA at least he would know which end of the FMK sub the bullets came out of. *Or so you would think* .... He gave Parks another passing glance. *Either way,* he told himself, this job was *on*. They were a couple of guys driving to work together.

Parks said without facing him, "There'll be an old fruit stand up ahead, take a right."

Dylan nodded, watching Parks strain forward, searching the side of the road ahead.

A half mile farther he slowed at the abandoned old roadside stand and turned on a narrow sandy trail. A few yards into an overgrown woodlands of wild palm, palmetto, vines and bracken the terrain engulfed them. Snakes slithered out of sight at their approach. They drove on over sandy potholes, Parks still forward in his seat, searching straight ahead.

"You'll see an old confederate lookout tower on my side," he said. "It's perfect for us." He touched the thick glasses up on his nose.

Dylan saw a recent stir of dust still settling on the foliage lining either side of the trail, but he made no comment. He drove another quarter of a mile and turned the surplus Jeep off the trail into a weed strewn clearing. He braked the vehicle to a halt beside a coral stone and split log watchtower. A hundred yards farther along the trail, above the tree line, gulls rose and dipped in the evening light. When he turned off the engine and looked all around something skipped away fast through the overgrowth.

"All right, get set up. I'll check things out," Parks said, picking up the submachine gun. They both stepped down from the Jeep. Parks looked all around the thick tropical growth surrounding the clearing. Dylan reached behind his seat and took out the long battered gun case sitting on the floor.

The two walked to a weathered lookout tower where a faded demolition notice and warning sign had been stapled to the entrance. A covered switchback stairwell reached up the center of the structure. Parks lagged back, looking all around; he waited for a moment before going up. Dylan continued on, rifle case in hand. At the top of the stairs he stepped onto a dusty framed landing covered waist high with brittle plank siding. Above the plank siding, he had a long view of Sanibel Island. Closer in lay Fisherman Key, Kitchel Key, Big Island, Pine Island, other smaller places. West lay Cape Coral and the mouth of the Caloosahatchee River. Places familiar to him.

Looking down and out a hundred yards, he saw the shoreline of Punta Rassa. Timeworn rows of dock posts still stood strewn out into the water, remnants of wharf and loading dock framing along the water's edge. He crouched down and moved around over to where a four inch wide plank had been conveniently loosened and left sagging down on one nail. Squatting, he opened the gun case, took out a rolled up straw mat and spread in on the landing floor. A pair of olive drab binoculars stood beside the opening in the plank siding. Beside the binoculars lay a steady-bag filled with sand for him to rest his rifle on.

Dylan moved both items aside—didn't need them, wouldn't be using them. He gave them a curious look and wondered why anybody would have left them here for him. *Good question* .... He studied the items a moment longer, then turned away from them when he heard Parks' footsteps on the stairs. He opened the gun case and raised an M40 *Quantico* modified Remington 700 rifle from inside. He uncapped and inspected the Unertl scope attached atop the barrel before laying the rifle on the mat facing the docks.

Flattening on the mat, he shouldered the rifle and looked down through the scope. He scanned the crosshairs back and forth along the old dock area, judging the distance from the tower to the shoreline to be a hundred yards—98 meters. Not much of a challenge for this rifle, this scope, this close in. But he moved the scope farther out on the water, another hundred yards, two hundred; and he watched the surface, judged the chop and sway. Out there would be a different story, targets moving away fast, over a loose body of water. Out there would be the money shots.

Interesting ....

He considered it. Then he laid the Remington back down on the mat and sat up. Inside the open rifle case he carried three box magazines, five .308 NATO rounds in each. He picked one of the magazines up, inspected it and slipped it into the rifle's belly. Five shots were more than enough. He slid the bolt shut, watching it pick up a long brass bullet from atop the magazine and level it into the chamber. Silky smooth. Quiet as a whisper.

There, all set up, he told himself. He flipped the corner of the mat over the rifle. He closed the rifle case and moved it aside. Crouched low, he walked back to the stairs where Parks stood watching from inside the covered stairwell.

"There's something about this I don't like,"

Parks said. "I can't put my finger on it." He gazed far out across the water and pushed his thick glasses up on the bridge of his nose. "You never told us much about yourself." He stared intently. Dylan caught some sort of veiled accusation in his words. But he wasn't backing off.

"You're right, I didn't." He held the stare, returned it until Parks gave up and looked away. Whatever this man and his boss needed to know, they should have asked two days ago when they'd met him. They were past the Q&A stage, Dylan thought.

Parks said, "The other day, you never really asked who referred you to us. I find that strange." He stared at Dylan with his huge magnified eyes.

Dylan didn't reply. He didn't have to ask. He *knew* who'd referred him. He wouldn't have been here otherwise. He wondered about this guy. Maybe he got a little jumpy before a job.

"Anyway …." After a tense pause Parks mopped a hand across his forehead and looked back at him, "Are you ready?"

Dylan only nodded. He was starting to like the way his silence seemed to keep the man a little put off.

"You don't talk much, do you?" Parks said.

"Not a lot," Dylan replied flatly. "Are we good here?"

Parks had made several attempts at asking him questions earlier. Dylan had fended them off. He knew he had been well recommended by a third party, his contact out of Chicago. If that wasn't good enough, he would keep the half payment he'd been given up front, re-case the rifle and call it a day.

Parks took a hint.

"Yes, we're good here. Just be sure you catch my signal," he said, "when I take off my glasses and wipe them with my handkerchief."

"Got it," Dylan said.

"Good." Parks gave him a nod, turned and walked down the shadowed stairs. Dylan watched until the tall gangly man spiraled down out of sight. Then he walked back across the landing in a crouch to where the rifle lay waiting. He stooped down, used his shirttail to wipe any prints off the binoculars he'd picked up and moved. *Just in case*, he thought. Then he uncovered the rifle and stretched out on the shooting mat beside it. He lay gazing out through the opening in the plank siding. And he waited, his hands steady, his mind clear and relaxed.

Leonid Volkov cursed to himself in Russian. Then instinctively, he glanced around as if to see if he'd been heard. *Not likely* .... Here on the strip of land below the city of Fort Myers. Still he had to be careful, even though most times he doubted anyone here would know the difference. He could speak Russian, or Zulu, or Martian, or whatever, these ignorant mongrels wouldn't know. They would likely bat their eyes, laugh like a braying ass, and offer him a can of beer.

Fucking Americans ....

This time he cursed to himself, in English, as good as any he'd heard in this sweltering pigsty.

He looked around again, this time in contempt. He hated this scalding inferno, this primordial bacterial *swamp,* even worse than he hated Cuba. Although not by much, he had to admit. True, he found both places equally repulsive, the heat, the insistent sweat, the stench of sewerage improperly treated. Fortunately the Cubans had learned from *his people* not to mix their natural odor with that of sickening sweet western cologne. His nose crooked a little at the thought of it.

At least in Havana there was no one out to kill him—he smiled faintly—that he knew of, that is. He took a deep breath. That might change quickly after today.

He stepped over to the water's edge and watched as the boat grew larger, moving toward him from the direction of Sanibel Island. The cruiser bobbed slightly, its bow tilted up, not rising up onto plane or even attempting to. Volkov shook his head and watched it for a few seconds longer. He turned at the sound of Parks walking through the foliage and bracken behind him, holding the submachine gun across his waist.

"Do you have our *hired help* squared away?" Volkov asked, liking the sound of his English, not realizing there remained a slight hint of an accent in it.

"He's waiting for my signal," Parks said, his English also good and clear, carrying only a shadow of Urban Cuban Spanish behind the vowel sounds. Two men well spoken, from opposite sides of the planet, each driven to master the language of a people they would destroy.

"He appears to be well prepared," Parks said. He nodded in agreement with himself. "I think we'll like what he does here." He looked out at the approaching boat. "Although, I have to say, my teenage sister could do this."

"Oh?" Volkov appraised him up and down. "Is

your sister a former U.S. Marine? Does she own a .308 sniper rifle?" His hard stare demanded an answer, no matter how obvious. "Is she a hired assassin, like our fellow here?"

"No, of course not, comrade," Parks said. "I apologize"

"Then she certainly wouldn't fit the bill to do this," Volkov snapped, turning his face away. He looked out at the cruiser, then back at Parks with a sharp stare and said, "Did you learn any more about him, make sure the assassin I *received* fits the assassin I *ordered?*"

"No more than he told us the day we met him. He does not say much, comrade," Parks offered.

"Please call me comrade again," Volkov said, "so I can examine your eye in the palm of my hand." He held his palm out as if Parks' eye was already in it.

Parks swallowed a dry knot in his throat. He'd seen enough of Professor Leonid Volkov to know this was not an idle threat.

"His rifle and scope are the kind Marine snipers use. They are difficult for civilians to acquire—especially the scope."

"But you did not find out if he was ever actually *in the Marines,* did you?" Volkov pressed.

"No, I did not, com— I mean, *Professor,*" Parks corrected quickly. "I tried to. But he would not answer. He only told me he is ready, but he hasn't said much else. He doesn't appear to like people."

Doesn't like people ....

Volkov grumbled under his breath and shook his head. As the sound of the approaching boat became audible he turned toward a patch of thick foliage and gave a barely noticeable hand sign. Parks looked surprised as a large man carrying an Uzi stepped from behind a cabbage palm and moved forward a little and went back out of sight.

"I didn't know you were bringing Gilbert Haas," Parks said.

"That's because I chose not to tell you," Volkov said in a crisp tone. "I also brought Thomas Moon. I want dependable backup on this." Dismissing the matter, he bent down and picked up the small leather case at his feet. As he straightened he saw Parks searching the foliage for the other man Volkov had mentioned. "Be ready, Randall," he said, drawing Park's attention back to him. "Our future is on the line."

Parks stiffened his stance. He watched Volkov snap a handcuff onto his own wrist and snap the other cuff on the case's handle. Volkov smiled a little and wiggled his cuffed hand at Parks.

"Image is everything, here in this land of simpletons and psychotics," he said with wry contempt. He held the case at his side. The two stepped onto a weathered dock and walked out and waited as the boat slowed and idled in toward them.

Other Books by Ralph Cotton

The Gun Culture Series

1. Friend of a Friend   2015
2. Season of the Wind
...More to Come...

Western Classics
The Life and Times of Jeston Nash

1. While Angels Dance*	1994
2. Powder River	1995
3. Price of a Horse	1996
4. Cost of a Killing	1996
5. Killers of Man	1997
6. Trick of the Trade	1997

* While Angels Dance *was a candidate for the **Pulitzer Prize** in fiction in 1994. This entire **Western Classic** series has been released and is available from Amazon.com and other retailers, as well as Kindle and other ebook formats.*

Dead or Alive Trilogy

1. Hangman's Choice	2000
2. Devil's Due	2001
3. Blood Money	2002

*The **Dead or Alive Trilogy** is available from Amazon.com and other retailers, as well as Kindle and other ebook formats, as part of **Ralph Cotton's Western Classics.***

Other Books by Ralph Cotton

Danny Duggin (Written for the Estate of Ralph Compton)

1. The Shadow of a Noose	*2000*
2. Riders of Judgement	*2001*
3. Death Along the Cimarron	*2003*

Gunman's Reputation (Lawrence Shaw)

1. Gunman's Song	*2004*
2. Between Hell and Texas	*2004*
3. The Law in Somos Santos	*2005*
4. Bad Day at Willow Creek	*2006*
5. Fast Guns Out of Texas	*2007*
6. Gunmen of the Desert Sands	*2008*
7. Ride to Hell's Gate	*2008*
8. Crossing Fire River	*2009*
9. Escape From Fire River	*2009*
10. Gun Country	*2010*
11. City of Bad Men	*2011*

Spin-Off Novels

1. Webb's Posse	*2003*
2. Fighting Men (Sherman Dahl)	*2010*
3. Gun Law (Sherman Dahl)	*2011*
4. Summer's Horses (Will Summers)	*2011*
5. Incident at Gunn Point (Will Summers)	*2012*
6. Midnight Rider (Will Summers)	*2012*

Other Books by Ralph Cotton

Ranger Sam Burrack (Big Iron Series)

1. Montana Red	*1998*
2. The Badlands	*1998*
3. Justice	*1999*
4. Border Dogs	*1999*
5. Blue Star Tattoo	*2000*
6. Blood Rock	*2001*
7. Jurisdiction	*2002*
8. Vengence	*2003*
9. Sabre's Edge	*2003*
10. Hell's Riders	*2004*
11. Showdown at Rio Sagrado	*2004*
12. Dead Man's Canyon	*2004*
13. Killing Plain	*2005*
14. Black Mesa	*2005*
15. Trouble Creek	*2006*
16. Gunfight at Cold Devil	*2006*
17. Guns on the Border	*2007*
18. Killing Texas Bob	*2007*
19. Nightfall at Little Aces	*2008*
20. Ambush at Shadow Valley	*2008*
21. Showdown at Hole-In-The-Wall	*2009*
22. Riders from Long Pines	*2009*
23. A Hanging in Wild Wind	*2010*
24. Black Valley Riders	*2010*
25. Lawman from Nogales	*2011*
26. Wildfire	*2012*
27. Lookout Hill	*2012*

Other Books by Ralph Cotton

Ranger Sam Burrack (Big Iron Series), *cont.*

Stand Alone Novels

Author Ralph Cotton

Ralph Cotton is a *Best Selling Author* with over *Seventy* books to his credit and millions of books in print.

Friend Of A Friend is the first book in his new series: **Gun Culture**. Look for the second book, **Season of the Wind**, to be released in the summer of 2015.

Known for fast-paced narrative and wry dark humor, Ralph's debut to the avid readers of Florida crime fiction will be well received in his **Gun Culture** series.

Ralph lives on the Florida Gulf Coast with his wife Mary Lynn. He writes prodigiously and his books remain top sellers in the Western and Civil War/Western genres. Ralph enjoys painting, photography, sailing and playing guitar.

Made in the USA
Charleston, SC
18 July 2015